Dedication

Kay, Bob, Clifford, Diane, Martha, Jim, Wanda, and Grace.

It's seldom we have long lasting friendships.
The Lord has blessed me with mine.

Love you,

—Sue

Acknowledgments

I give all praise, honor, and glory to my Lord and Savior, Jesus Christ. Without Him, this book would not be possible.

I want to thank Jeff Disend for your culinary expertise. It is greatly appreciated.

Hillary, without your editing expertise I would have drown in a sea of words. Thank you so much and to all who have helped me in bringing this book to reality, a big thank you.

Martha, your input, humor, encouragement, and support has helped me to keep my sanity during this process. We'll rejoice together.

Many have prayed for me during the writing of this book, and may God bless you. Thank you.

Other books by Sue Cass:

Laying Down my Net–
A Walk of Faith

. . .

Sacrifices of a Saint

. . .

Seek My Face

Chapter 1

The long driveway leading to the house is lined on both sides with dogwood trees in full bloom, and they leave a trail of beauty as Chris and Teri slowly drive between them. It's almost like a fairy tale come true, with two sisters traveling down a wonderland of beauty and heading for the magical castle.

Chris and Teri aren't able to come back to their childhood home as often as they would like, but this is a special occasion, and they wouldn't miss it for the world. Margaret and Clay are celebrating their thirtieth wedding anniversary.

Parking the car on the circle drive in front of the house, Chris and Teri sit looking at their childhood home. "Teri, do you remember Grandma?"

"Yes. Why?"

"I just miss her sometimes. I'm glad Mom and Dad fixed up her old house after she went to be with the Lord. I think she'd be pleased to see what they've done."

"I think the thing I remember the most is how she would sit me on her lap and tell me stories. Do you remember the tire swing?"

"Yes. You really loved spinning around on it."

"I remember doing that. I think it would still be fun."
Teri says, as she points to the old oak tree at the side of
the house. Each is lost in her own thoughts for a moment. "Come on. We better get inside and see what Mom
is up to," Chris says as she opens the car door.

Walking to the front porch, the wicker chairs and
settee facing the front yard greet them. Wooden rock-
ers, with flowered cushions, rock slightly in the breeze.
A porch swing sways gently on the opposite end of the
porch, and several potted plants hang from their hooks,
soaking up the afternoon sun. Of course, the old furni-
ture Grandma had has been replaced, and the new furni-
ture is as welcoming.

Walking up the four wide steps reminds them of
their growing-up years and how they played with their
dolls on these very same steps, chasing each other around
the front yard and petting stray dogs or cats that would
show up on occasion. Reaching for the door handle,
Chris looks at Teri.

"Something smells good. I thought Mom wasn't supposed to do any cooking."

"Mom not in an apron? Dream on, sister."

As expected, Margaret is in the kitchen. Her bibbed
apron with its flowers, ruffle-trimmed edges, and em-
broidered with "Best Cook, Be Nice to Me" is tied in the
rear. Hearing the girls enter, she spins with outstretched
arms. "Oh, my girls are home!" Grabbing each daughter
at the same time, she gives each a big hug.

"What's all the ruckus going on in here? Are my two

beautiful daughters home from the big city?" Grinning widely, Clay knows full well his children are home and gives each a big kiss on the cheek.

Laughing and waving a dish rag at them, Margaret says, "Are you going to go to the store and pick up the few things I need, or are you going to stand here smothering your children in kisses?"

Winking at his wife while grinning, Clay asks, "Chris? Teri? Would you like to ride into town with me? You never know what handsome guy we might run into."

"Teri, why don't you go with Dad, and I'll stay here and help Mom with whatever it is she's cooking that smells so good."

"Okay. Dad, I'll ride along. Just point out the good-looking guys in case I miss one."

Laughing, they walk toward the front door teasing each other. As they leave, Margaret is stirring her famous stew meat in the cast-iron skillet that's sizzling on the stove. An apple pie is in the oven, and the aroma fills the kitchen.

"Mom, can I help you with anything?"

"No, sweetheart. I think most everything is done."

"Don't you want these veggies cut up?"

"Oh dear! I was so excited about you girls coming home that I completely forgot about them. Would you mind?"

"Happy to do it."

Leaning against the kitchen cabinet, Chris feels right at home with the aroma of meat sizzling, a pie baking, and Mom in her apron. Clay and Margaret agreed from the onset of their marriage that Margaret would be a stay-at-home mom. She has never regretted being home for her children as they grew up. Baking, chasing them around the yard, playing games with them, reading stories to them before they go to sleep, and listening to their prayers have been blessings she never dreamed possible.

As Chris leans against the counter, watching her mother, she thinks, *That little bit of gray showing in her hair doesn't age her a bit. She's still as slender and active as she was when I was growing up.* She smiled. *As ornery as we were, I don't remember her or Dad ever yelling at us or spanking us.* She laughed out loud. *I can't remember her cooking without an apron. I don't think she'd know how!*

Smiling as she turns from the stove, Mom says, "Chris, a penny for your thoughts."

Startled, Chris hasn't realized she was so deep in thought, and feeling a little guilty, she quickly picks up the knife. "I was just thinking how good it is to be home and how much I love you."

"I love you too, honey. Now the veggies?"

Margaret turned back to the stove. "Dad and Teri will be back soon. We need to add those to the meat. The meat is finished cooking, and everything will be ready as soon as those are done."

Finished slicing the vegetables, Chris says, "Is there anything else I can do, Mom?"

"I don't think so. You're probably tired from the drive. Why don't you go lay down. I'll call you when dinner is ready."

"Are you sure? I can set the table if you'd like."

"No, honey, you go rest."

"What time do you think dinner will be ready?"

"Oh, in an hour or so."

"Okay, if you're sure there's nothing else I can help with. I have some briefs I need to work on. I have a trial next week. Call me if you need some help," Chris answers as she steps out of the kitchen.

"I will. Go work on your briefs." Margaret says, removing the pie from the oven.

Now thirty years old, Chris has always wanted to be an attorney, and after getting her law degree, she is now a prosecuting attorney in Atlanta. She's tall like her father, five feet ten inches, and slender, with flowing brown hair reaching just past her shoulders. She is highly respected in her field and has a heart for victims of crime. When she enters a courtroom, she has full confidence she'll win the case. Some have said, "Don't mess with Chris. She'll eat you alive."

Many have told her she takes after her father. Clay is six feet two inches tall with dark hair and sparkling brown eyes. He's quite ambitious, and being the CEO of a large company in Atlanta hasn't dampened his lust for life. His motto is: "Live for the Lord but have fun doing it." He and Chris alike have quick smiles and a sense of humor everyone enjoys. Chris is just as ambitious and, like her father, has an air of authority. When Clay enters the conference room, others sit up straight. When Chris enters a courtroom, even the judge takes notice.

Teri, on the other hand, is more like her mother. She isn't as tall as Chris but only by a couple of inches. Like her father, though, her favorite sport is tennis, and it has kept her slender and tanned. She and her father love to square off on the tennis court. Her stylish, short brown hair enhances her tanned face.

Teri has a gentle spirit. She's soft-spoken, and her heart is for children, just like her mother. She's just finishing up her master's degree in sociology at Emory University and will graduate this month. When her friends tease her and tell her she'll be an old maid, she merely smiles. "If the Lord wants me to marry, He'll bring the right man into my life. For now I'm quite content being single, and besides, first thing's first. Graduation is on the top of the list."

Chris climbs the stairs that lead to the second floor where the bedrooms are and enters her room. This has been her bedroom since childhood. The childhood curtains with the *Cinderella* print have been replaced with floor-length drapes; large red hibiscus and green leaves scattered in a unique design bring an air of the tropics to the room. Sheer curtains rustle slightly against the open window. The bed has a matching comforter with throw pillows piled against the headboard. It too has been replaced. The small twin-size bed is now a queen. The childhood dresser and chest of drawers are gone.

Chris stands, for a moment, looking at the copy of her law degree, a framed newspaper article announcing her win in a well-publicized criminal case hangs beside a portrait of her family. Grandma smiles brightly from the gold filigreed framed portrait on her dresser. Chris stretches out on her bed and leaning back on the pillows, she allows herself to reminisce about her growing up years. *I love this house. Mom and Dad did a beautiful job fixing it up. I wish Grandma could see it now.*

Kicking her shoes off and stretching her long legs across the bed, she smiles to herself, remembering how she and Teri would fight over who gets to ride the bicycle first. *Dad had to buy one for Teri just to keep us from fighting and that old tire swing is now gone. Dad said he wouldn't replace it; it's too dangerous. Oh, how we cried!*

Chris shifts slightly as she places her arms behind her head and crosses her legs at the ankles. *Dad always wrapped us in his arms as soon as he walked through the door. He always said he couldn't love just one, so he'd grab us both as he knelt down, plastering kisses on our cheeks.*

Clay never kissed the same child first. He would alternate each time when entering his home. He wanted no feelings of, "He loves her more." Chris didn't know that's why he did that until many years later when he told her, "God doesn't love one more than the other, and neither do I."

Snuggling down into her pillows, her eyes begin to droop. Soon she is fast asleep and doesn't hear her father and sister in the kitchen teasing her mother.

"Chris, dinner is ready." Margaret shouts.

I must have really slept! Chris thinks as she slowly rolls to the edge of the bed.

"Chris? Dinner's ready. Come on down, honey, before everything gets cold."

"I'm coming, Mom. I'll be there in just a second."

With a large yawn and rubbing her eyes, Chris slips her feet into her loafers and heads for the dining room.

A beautiful cherry table with eight straight-back chairs sits comfortably in the center of the large dining room. A china cabinet stands tall, against one wall, filled with the china Clay gave Margaret as a wedding gift. Family photos are framed and hung above the buffet, the girls in swimsuits, dad holding Teri precariously on the back of a pony, a wedding photo of Margaret and Clay, Grandma sitting on the front porch, Clay's parents standing beside a 1938 Ford, Margaret's parents peeking around the big oak tree. A wall filled with memories.

"Honey, this looks absolutely wonderful. It sure smells good, and I'm hungry as a horse." Clay says as he sits down at the table.

Each taking their place, it goes without saying that a blessing will be offered for the abundance of food and gratitude for having it as well as each other. Reaching for each other's hands, a circle is made that represents their never-ending love of God and each other.

Clay, taking another refill of stew, "Teri, will you pass the cornbread, please?"

As Chris cuts through a piece of meat, "Dad, how is that big contract you've been working on going?"

"It's going well. We should have it closed sometime in the next week or so. What about that trial you have coming up? Are you going to nail the bad guy?"

Chris smiles. "You bet I am, Dad! With me prosecuting, that guy doesn't have a snowballs chance."

Rising early the next morning, everyone is excited about the day. Today is the celebration of a marriage made in heaven. "Mom, are we going to have balloons and all of that?" Teri asks, feigning ignorance.

"Teri, if that's what you girls want, then that's what we'll have."

Clay walks into the room. The excitement is palpable. "Did I hear balloons?"

"Yes, Dad. You heard balloons and a bunch of other stuff, too."

Both girls grin as Clay takes Margaret in his arms and dances her around the living room floor singing "Everything is Beautiful."

Chris, standing on a ladder, laughs. "Okay, you two lovebirds. It's time you leave everything up to us. Go! Go!"

Twirling Margaret under his arm, they two step out of the living room and out to the car. The girls have ordered them out of the house until six o'clock while they do the decorating. They knew long before this day what the decorations, meal, guests, and music would be. They spent many hours planning it together. Invitations were sent to neighbors, church members, friends, family, and colleagues. Jeffery Coleman, "Chef Jeff," has been called to prepare a special meal. The photographer is lined up, champagne is ordered, a very large sheet cake is ordered, and the music has been taken care of.

Chris and Teri decided to play a joke on their mother and father. While everyone is to be served roast duck with wild rice, grilled baby heirloom vegetables, and an Asian pear and prosciutto salad with a citrus vinaigrette, their mother and father will be served a hamburger, French fries, and a Coke each.

Clay had told them many times that when they married, all they could afford was a hamburger, French fries, and a Coke. They had lived on those for so long that they almost hated to even smell a hamburger or French fries. The Coke they could still tolerate. Of course they would join the others, after a good laugh, in the succulent meal.

A small band has agreed to play some of the songs that were popular when Clay and Margaret took their vows: "Walk like an Egyptian"; "In the Still of the Night"; and "Hit the Road Jack." Chris and Teri have figured it all out to a T, and the night will be closed with Margaret and Clay's favorite two songs of that era, "Every Time You Go Away" and "Lean on Me."

"Chris, how many from church do we have that are going to help set up?"

"Ten men are bringing chairs and those nice round tables in the food court, and from what Mrs. Kindle said, there's a bunch of women that are coming to decorate them. I'm not even sure how many. She just said, 'Leave it to us.'"

"Who's going to set up the back patio for the band?"

"Teri, it's all been coordinated. Please don't worry. The soundman from church is doing all of that. He's contacted the band to see exactly what they need."

"I'm not really worried. I just want this to be so special and perfect for Mom and Dad."

"I know. I do, too."

The lawns have been mowed and trimmed to perfection. The flowers, dogwoods, and azaleas are still in bloom, which gives an even lovelier touch to their outdoor celebration. The tables will be strategically set, leaving an area for dancing.

Several pickup trucks pull up to the edge of the lawn filled with tables and chairs. "Hey, Chris, where do you want these?"

"Frank, I didn't know we had *that* many tables and chairs in the whole church! We'll be positioning them in a little while, so why don't you bring them all over here?"

"Okay, but we're going to help you place them wherever you want them."

"Thank you. You're an angel sent from God."

Before the men have unloaded ten tables, three minivans pull up, and like small circus cars with clowns filing out, women begin emerging, including Mrs. Kindle, Bertha, Mary, Lou Ann, and several others.

"Hi, Chris. Hi, Teri. We're all here to set the tables for you," Mrs. Kindle shouts.

"Oh my gosh. Chris, did you know *that* many were coming?" Teri exclaims.

"No, but we can sure use them."

With all the women bustling around with their assigned jobs, the air is filled with excitement. The men are working quickly to unload the pickups and set tables where specified.

Mrs. Kindle seems to be the table coordinator, "Joe,

put that table over here. Frank, that one should go over there. No, Mark, it needs to be closer."

Chris and Teri watch for a few minutes and, smiling, they have to walk away, or they'll burst out laughing. Mrs. Kindle is taking her assumed job quite seriously.

"Mrs. Kindle certainly has her job cut out." Chris says as Teri covers her mouth and giggles.

As the afternoon wears on, the large, round tables that seat eight people have been covered with violet satin tablecloths. Candles are centered with champagne glasses ready for each guest at the table. Soft lights have been strung; the patio is ready for the band. Looking around at everything that has been done, Teri and Chris are amazed.

"Oh, Chris, everything is so beautiful." Teri states with tears welling up in her eyes. "Yes, it is. Now don't start me blubbering before it even starts!"

. . . .

Chef Jeff is bustling around the kitchen, finishing up the last-minute preparations before the servers arrive to serve the meals. That was another small task that needed to be handled. Ten of the church's teenaged girls offered to be servers. Chris and Teri insisted they pay them.

"We don't need to be paid, Miss Chris."

"You have school expenses, and I know you want extra spending money. We *will* pay you, but we expect you to be gracious hosts."

The girls all gather around Chris and Teri. "What are we supposed to wear?"

Chris shrugs. "Oh gee, I didn't think of that."

The girls look to Teri, waiting for an answer. "Ladies, and you are ladies, why not wear a pretty sundress if you have one? It's going to be warm."

Smiling, the girls all agree and, giggling, walk away acting quite important for being part of the festivities.

Margaret and Clay are absolutely flabbergasted when they return from their day in Atlanta. Margaret can't hold the tears back. "Oh, Clay! Look at what our children have done. It's absolutely *beautiful!*"

Turning his head slightly, Clay fights back a tear. "This is so much like our daughters, Margaret. It *is* beautiful! Come on. We better start getting dressed."

Meeting them at the door, Chris ushers them toward the stairs before they can see what is being done in the kitchen.

"You just need to get dressed, Mom. Everything is under control."

"Honey, I just want to see what they're cooking."

"No, Mother! It's all a surprise. Now go join Dad and get all pretty."

Saluting her daughter like a marine sergeant, Margaret climbs the stairs, trying very hard not to sneak back down when the girls aren't looking. *All I want to do is take a peek.*

Guests begin arriving, and thank goodness there are twenty-five acres to handle all the vehicles. Margaret had no idea there would be so many people to help them celebrate. Shocked, she sees car after car parking in the open field.

"Teri, how many did you girls invite?"

"Oh, just a few, Mom. Two hundred."

"Teri, we don't *know* that many people!"

Laughing, Teri goes to find Chris as Margaret continues to greet their guests. Margaret and Clay make a point of visiting with as many guests as they possibly can. "I didn't know we knew this many people. Where in the world did Chris and Teri find them?" Margaret whispers to Clay.

Laughing, "Honey, I don't know, but we know most of them."

Turning and reaching out his hand, Clay sees an old friend. "Hello, Ralph, it's good to see you. How's the new company coming along?"

As the guests mingle, the servers are passing through the crowd, offering hors d'oeuvres. Since wine is being offered, the high-school girls cannot serve it due to being underage. Teri and Chris realized this and hired ten college seniors to carry the serving trays with glasses of wine.

With the soft music, the warm weather, and guests all over the place, Clay and Margaret feel like they've been crowned king and queen. Chris and Teri are making sure everything is going as planned yet have time to mingle with friends and family. Walking up to Chris and after waiting for her conversation to end, Teri pulls Chris aside.

"They just delivered the cake. Chris, you should see it! It's *huge* and beautiful. It has white icing with 'Congratulations, Margaret and Clay' and a thirtieth anniversary decoration in the center."

"I know, Teri. I ordered it, remember? Where did they put it?"

Glancing around quickly as though she's a secret agent, with her hand cupped to one side of her mouth so no-one can read her lips, she whispers, "It's on the dining room table. We can't let anyone go to that side of the house, or they'll see it."

Chris can't help it; she bursts out laughing. "Teri, you are such a drama queen!"

"I am not!"

Clay's brother, Richard, reaches for the microphone and gently taps it to make sure it's on. "Ladies and gentleman, welcome to our celebration. If you will take a seat, we'll be serving dinner soon. Thank you."

As the guests are finding their way to seats, the band suddenly begins playing, "Walk like an Egyptian," and the crowd bursts into laughter. Margaret stops in her tracks with a shocked look on her face.

"Clay, did you know they were going to play that?"

Laughing so hard tears come to his eyes, "Honey, I had no idea, but I love it!"

The music continues on a softer note as the servers prepare to start serving, and the college students pour champagne to all the guests. Clay and Margaret are seated in front of the musicians and are the focal point of the evening. When it appears everyone has champagne, Richard steps up to the microphone to offer a toast to the happy couple.

Lightly tapping his champagne glass to get everyone's attention, "Ladies and gentlemen, I would like to offer a toast to my brother and his beautiful wife. Clay, what in the world did you do to deserve her?"

Laughter ripples through the audience.

"I remember when Clay was in high school, and when he met Margaret, he fell head over heels. We teased him mercilessly and told him there were more fish in the sea. He's stubborn, and here they are, thirty years later. My best to you both, and may you have another thirty years."

"Hear, hear," is spoken throughout by the guests as glasses are clinked together.

Two of the high-school girls, Sherry and Candice, come forward, each carrying a large covered serving platter. As they stop at Clay and Margaret's table, Richard takes the microphone again. Signaling Pastor Mike to come forward, "Pastor Mike, would you say a *quick* blessing over the food?"

"Lord, we thank you for this auspicious day of celebration," Pastor Mike begins. "We thank you for all the wonderful guests that have come to celebrate Margaret and Clay's thirtieth wedding anniversary. What a wonderful couple and we're so thankful for their marriage filled with love. We ask that you bless every person here and fill their hearts with your love. Thank you for this wonderful gathering on such a beautiful day. Thank you for allowing us to partake in your glorious presence."

Peeking out from his closed eyes at the pastor, Richard clears his throat.

Quickly, he continues, "Lord, we thank you for this

wonderful food and ask that you bless it as we partake of it and for the nourishment of our bodies. In Jesus's name. Amen."

"Thank you, Pastor Mike, and now, ladies and gentlemen, in honor of Clay and Margaret and their special night, we have a very special meal prepared just for them."

The crowd cranes their necks to see, and all eyes are on Clay, Margaret, and the two high-school girls. The band plays a soft drumroll, and with a flourish that Teri taught them, the girls uncover the meal and set one paper plate filled with a hamburger, French fries, and a packet of catsup before each one. They then set a glass of Coke beside their plates. Clay is roaring with laughter, and Margaret is stunned and silent.

Richard knew ahead of time what was going to take place, so he held on to the microphone. He announces to the guests, "In honor of the old days," and tells the guests what is on the paper plates and why they've been served hamburgers. The band quickly starts playing, "Hit the Road Jack," and everyone is howling with laughter. Margaret has come out of shock and is laughing along with everyone else. Clay can't seem to stop laughing and reaches for a napkin to dry his eyes. Chris and Teri can't give each other enough high fives as they laugh and cheer with the others. Clay, finally able to control his laughter, picks up his hamburger and feeds a bite to Margaret.

As the guests are eating, servers gather in the dining room to eat their share of the fine food while keeping an eye out for Teri to signal to them that it's time to clear dishes. The girls clear the dishes as the young men serve coffee. As dishes are cleared and the guests continue to visit, the large cake is rolled out and set before Clay and Margaret. The photographer, with one camera hanging on a strap around his neck and another in his hand, has been running from one position to the next taking pictures. Kneeling on one knee, he aims his camera as Clay and Margaret stand before the cake, holding a knife just as they did at their wedding, ready to cut the first slice. Slicing the cake together, the photographer snaps a close-up of them kissing while Margaret holds the first piece on a plate in one hand and Clay holds a champagne glass with bubbling champagne.

The teenage servers are busy passing out cake, and coffee is offered as the festivities continue. The band is playing "In the Still of the Night," and soon some of the guests begin dancing. The mood has changed, and several couples join in as the band continues to play softly. Clay takes Margaret's hand and valiantly bows. "May I have this dance, you beautiful specimen of womanhood?"

"Of course, my knight in shining armor."

It's almost midnight, and couples are still dancing, but the revelry has toned down considerably. The servers are now standing back, watching the elders dance.

Yawning, Charlotte asks, "Judy? Are we *ever* going to get to go home? I'm bushed!"

Judy yawns. "I didn't realize it would be *this* much work when we said we'd help."

Chris walks up to the group of girls, smiling. "I'll bet you ladies want to pack it in." Chris hands each one an envelope with their name on it. "Thank you so much for all your help. You were all wonderful. We really appreciate it."

Each girl can't help herself and opens the envelope she's been handed. Gasps rise from the group.

"Miss Chris! We *never* expected *this* much!"

"Charlotte, you ladies have worked very hard tonight and deserve every penny. Now take your stash, and go home and get some rest. Church is tomorrow, and I hope to see each one of you there."

Turning to the group of college students, she hands each his envelope and thanks them profusely as she points to the envelopes. "No partying with that now!"

Laughing, the boys walk away, headed back to their cars to return to their dorms.

The band begins to play "Every Time You Go Away," and the dancers instinctively move aside, leaving Clay and Margaret dancing together alone on the plush, now trampled lawn. Chris and Teri are standing on the sidelines with tears streaming down their cheeks. Chris turns to Teri, taking hold of her hand. "Now I can blubber!"

The song changes, and tears and misty eyes are seen throughout the bystanders. As "Lean on Me" is softly played, even Candy, the singer, has tears in her eyes. Clay and Margaret are in their own private world as each step is taken to the music. When the song ends, the crowd bursts into applause.

When the last car pulls away, Clay looks at his watch and, loosening his tie, gives a large sigh. Looking at Margaret, he can see she's happy and exhausted. "Honey, it's after midnight. We better go in."

Chris and Teri walk up to them and give each a hug.

"I love you, Mom."

"I love you, Dad."

Together, Clay and Margaret look into their daughters' eyes. "We love you, too."

"Thank you for all of this. It has been more than wonderful." Clay says as he hugs each daughter.

Margaret swipes at a tear as she thanks her daughters and states. "Okay, you girls, we have cleaning up to do!"

Clay spins to face her. "You don't mean it! We can do all this tomorrow after church."

Chris and Teri grin. Chris moves beside her father and takes hold of his hand. Teri moves to Mom's side and takes her by the hand, and they begin pulling them forward toward the house. Margaret stops suddenly.

"Girls, we can't just leave all this out here!"

Chris laughs and Teri snickers. "Mom, we've got it covered."

"Chris, what do you mean, you've 'got it covered'?"

"Mom, go to bed. A cleaning crew is coming at six tomorrow morning. By the time you get up, you'll never know there's been a party."

Clay claps his hands, says "Hallelujah!" and quickly hugs Chris.

Margaret hasn't budged an inch.

"But—"

Teri cuts her off, "Go to bed, you two! We'll see you in the morning."

Chapter 2

Entering the Fulton County courthouse and passing through the security checkpoint, Chris walks with purpose and confidence. Her silky brown hair has been trimmed and styled. Her white blouse is neatly tucked into her knee-length, soft blue skirt. Her dark-blue fashionable jacket sets off the entire ensemble. Her black high heels clicking on the marble floor echo throughout the long hallway leading to courtroom number seven.

Opening the door, she sees the defense attorney, Mr. Doe, sitting at his table. His table is to the left of hers across the narrow aisle. People have already started wandering in and taking seats. Stepping around the corner of her table, her smile is genuine as she nods in Mr. Doe's direction. She already knows she'll win. Without a doubt in her mind, she sets her briefcase gently on the table.

Mr. Doe looks over at Chris; his face contorts into a sneer. Looking away, he opens his briefcase and places papers in front of him. He's never liked Chris and knows full well he has an adversary that won't back down and has lost very few cases. Chris looks up as the defendant is being brought into the courtroom from a side door.

Shuffling between two Fulton County deputy sheriffs, with shackles and handcuffs tightly in place, he grins as though those in the courtroom will stand and cheer.

Looking gaunt, his shaggy hair and unshaven face make him appear much older than his thirty-four years. The orange jumpsuit, with "Fulton County Corrections" imprinted on the back in large black letters, sags on his body. Normally the shackles and handcuffs would be removed while in court, but not with this killer!

A smirk crosses his face as he looks at Chris. His eyes roam ever so slowly up and down the full length of her body as though he can see right through her clothes. Mr. Doe grabs him by the arm and pulls him down onto the chair next to him. Chris is used to this disgusting display from hardened criminals. It doesn't bother her. If she has anything to say about it, he'll get the death penalty.

Taking her seat behind the prosecuting attorney's table, she begins laying out papers before her. More spectators have gathered in the courtroom and crane their necks to get a better look at the defendant.

Whispers are heard, "Do you think he really did it?"

"I just can't imagine someone doing those horrible things to another human being."

"I hope they nail his butt to the wall!"

"From what I've read, the death penalty is what he deserves!"

A long, polished wooden railing separates the spectators from the attorneys. Directly behind Chris, the family members of the victim sit in the front row: mother, with hanky waded in her hand and father, with his arm around his wife offering support, and a sister whose tears are already flowing.

The courtroom is shoulder to shoulder with spectators. This has been a highly publicized murder. The media has had a heyday with it, and it took just under two months to finally find an unbiased jury after an appeal to move the trial elsewhere was denied. Because of the magnitude of this case, the largest courtroom is chosen. Any time a high-profile case comes to court, it always attracts a crowd, including dozens of reporters.

A deputy sheriff, dressed in his starched and ironed brown uniform, approaches the judge's bench. Displayed on the wall behind it, "In God We Trust" hangs prominently. On the left, in the corner, stands a freestanding pole with the American flag. On the right in the corner is the Georgia state flag.

The deputy looks out over the filled benches and attentive faces. "All rise."

A rustle fills the courtroom as everyone stands.

"Hear ye, hear ye, the Honorable Judge Nelson presiding."

Judge Nelson enters with his long black robes flowing about him. The courtroom is silent as he steps up, taking his seat behind the large mahogany bench. "Be seated," the deputy instructs. As the people take their seats, the deputy walks away from the bench, joining three other deputies standing near the wall; their badges and guns are obvious to those who look.

Judge Nelson is an imposing man with gray hair. His face is a story of the pain, suffering, and horrors he has heard over the thirty years he has presided over the many cases that have come before him. His reputation is as one of the toughest judges in Fulton County. He runs a strict courtroom and will take no nonsense from the attorneys. Picking up the large cherry-wood gavel, he slams it down. "This court is now in session. Bring in the jury."

One by one, men and women from all walks of life file into the jury box. A retired teacher, a carpenter, a plumber, a doctor, and a homemaker are among the twelve peers who will decide this man's future. Both attorneys are watching closely as the jury files in and takes their seats. So are the spectators. Taking their seats, none have so much as glanced at the defendant. Judge Nelson waits patiently as they seat themselves.

Chris stands. "Your Honor, may I approach the bench?"

"Yes, come forward."

Someone in the crowd whispers, "Oh, this is going to be good. They haven't even started yet!"

A "shhh" is heard from someone nearby. Mr. Doe quickly leans over and whispers something in his client's ear then stands and follows Chris to the judge's bench.

Judge Nelson, placing his hand over the microphone before him, leaning forward, "Isn't this a little early, Ms. Wilson?"

"Yes, it is, Your Honor, but I think it is of the utmost importance before this trial starts."

Judge Nelson gives Chris a stern look. "Really!"

"Yes, Your Honor."

Mr. Doe stands with his hands lightly holding the

edge of the bench, looking at Chris. Glancing at Mr. Doe, Chris continues. "Your Honor, Mr. Doe's client has taken a life in the most brutal and heinous possible way." Pointing to her opponent, "It has come to my attention that Mr. Doe was not only aware of the murder but was a part of it!"

Mr. Doe, shocked, "Your Honor! That's outrageous!"

Judge Nelson glares at the two standing before him. "Silence! In my chambers! Now!"

Both counselors follow Judge Nelson into his chambers, and he throws off his robe.

"Your Honor!" Mr. Doe shouts.

The judge glares across his desk. "Mr. Doe, quiet!" He then turns to Chris and glares at her also. "Ms. Wilson, is there any evidence you can produce to back up this accusation, which, by the way, is extremely serious? I hope you know that and are aware of the consequences if it is proven to be untrue!"

Chris stands silently. The judge's warning does not detour her. "Your Honor, I am very aware of the consequences and, yes, I have absolute proof that Mr. Doe and his client were in this together!"

Flinging his arms wildly and shouting, "You're crazy, Chris! I have no idea what you're talking about, and I am highly insulted by your crazy accusation! I am respected in this town and have a very good reputation, and—"

"Mr. Doe, calm down! We are quite aware of your *reputation!*" Judge Nelson says as he turns his attention back to Chris. "You better have very solid evidence, or you'll be selling hot dogs at a Braves game! You have until nine o'clock Tuesday morning to have it on my desk! This better not be an underhanded tactic to gain more time! Doe, I want you here at ten! Now get back in there!"

Chris and Mr. Doe exchange looks as they leave the judge's chambers and reenter the courtroom. After taking their seats at their respective tables, Mr. Doe glares daggers at her. He then turns to his client and whispers something in his ear. Judge Nelson has donned his robe, and he enters the courtroom, taking his seat behind the large bench; his eyes are flashing. "We will resume Tuesday morning after the Memorial Day weekend at eleven o'clock sharp! You are not to discuss this trial with anyone or within yourselves!" He states to the jury. "Court dismissed!" Slamming the gavel onto the bench top, he angrily leaves the courtroom.

The reporters storm the doors. As the rest of the people leave, the chatter is almost deafening.

"Can you believe that? I wonder what *that* was all about!"

"I like that prosecutor. She's one to be reckoned with!"

"That defense attorney didn't look any too happy."

Chris gathers her papers, ignoring the comments, and lays them neatly in her briefcase.

Her opponent isn't as calm. As soon as his client has been removed from the room, he slams his briefcase shut with papers sticking out the sides. Taking a step across the narrow aisle, he jams his index finger close to her face. "That's about as low as anyone can go! You have no idea who you're dealing with, and you'll not get away with this!" His face is contorted with anger, but Chris smiles, undaunted.

"Really? Are you threatening me? If you are, that's only more proof of your guilt."

Turning on her heels, she calmly walks down the short aisle and steps through the large double doors without so much as a glance back.

• • • • • • • • • • • •

With the long weekend ahead of her, Chris plans to work diligently on the trial preparations. She is determined more than ever to prove, without a shadow of a doubt, Mr. Doe and his client were partners in this crime. At home in her apartment, her kitchen table is littered with papers she's been going through and studying. Pretrial hearings, witness reports she's gathered from the police investigation, eight by ten glossy pictures, one videotape taken during a statement of her key witness, and of course a taped conversation of Mr. Doe and his client planning the murder are scattered about her table.

Holding the recorder with its damning evidence in front her, *This will prove it if nothing else will.*

Laying the recorder aside and shuffling through the stack of papers, she pushes the pictures to the side, finding what she's looking for: the videotape. Chris takes her glass of tea and gets comfortable on the couch as she picks up the remote control, clicking the *play* button. The large-screen television lights up with a scene of an interrogation room.

The room is small; the walls need fresh paint; and

the table could use replacing. Detective Gordon has spoken to Chris and wants this guy behind bars as much as Chris does. There have been many people he has interviewed, but this one he wants on a videotape. He's had "gut feelings" about her from the first. Sitting across from the witness at the worn-out table, he has explained her statement will be recorded and is ready to begin.

"Now, Ms. Dawson, just tell me everything you saw."

"I saw Mr. Doe and that man, I don't know his name, but I've seen them together several times." She begins.

The detective remains silent.

"Mr. Doe handed the man a big gun and said, 'Don't miss!'"

Chris is intently listening. *That part doesn't prove anything, and how does she know Mr. Doe's name? Where has she seen them together?*

"Then the man took the gun and checked to see if it was loaded. They walked over to Mr. Doe's car, at least I think it was his. He was driving when they were leaving."

Chris pushes the *pause* button as she stands and walks to the sliding glass doors that lead out to the sixth-floor balcony that overlooks downtown Atlanta. *Where were they when this took place, and where was she to witness all of this? I think I need to call Frank.*

Walking past the matching couch and love seat, the designer end tables and fifty-gallon aquarium with her favorite colorful saltwater fish, she enters the kitchen for a snack.

Picking up her cordless phone and dialing, she says, "Frank, Chris here. How are you?" Listening for a second, she answers, "I know its Memorial Day weekend, but this is important." Sitting down on the couch, she says, "I know, I know, but you are my very special investigator, and I really would appreciate you sacrificing part of your weekend plans to help me out." She moves to the edge of the couch. "You know me too well. Frank, there's a woman who claims to have actually witnessed the murder." Standing up and slowly walking back and forth, Chris explains what she needs. Hanging up while pacing back and forth in front of the television, with it still on pause, her phone rings.

"Hello. Hi, Dad." Walking over to her aquarium, she leans over to gaze at her fish. "Oh my gosh! I forgot all about our luncheon date." Glancing at the clock, she says, "I'll be there in fifteen minutes. Yes, I remember which one." Hanging up, she grabs the remote control, clicks off, and the television goes dark.

· · · · · · · · · · · ·

Entering the oriental restaurant, she has always enjoyed watching the chefs standing in their pits, flipping shrimp or vegetables as the customer sits on floor-level cushions in front of the pit, smiling and cheering him on. The oriental décor and calming atmosphere is, to her, not only enjoyable, but relaxing. Seeing her father across the room sitting at a table, instead of on the floor-level cushions, she waves and walks to him.

Leaning over, she gives him a quick kiss on the cheek and takes her seat across from him. "I'm sorry I forgot. I really have a lot on my mind with this trial. Forgive me?"

"Of course I forgive you."

Ordering their meal and pouring the hot tea from the decorative teapot, Chris can tell there's something bothering her father.

"Are you okay, Dad?"

"Yes, honey, but I'm concerned about you."

"You're talking about the trial, aren't you?"

"Yes."

"What about it?"

"Chris, I have some concerns. I've heard some things about that attorney, Doe."

"Like what?"

"I don't know if any of this is true, but rumor has it that he's quite shady."

"In what way?"

"I've heard he's connected in some way with the mob. Now like I said, I don't know if any of this is true."

"I haven't heard anything like that, but I'll get Frank to check it out."

Clay hesitates before continuing. "I'd like for you to recuse yourself from this case."

"Recuse myself! There's no reason, no ground for me to do that. No way, Dad! This guy, if anyone, deserves the chair. That poor family needs justice, and I'm just the one to give it to them so they can move on."

The server arrives with their plate of grilled shrimp and vegetables. Giving each their meal, "Do you need anything else?"

Chris smiles. "No, thank you. This is fine."

Taking each other's hands across the table, Clay says

a quick blessing over the food. For the first few minutes, there's an awkward silence between them. Each is hesitant to bring up the subject again.

"How's Mom?" Chris finally asks.

"She's fine. Please don't change the subject, Chris. I'm really concerned for you. You just don't know what these people can or will do."

On the drive through Atlanta to the restaurant, Clay already knew what Chris's answer would be. *Maybe I shouldn't say anything. No, darn it! I'm her father, and I'm concerned for her safety.*

"Dad, I'm sorry. I just can't do that. I didn't mean to jump down your throat, but these people need closure, and he needs to be off the streets."

"Chris, I love you very much, and I couldn't stand it if something happened to you."

"Dad, please don't worry. I'll be fine. I have to go. I have a lot to do before Tuesday. Tell Mom hello. I love you."

· · · · · · · · · · · · ·

Returning to her apartment, Chris is deep in thought, not just about what her father said, but some of the statements witnesses for the prosecution have given. Kicking off her shoes, sitting back down on the couch, she clicks the *on* button on the television then the *play* button. Ms. Dawson's face reappears.

"I knew something bad was going to happen, so I got in my old clunker and followed them, just like I've seen them do on TV. You know, staying back far enough so they can't see you and all that."

Detective Gordon places his big bear claw-sized hands on the table. "Go on," he says.

"Well, at the Shell station about a mile or so down the road, they pulled in behind the gas station and got into a black van."

Chris leans a little closer to the TV. *"Where was she that they didn't see her?"*

Ms. Dawson wrings her hands. "When they pulled out from behind the gas station, Mr. Doe was driving. I kept following them, being *very* careful so they wouldn't see me."

Having been a bit nervous in the beginning, she is now warming up to her story and smiles at the detective. Detective Gordon shifts in his seat, crossing his legs.

"What happened then?" the detective asks.

"I saw them pull over to the curb and grab this man and shove him into the van. Boy, was he fighting! Then they sped off, and I just kept following them almost to Palmetto! They pulled into some old warehouse out in an open-field kind of place."

Detective Gordon leans forward. "Was it dark?"

"Oh, no, sir! It was almost dark but not dark yet."

"Did they have their headlights on?"

"Yes."

"Did you?"

"Oh, no! They show on TV to turn them off so they can't see you!"

Pressing the *pause* button, Chris jumps up and runs to the table. Flipping through the glossy pictures, she sees the one with the warehouse. Picking it up, she studies it closely. A small, dilapidated warehouse, with weeds and grass growing at its base, sits in an open area. A chain-link fence is bent and tipped over and surrounds the warehouse. Its posts are pulled partway out of the ground, and a rusted No Trespassing sign hangs from one hook. The fence gate has been torn off and is nowhere to be seen. *I wonder how they knew about this place?* In the distance, trees are scattered behind the warehouse. *Not close enough for someone to hide in and see what's going on.* Laying the picture back on the stack, *That is so wide open. Where was she that they couldn't see her?*

Walking back out onto the balcony deep in thought, Chris hardly notices the street sounds floating up. She'd rather be living in the country like her mother and father, but it's necessary for her to be close to her office and the courthouse. Returning to the table, she picks up another picture. Looking at it, she lays it back down and walks back to the couch. Pressing the *play* button, Ms. Dawson continues.

"It wasn't real dark yet, so I could see everything they were doing to that poor man! It was horrible! I just wanted to get out of there as fast as I could." She picks up the glass of water the detective previously gave her and takes a sip then continues, "I ran back to my car and high-tailed it out of there just as fast as I could. I went home and couldn't stop shaking for two days. Y'all don't know how scared I was! I didn't tell anyone because I was afraid it would get back to the killers, and they'd come after me."

Chris looks at the clock. *It's almost eight o'clock. I need to get through this and move on to others.* She continues watching the video.

"I keep picturing it all in my head, you know. I can't shut it out. The first thing they did was drag the man out of the van. He was gagged, and his hands were tied. Then they—" Feeling sick to her stomach at what she's hearing, Chris presses the *mute* button for a second.

After watching the rest of the woman's statement, Chris turns the TV off with tears in her eyes. Bowing her head, "Lord, help me to bring these two to justice. They don't deserve your mercy! Neither do we, but please help me to convict them and give his family closure. These two don't need to be out killing other people. You know that. Please help me, Lord. Amen."

Wiping her tears, she wearily leaves the couch and walks to the phone and dials Frank's number. "Frank, it's me again. I've been watching this video with Ms. Dawson's statement, and something just doesn't add up. Will you check it out? I can't figure out how she was able not to be seen." Continuing on, "I just don't trust this woman, and I think she's lying. See what you can find out about her, please."

The entire weekend, Chris and Frank are burning the midnight oil. She is studying witness statements and looking for any inconsistencies; Frank is out gathering as much evidence as he can. Over and over, Chris listens to the incriminating tape, taking notes after notes. The video of her key witness is watched over and over and over. Chris writes down her impressions of Ms. Dawson's body language: how her eyes won't meet the detectives at certain areas of her story, the wringing of her hands, and the inappropriate smiles.

Several phone calls go back and forth between Chris and Frank, and many meeting of the minds are done in her apartment. Neither has slept more than a couple of hours a day during this whole process, and fast-food sacks and cups litter the kitchen counter. The coffeepot has burnt coffee in the bottom, and still they continue laying out what has been found. Monday afternoon, both are worn to the bone.

Chris is searching through more pictures and, without looking up, she asks, "Frank, do you know where the picture is of the van they drove?" He doesn't answer. She hears soft snoring. Frank is asleep in the recliner. She hates to wake him up but thinks, *If I don't wake him up, he'll have a sore back.* "Frank, wake up. I think we have enough to nail them for life. Go home and get some sleep."

"Yeah, and you do the same." Frank says through a yawn. Walking toward the door, he grabs his jacket off the sofa corner. Reaching for the door handle, he turns to look at Chris. "Chris, you're one heck of an attorney! Once you get your teeth into something, you don't let go or back down. I hope I never have to come against you if I ever get in trouble."

Chris covers her yawn with her hand. "Thanks, Frank. Now get out of here."

Gathering up the pictures and a small Ziploc bag that contains more evidence and the tape recording, Chris pulls on her tan jacket. Straightening the collar as she checks her appearance in the mirror, *Hmm, this does look nice with my new brown skirt.* Smiling at her image and giving a thumbs-up, *You did good, ole girl.* Returning to the kitchen, she places her evidence in her briefcase and leaves for the courthouse.

Judge Nelson is waiting in his chambers, and when he hears her light knock on the doorframe of the open door, he swivels his large leather chair around to face her. He signals her to come in without saying a word. His large walnut desk dominates the room. Floor-to-ceiling bookshelves line both sidewalls and are filled with law books. This isn't the first time Chris has been in the Judge's chambers but it always amazes her at the number of law books he has. *I'll bet some of those go clear back to the '30s.*

Judge Nelson says nothing while watching her glancing about his office. Without picking up the photo on a side table, she's looking at it as he watches her. She studies the photo of his wife, three sons, and one daughter. Turning back to face him, she sees the small, wooden gavel paperweight.

"Take a seat, Ms. Wilson."

Chris complies.

"I want to see this proof you claim to have, and it better be good!"

Reaching down to pick up her briefcase off the floor

next to her chair, she gently sets it on the corner of his desk. Calmly opening it, she holds up four eight-by-ten glossy photos. Laying the first one down in front of him, "This is tire tracks from the murder scene." Placing the second one next to it, "These are the tire treads on Mr. Doe's car." Judge Nelson says nothing but is studying the two photos. Chris lays down the two left in her hand side-by-side in front of him. "As you can see, Judge, they match!"

While Judge Nelson studies the photos closely, Chris reaches into her briefcase and pulls out the Ziploc bag and holds it while he continues to study the photos. "What else?" he asks as he lays a photo down.

Chris lays the Ziploc bag in front of him. "Those, Judge, are cigarette butts my investigator found at the murder scene. The wind must have blown them up under a piece of wood siding, and the police missed them."

"Get on with it!"

"Yes, sir. Sir, one of these butts has Mr. Doe's DNA, and the other belongs to his client. DNA has proven both."

"You're sure about this?"

"Yes, sir!"

"Is that it? Any more evidence you have hidden in that briefcase of yours?"

"Oh, yes, sir, Your Honor!" Chris can't help but grin.

Chris wants to jump up and dramatically present the tape but refrains from doing so. Setting the small hand-held tape player she brought to make sure he didn't put off until a later date to listen to, she presses the *play* button. When the tape player clicks off, Judge Nelson jumps up out of his chair, and as he storms out the door, he commands Chris, "You stay here!"

Chris can't help it. "Gotcha!" She smiles from ear to ear.

Judge Nelson returns with a deputy sheriff and tells him to stand in the hall near the door. Returning to his desk, he plops down in his big leather chair. "Put that stuff back in your briefcase. You'll need it for his trial!"

Chris does as he says and closes her briefcase.

"You stay right where you are, Ms. Wilson!"

I wouldn't miss this for the world. Thank you, thank you, thank you, Lord. I can't wait to see what the judge is going to do.

Mr. Doe greets the deputy as he's walking toward the judge's door. "Good morning. Nice morning, isn't it?"

Chris wants to keep from grinning like a Cheshire cat. Mr. Doe knocks lightly on the doorjamb of the open door and steps into the office. Seeing Chris, his smile disappears, and he glares at her. She merely nods.

"Good morning, Judge Nelson."

"Sit down!"

At ten forty-five, the judge stands and shouts, "Deputy!"

The deputy sheriff steps to the door.

"Arrest this man, and get him out of my sight!"

Chris remains seated but wants to jump up, throwing her hands in the air and dancing around the room shouting, "Hallelujah," but she once again refrains, at least until she gets home. As the deputy draws Mr. Doe's hands behind his back, Mr. Doe hangs his head, looking down at the floor.

He's facing Judge Nelson but won't look at him. Judge Nelson, with much sarcasm, says, "I suggest, *Mr. Doe,* you get yourself an attorney and one with a better reputation than yours!"

The deputy turns his prisoner around and marches him out the door. Chris has seen judges angry before but never has she seen one as angry as Judge Nelson at this moment. Judge Nelson leans back in his chair, looks at Chris, swivels his chair turning his back to her, and looks out the large window behind his desk. Quietly picking up her briefcase off the floor by her chair, she quietly slips out of the room.

People have already filled the courtroom, and there's an air of expectancy that has filled the room. Chris is seated at the prosecutor's table, and looking across the aisle, there is one chair empty next to the defendant. He isn't smiling and undressing her with his eyes this time. He keeps glancing over his shoulder, looking at the large double doors, and watching for his attorney to come rushing down the aisle.

The same deputy walks to the left of the judge's bench. "Hear ye, hear ye. The Honorable Judge Nelson presiding. All rise."

As the spectators and reporters rise to their feet, the rustle within the courtroom drowns out the whispering and speculations about what will happen this morning in courtroom number seven. Judge Nelson, with black robes flowing, enters the courtroom and takes his seat.

"Be seated," the deputy says and moves to the wall where the other deputies are positioned.

"This court is now in session. Bring in the jury," Judge Nelson declares.

Instead of watching the jury file in, Chris is looking at the judge. *He is not a happy camper!* Chris glances over at the defendant and sees he is once again looking back to see if his attorney is coming. The courtroom is hushed; not a word is spoken from the crowd. Judge Nelson looks at the defendant without saying a word for a few seconds. Finally he says, "I suggest you find yourself another attorney, and you have five days to do it in. This court will resume—" looking down at his calendar "—June the sixth at nine a.m." Judge Nelson turns to the jury. "You are still sworn in, and be back here June sixth to resume your duties. Court dismissed!" Standing, he angrily strides out the room.

As the crowd disperses and the reporters charge the door, Chris turns to the parents and sister that have sat behind her throughout the procedure.

"What does this mean?" the father asks.

The mother grabs hold of her husband's arm, and the sister leans slightly over the railing that separates the attorney from the spectators. "What's going on, Ms. Wilson?"

Chris smiles as the mother clings to her husband. "It means one down, one to go."

The sister is puzzled. "What exactly does that mean?"

Chris places her hand gently on the sister's shoulder. "It means that Mr. Doe is going to jail."

The mother gasps and holds her hanky to her mouth, and the father looks shocked.

Chris continues to explain, "Mr. Doe and the defendant planned the murder of your brother." She places her hand gently on the mothers arm and says, "And your son." The mother begins to sob as her husband tightens his arm around her shoulder. "It's all going to turn out in your favor. Go home, and don't worry. Try to get some rest if you can. I'll see you in a week." Chris reassures them.

When everyone leaves, Chris closes her briefcase and turns to leave. "Nice job, Counselor." Looking up, Detective Gordon is standing in front of her.

"Detective Gordon, what brings you here?"

"You do."

"Oh? How's that?"

"We have some information I think you might like. Do you have a minute to spare?"

"Oh, you bet I do!"

Walking out of the courtroom, the deputy leads her to his office.

"Have a seat, Counselor."

"Detective, I have something I want to ask you before you give me the surprise you have for me."

"Shoot," he says as he smothers laughter.

"How were you able to tape the conversation between those two?"

"We've been watching Mr. Doe for some time now. When we saw him with his client over and over before any killing was done, we knew they were up to no good."

"Really?"

"We were finally able to get a warrant to bug his place. The result of that bug is what we gave you the copy of."

"Thank God you did, or we would never have known. Not with him being an attorney and, as he said to Judge Nelson, 'highly respected and a reputation to be upheld.'"

Detective Gordon bursts out laughing,

"Is that so? Well, I wonder where that *upright* reputation will take him now."

Detective Gordon, leaning his chair back on its two back legs, throws his long legs out in front of him and places his feet on his desk, with his arms behind his head.

"Chris, we have interviewed Ms. Dawson several times, and after six hours, she finally broke."

Chris sits up straighter in her chair. "What did she say? Was she in on it? I knew something wasn't right with her!"

"She said she was Doe's ex-girlfriend and really needed money. He paid her ten thousand dollars to be the third 'guy.'"

"Third guy? How so?"

"She agreed to be in the back of the van, and when your victim was shoved into the back, she put the gag in his mouth while your killer held him down and tied him up."

"Go on."

"When they were done torturing him—and, you know, she shot him but apparently didn't kill him. Then Mr. Killer finished him off by shooting him in the head. By the grace of God, it ended his suffering."

"And?"

The detective hesitates. Not wanting to be graphic, he finally says, "The rest they did after he was dead. She helped."

The images on the photos she saw race through her mind and make her want to cry once again. "Have you taken all of this to the district attorney?"

"Yeah, Ms. Dawson is in jail right now awaiting trial."

Chris shakes her head and stands. "Detective, I thought, at some point, I would get used to all of this, but I guess not. I think I'll go home and cry, vomit, or both."

"Chris, you never get used to it. Go home, but get some rest. You did one heck of a job with that attorney. It took guts to take that stuff before the judge."

"Thanks. It isn't over yet. We still have a killer to try."

The next five days, Chris tries to get as much rest as possible, but her drive and determination won't allow her to rest much. Going back over the witness statements yet again, she wants to make sure every "T" is crossed and every "I" dotted.

. . . .

Walking into the courtroom, Chris isn't surprised to see standing room only. The press has promised not to print the photos of the crime. They agreed with the attorneys they were too gruesome to show the public. It was also agreed the jury would not see them. Chris takes her seat at her table, opening her briefcase. She is more than prepared and more confident than ever that this killer will go to jail for the rest of his life, if he doesn't get the death penalty. There had been requests for a plea bargain, but she absolutely refused. She told her assistant, "Now it's time for him to face the full consequences of his actions."

Brought in with shackles and handcuffs, his orange jumpsuit seems to sag on his body even more. His cocky attitude is long gone, and he looks straight ahead. He has a court-appointed attorney that looks like he's fifteen years old sitting beside him. Chris can't help but turn her head to hide her smile. *I have this one nailed!*

"Hear ye, hear ye. The Honorable Judge Nelson presiding. All rise."

Once again the court becomes quiet as Judge Nelson takes his seat. "This court is now in session. Bring in the jury." When all are seated, he looks at the defendant and his young attorney. "Will the defendant please rise."

Attorney and his client rise, standing behind the defense desk.

"You are charged with first-degree murder. How do you plea?"

The attorney turns to his client, shaking his head no. "I plead guilty, Your Honor."

The courtroom bursts into havoc.

"There will be order in this court!" Judge Nelson yells.

The noise quiets. Chris sits with her mouth hanging open. *I don't believe this! What happened?*

"Have you conferred with your attorney about this decision?"

"Yes, Your Honor."

"Mr. Boyd, do you agree with this decision?"

The attorney glances at his client and shrugs. "Not really, Your Honor."

Chris refrains from laughing.

Looking at his calendar, "Your sentencing will be handed down three days from now. The jury may be excused. Thank you for your service. This court is adjourned."

Once again, with robes rustling about his legs, Judge Nelson leaves the room.

Chris can't get out fast enough to find out what in the world made him suddenly plead guilty. Grabbing her briefcase, she almost runs to the wooden double doors. Throwing them open, she suddenly has a barrage of questions thrown at her while microphones are shoved into her face and flashbulbs blind her.

"No comment, no comment," she says, as she tries to shove through the reporters.

Suddenly she is taken by the arm and spun around.

"Come on. I'll get you through the back door."

Without even looking to see who has grabbed her arm, she's more than willing to be led back into the courtroom. When the double doors are fully closed, she stops and looks up. Detective Gordon is smiling down at her. "Oh, Detective! You are now my knight in shining armor!"

The detective can't help but laugh as he says, "Come on. I'll get you out of here."

Helping her into his black sedan and closing her door, he walks around to the driver's side and squeezes his six-feet, four-inch body behind the wheel. As he turns the ignition key on, he grins, "You're a little thing, but you sure have guts. Didn't you realize you'd be swamped by reporters?"

"I was so intent on finding out what happened in there that I just didn't think."

"Well, if you'll have dinner with me tonight, I'll tell you all about it."

Surprised, Chris can't answer for a moment.

Detective Gordon watches her, waiting for an answer. "Well?"

"Sure, okay. That would be nice."

How does he know when no one told me anything about it?

• • • • • • • • • • • •

Sitting across from each other with a glass of wine beside each plate, Chris looks across the table at him as she takes a bite of her rib-eye steak. "Okay, are you going to tell me what happened before I finish this wonderful meal?"

He better not have lied to me just to be able to take me to dinner!

Setting his glass down and wiping his mouth with his napkin, "Well, it's like this. Your killer found out that Doe was arrested. You know news travels fast in prison."

Picking up her glass of wine and taking a sip, she can't take her eyes off the detective. Smiling, the detective knows she's going nuts wanting the whole story. Chris very slowly sets her glass on the table, never looking away.

"Are you going to tell me, or are you going to drag this out until next week?"

"Don't get your panties in a wad. I'm getting there."

Chris looks at him impatiently for the rest of the story.

"Oh, by the way, I guess you know Doe was found hanging in his cell."

"No! Why haven't I heard any of this?"

The detective shrugs. "Then when your killer found out that dear Ms. Dawson had spilled the beans and was now in jail, he decided it was in his best interest to plead guilty, hoping not to get the needle in the arm."

"Do tell!"

"Dessert?"

"No, Detective. I think I've had enough, but thank you."

"Why don't you call me Jack?"

. . . .

Chris is running late and as she hurries down the courtroom isle to her table, the judge gives her a disapproving look. He says nothing for a moment then turns his attention to the defendant. "I find you guilty of murder in the first degree and sentence you to the fullest extent of the law that I could find! You will serve your sentence beginning today in the Maximum Security Institution in Nashville, Tennessee. You will serve a life sentence with no parole plus one hundred years consecutively."

A gasp ripples through the crowd.

Judge Nelson leans forward over the edge of the bench as far as he can, without actually climbing up on it. "I find you to be one of the lowest, most malicious, and most contemptible kind of human being I think I've ever encountered in my thirty years on this bench! By law, if I could give you the death penalty, I would do it without hesitation!" Court dismissed!" The defendant is led from the room.

. . . .

Slowly driving down the dogwood-lined driveway, Chris gives a long sigh. Pulling up to the front door, she sits looking at the home she was raised in. *Lord, it's so good to be home. Thank you for this time away.*

Her cell phone rings. She flips the cover open, checking the caller I.D.

"Hello."

"Chris? I hate to bother you. It's Jack Gordon."

"Yes, what is it?"

"I just thought you'd like to know that the judge didn't have to sentence your killer to death. Someone else took care of it for him."

"You're not serious! What happened?"

"He got in a fight almost as soon as he entered the prison. Apparently he already had enemies waiting for him. He's dead."

"I guess justice has been served. Thanks for letting me know, Jack."

"Enjoy your time off. Bye."

Margaret steps out onto the porch. "Chris? Are you coming in?"

Turning the ignition off and opening the door, she retrieves her suitcase that she has packed for the week.

Clay joins them, giving her a kiss on the cheek. As Chris enters the house ahead of them, Margaret whispers to Clay, "She is absolutely exhausted! I'm so glad that trial is finally over."

Clay nods in agreement, and they enter the house together.

Chapter 3

The day of graduation is yet another celebration. Chris, Mom, and Dad are there to watch Teri receive her master's degree certificate. There are gifts and Teri's favorite meal waiting at home—spaghetti with meatballs, a tossed salad, and garlic French bread. Although they seldom drink wine, red wine is poured to add a little special touch to the dinner. Peeking at the others, Teri slurps a strand of spaghetti like she did as a child, making everyone laugh when the end of it hits her nose.

"Teri, I thought you weren't doing that anymore." Clay laughs.

"Oh, Dad, she hasn't grown up like the rest of us."

The kidding and joking around the table continues, just as it does each time they come home. As the meal comes to a close, Margaret leaves the table and returns with a cake. Across the top of it, "Congratulations, Teri" is written in green icing, Teri's favorite color.

Margaret leaves to get utensils, saucers, and coffee cups. While she's gone, Clay reaches behind him and opens a drawer in the buffet. As Margaret sets coffee cups in the center of the table, with the saucers and silverware, Clay lays a small gift-wrapped box in front of Teri. Chris reaches in her lap and brings up a gift from her, setting it in front of Teri.

"What is all this? I never expected any gifts."

As Margaret picks up the knife to cut the cake, "You deserve a little something. You've worked very hard for a long time."

Reaching for the gift from her mother and father, she grins widely, eyes sparkling. "Oh, this is like Christmas!" she says, as she rips the paper off and opens the small lid. Looking puzzled, she removes a key.

"It's from your mother and I. We're so proud of you."

"What's it for?"

"It's a key to the outhouse, you silly girl!" Chris says.

Bursting out laughing, Clay picks up a blindfold. "Close your eyes."

"What?"

"Teri, just close your eyes!" Chris commands.

Placing the blindfold over her eyes and standing her up out of her chair, Clay leads her toward the back door.

"Where in the world are you taking me?"

Holding her arms out and feeling around to make sure she doesn't bump into something, nervously, she says, "Dad, I don't know where you're taking me, but I *think* this might be fun?"

Laughing, they lead her out onto the patio facing the backyard. Chris stands on one side of her and Margaret stands on the other, with Clay behind her; he removes the blindfold. Teri lets out a loud scream while she runs to her green 2012 sedan. While she was helping her mother set the table, Clay snuck out; not wanting her to hear the car engine running, he pushed it into the backyard.

Ripping the huge red bow off the roof by its ties so she can open the door, she's still screaming, and tears are flowing down her cheeks. "I can't believe this! I can't believe this! Oh my gosh, I can't believe this!"

The three walk over to her, and Clay lays his hands on her shoulders.

"Oh, Dad. Oh, Mom," she says, as she spins around and gives each a hug. Tears still flow as Teri wipes her arm across her face.

"Well, daughter, are you going to get in it or stand there crying?" Clay laughs.

Chris is standing silently, but tears have filled her eyes. *Teri has worked so hard. I'm glad Mom and Dad replaced that piece of junk she's been driving.*

Teri jumps in behind the wheel, running her hands over the soft, brown leather seats and the dashboard and twisting around to check out the backseat.

Laughing, Margaret points to the car. "Teri, we didn't give you the key to hide in your room. Start the car, honey!"

Taking hold of the steering wheel, looking out the open door, she says, "Va-room, va-room," laughing as though she's a kid in a play car. Placing the key in the ignition and starting the car, she says, "Chris, hop in, and let's go for a ride."

Chris walks around to the passenger side. Wiping the tears from her own eyes, she slides in and sits back. Closing her door, Teri races the engine.

"Teri Ann, don't you go racing up and down that road now!" Margaret warns.

Chris busts out laughing and leans toward Teri. "Now doesn't that just sound like it did when we were kids?"

Returning home after a thirty-minute drive, Chris and Teri enter the dining room. One lone gift sits where Teri had been sitting. Looking at Chris, she says, "Oh, Chris, I'm so sorry! I didn't open your gift!"

"Hmm, I wonder why not."

Laughing, she shoves her cake plate off to the side and begins ripping the paper off the gift Chris has given her.

Watching her, she says, "Teri, it isn't *anything* like what Mom and Dad gave you. I hope you aren't disappointed."

Teri places her fingers on the lid of the small box. "Well, if it isn't another car so I can have a variety, I just don't know."

Laughing, they all watch as she lifts the lid. Gasping and grasping the small box in her hand, tears well up in her eyes again. Running around the table to Chris, as she hugs her, she says, "I don't need another car. I *love* this! It's absolutely *beautiful!*"

Margaret can't stand it because she has no idea what Chris has given her. "We want to know what it is, too!"

Walking around to her mother and father, she holds the box out so they can see inside. Margaret throws her hand over her mouth. "Oh, Teri, it's beautiful!"

"Wow!" Clay exclaims, giving Chris a thumbs-up.

"Well, are you going to put it on?" Chris asks.

Chris is pleased that she likes it; she knew she would. She knows her sister well. Reaching into the box, Teri gently pulls out a beautiful chain with a one-carat, brilliant diamond hanging on it. "Mom, help me put it on," she says, holding her hair to the side and turning her back to Margaret. Running to the mirror hanging in the hall, she examines the necklace around her neck. Turning back to Chris, "It is so beautiful, Chris. You shouldn't have."

"Well, take it off, and I'll take it back."

Teri grabs the diamond in her hand. "The heck you will!"

. . . .

Teri and Chris have slept in late. The excitement from the day before and their previous schedules have worn them out. Clay and Margaret sit at the kitchen table, having their second cup of coffee.

"Clay, those girls are so tired, and they really need time to rest. I wish Chris could stay longer."

"I know, honey, but didn't Chris say she has more trials coming up that she has to prepare for?"

"Yes. She works too hard! She needs to take time and enjoy herself."

"That's what she's doing now, taking time to rest and enjoy herself."

"I suppose, but how much rest and fun can she have in just a weekend?"

Chris enters the kitchen in her pajamas. "Good morning. Is the coffee still hot?"

"It sure is, honey. Let me get it for you. Clay, do you want a refill?"

"Mom, I can get it."

Clay replies, "I've had two cups now, and I think that will do me."

"So what do you two have planned for today?"

"I think we're going to play in the dirt today," Margaret answers.

"Okay, Mom, do you want me to fill the sandbox?"

Bursting out laughing, Clay almost spits coffee all over the table. Margaret winks at Clay. "Okay, will you bring our little bucket with the duckies on it and the two little shovels, too?"

"What's so funny?" Teri asks as she enters the kitchen yawning.

"Oh, Mom and Dad want to play in their sandbox today."

"Huh?"

The laughter continues. "Teri, I'll explain later. Would you like some coffee or are you drinking that herb tea now?"

"If Mom has tea, I'd like some of that."

"It's in the pantry, third shelf."

"Chris, do you want to walk around and see all the improvements Mom and Dad made after we left last time?"

"Sure. Can we get out of our pjs first?"

"Very funny, sister. Of course."

The day is warm, but a light sweater is needed. The wind has kicked up a bit, and in the shade, it's still chilly.

Teri looks at Chris while passing through the large arbor with wisteria vines twisting and curling around the top and sides, reaching out in every direction. Their aromatic, purple grape-like clusters hang loosely with an invitation to be cut for bouquets.

"Let's sit in the gazebo," Teri suggests.

Following the brick path, a variety of blooming flowers line the edges. Small ceramic decorations add accent and variety within the flower beds. A ceramic frog holding a rake has his gardening hat on and sits at the edge of a Firebush. An angel, with her wings spread, welcomes visitors as they pass the weeping willow tree. Walking farther down the path, a birdbath's clear water glistens in the sun, and a frog sits at its base.

"Did Mom and Dad do all this themselves, Teri?"

"From what Mom said, they laid the brick path themselves, and you know Mom, she chooses all the flowers and does most of the planting."

Chris touches an iris as she passes. "They really made it pretty."

Looking beyond the blooming cherry tree, Chris points toward the gazebo. "Look, she even put an azalea on each side of the gazebo entrance."

The entrance welcomes any who enter to sit on its benches that curve around the center. Many guests, as well as family, retreat to the gazebo with their Bible, a novel, or to merely enjoy the quiet time with nature's sounds. As kids, their friends would join them for the shade and sharing Kool-Aid and peanut-butter-and-jelly sandwiches. Stepping into the gazebo with its mixture of hanging baskets, some are filled with petunias and others long stems, with small white flowers, hang from the spider plant. Chris and Teri take a seat. Teri hesitates for just a moment. *Should I ask her?*

"Chris? I want to ask you something."

"Okay, this sounds serious."

"When you were working on that big trial you had right after the anniversary party, were you scared of those people?"

"Teri, why would you ask that? No, I wasn't scared! Why would I be?"

"Mom said they might have been connected with the mob or something. Were they?"

"Mom worries too much. No, they weren't connected to any mob, Teri. They were just bad people, and we got them."

"What happened to them?"

"Well, the defense attorney, Mr. Doe, was in on the murder."

"You're kidding!"

"They found him hanging in his jail cell a few days after he went to jail."

Teri's mouth hangs open with disbelief.

"My so-called eyewitness lied through her teeth, and as it turned out, she was also in on it, too."

"No way!"

"She was Mr. Doe's ex-girlfriend and he knew she needed money badly, so he paid her ten thousand dollars to help him and the defendant."

"What happened to the other one, the one who you convicted?"

"The judge sentenced him to life plus one hundred years, but justice was served after all."

"They can do that?"

"Sure."

"So what do you mean justice was served if he didn't get the death penalty?"

"He walked into prison, and some enemies were waiting for him and killed him on the spot. End of story."

Chris walks over to one of the spider plants hanging from a hook and, fingering one of the small white flowers, she remembers the horror of what the pictures had shown and what she knew to be the facts of what they did to their victim.

"Chris? Do you want to talk about it? Mom said you wouldn't even tell them what they did."

"No, Teri. I'll never forget what I saw, and no one else needs to hear the gory details. It's enough that I still have nightmares about it. You don't need to, either."

"Okay, but I wish you hadn't taken that case."

"I'm not sorry for a moment that I did! Had I not, that attorney would still be doing the same thing and probably getting away with it, and the ex-girlfriend would be ten thousand dollars richer."

"What happened to her?"

"She's in jail."

"Chris? Teri? Lunch is ready."

Chris is happy the conversation is coming to an end. "We're coming, Mom." Chris pulls her sweater closer around her as she steps from the gazebo. The chill is not only from the shadowed gazebo but from the memories that are still very much alive.

Walking into the kitchen, "What delicious meal have you prepared for us, Mom?" Teri asks as she takes her seat.

Margaret, in her apron as usual, smiles to herself. "Oh, nothing really special. Just something light."

Chris takes her seat and places a napkin on her lap. Margaret turns her body so they can't see what she's about to put before them.

Cutting the sandwiches diagonally then looking over her shoulder before turning back around, she sees the girls are talking and not paying attention to what she's doing. Smiling, she sets a paper plate with peanut-butter-and-jelly sandwiches on it and two glasses of grape Kool-Aid on the table.

Stopping their conversation and looking down at the plate, confused at first, the memories begin to rush back, recalling the childhood lunch with their friends in the gazebo. Chris bursts out laughing, and then Teri realizes the significance and joins in.

Stepping behind them, Margaret leans over between them. "Gotcha! Now it's your turn!"

The girls can't stop laughing. Teri takes a sip of her Kool-Aid and chokes on it. Coughing, she tries to stop laughing.

"Teri, are you all right? I didn't mean to—"

Chris cuts her off. "Mom, this is wonderful!"

The worried look on Margaret's face turns into a smile. "I've been waiting for the perfect opportunity for this. When I saw you girls talking in the gazebo, I knew it was the perfect time."

Later, Margaret has aprons ready for Chris and Teri when they walk into the kitchen to help prepare dinner; she slips one over each of their heads. "Turn around so I can tie it for you."

"Mom, we don't—"

Margaret cuts Teri off. "You two have said you want to be like me." She is standing back to gaze at them. "Now you are!" She leaves to greet Clay at the door. The girls stand looking at each other.

. . . .

Teri turns from the window and sitting down on her bed, she thinks, *I think my happiest years were spent right here! I am so very, very blessed.* Removing her pajamas and putting on her pink terrycloth robe, she remembers how she insisted on having the big armchair, now sitting next to the wide window overlooking the grounds. "Mom, it's perfect for when I study!"

She smiles as she enters her private bathroom. Picking up the flowered hand towel, she hangs it back in its place and begins to apply her makeup. Reentering her bedroom, Teri rummages through the several dresses, skirts, slacks, and jackets hanging neatly in her walk-in closet. *What should I wear to church this morning?*

Margaret, holding onto the banister, looks up while standing at the foot of the stairs. "Chris? Teri? Are you ready? We need to leave for church in a few minutes."

Chris yells, "We're on our way down."

• • • • • • • • • • •

After finding a parking place in the large parking lot of the church, Margaret, Clay, and the girls greet several of their friends. Entering through double stained-glassed panel doors at the front of the sanctuary, a large wooden cross faces the congregation.

A piano, with its lid propped open, sits on one side of the stage with the praise band drums, guitar stands, and a trumpet hanging on its stand taking up one corner. The podium has been set aside for now. Three microphones, on their slender poles, are positioned near the front of the stage for the praise band's use. At the top of the side wall's stained glass windows are pictures of Jesus kneeling at the rock in Gethsemane, Jesus kneeling down with children gathered around Him, all depicting the love of Jesus allows the sun to shine upon Him as well as the congregation.

Piped-in music, as a calling for the service to begin, begins playing, and people begin filling the seats and the balcony. The musicians take their places, and the praise team leader steps forward. "Let's all stand and rejoice in the Lord. For this is the day the Lord has made. Am I right?"

The congregation shouts, "Yes."

As the praise band begins playing, those who have not sat down rush to take their seats. Everyone begins singing, raising their hands to the Lord, and some do dance movements at their seats. The tempo of the music changes to worship songs. To begin the worship segment of the service, the choir sings, "Amazing Grace." Some within the congregation have tears in their eyes as the song's words convict them.

Pastor Mike walks to the microphone. "Let's pray." As usual, the prayer goes on and on and on. Finally everyone is allowed to be seated, and he begins his sermon. "Please open your Bibles to Romans chapter ten verse nine and read with me, 'That if you confess with your mouth the Lord Jesus and believe in your heart that God has raised Him from the dead, you shall be saved.'" Laying down his Bible, he proceeds with his sermon.

When the sermon ends, the music once again starts playing, and all sing, "From the sky to the cross to make the way, from the cross to the grave, from the grave to the sky, Lord, I lift your name on high."

People congratulate Teri on her graduation after the service. Mrs. Folsom walks over to Teri. "What will you do now that you've graduated? Will you stay in this area, or are you looking for another area? Do you have any plans?"

"No, I'm just enjoying the summer right now and time away from school."

Mary Lou sees Teri amongst the crowd and runs to her with outstretched arms. "Oh, it's so good to see you. You're home!" Mary Lou says as she hugs Teri.

"Yes, I'm home for the summer."

"Good, Sally and I are going to Tybee Island in two weeks. Why don't you and Chris come, too? It will be fun with the four of us."

"That sounds great, but I'll have to see what plans Chris has and if she can take time from work."

• • • • • • • • • • • • •

As Chris, Teri, and their parents sit having lunch on the back patio, Clay, chewing the last of his sandwich, "Teri, I heard Mrs. Folsom ask if you have any plans now that you've graduated. Do you? Have you thought that far in advance yet?"

"There are a lot of possibilities, Dad. I'm not exactly sure which one I want to choose as a career yet."

"Honey, I never have really understood exactly what you do with sociology. Is it like teaching or out in some desert digging in the dirt for fossils? What exactly do they do?" Margaret asks.

"Well, Mom, there's several areas that sociology covers. I could become a psychologist, a teacher, or go into anthropology or archeology. I have a lot of different choices."

Chris sits quietly, finishing her meal.

Clay interjects, "Have you one in particular you're leaning toward?"

"Not really, but I am considering teaching, either that or counseling, maybe seminary. I'm just not sure what the Lord wants me to do yet."

Chris picks up her glass of tea. "If you go into teaching, what will be the subject you want to teach?" She sings, "The hipbone's connected to the leg bone. The leg bone's connected to—"

Everyone laughs, cutting off Chris's singing.

"There was a semester that we got into the various beliefs of different religions. I found that really interesting and have thought about teaching on that subject."

Leaning forward, Clay places his elbows on the table. "That sounds interesting. Tell us about it."

"It's really involved, Dad."

"Then just give us a snippet if you can."

"I'll try. Of course, Christianity believes in the Holy Trinity, God, Jesus, and the Holy Spirit being one. We believe in grace, as you know, in heaven, hell, and eternal salvation by the death and resurrection of Jesus."

Everyone nods in agreement.

"But not all believe as we do. The Jewish people, the Orthodox Jews, believe the Torah. They follow Jewish Law and strictly follow the commandments given to Moses.

Then there is Messianic Judaism. They believe like we do, the Holy Trinity and salvation because of Christ dying on the cross.

The Mormons don't believe in the Holy Trinity or that there is a hell. They don't believe in grace. They believe we work our way to heaven."

Margaret raises an eyebrow and interrupts. "How much work do they have to do to repay Jesus for dying on the cross for our sins? It isn't possible to repay Him!"

"Well, they base their beliefs on the *Book of Mormon* that Joseph Smith wrote. Many cults believe as they do. Another cult, like Jehovah's Witnesses, believe much like the Mormons. Then you have the New Age beliefs. They believe we all are our own god and something about our conscience being god."

Taking a sip of tea, she continues. "The Muslims believe the Quran. They worship their god, Allah. They call

all other religions 'false religions,' and anyone who is not of their faith is the enemy and must to be exterminated."

"That can't be true!" exclaims Margaret.

"Yes, I'm afraid so, Mom. They want to take over the world because all others are considered infidels. Now the Hindu beliefs hinge on Karma and astrology, and Buddhism believe in developing their mind through meditation."

Hearing the phone ringing, Margaret jumps up and runs to answer it.

Clay stands. "Let's continue this later. It's really interesting, but I promised Ralph I'd come over and help him. Maybe he'll be interested in hearing this, too."

· · · · · · · · · · · ·

As the sun is setting, the sky is filled with streaks of purple, mingling with pink, blue, and yellow, creating a tapestry of color.

"Clay, just look at this sky! It is so beautiful. How can anyone say there is no God? I don't understand how they can believe like that when all we have to do is look around us."

"It is beautiful, and that's a fact. I don't understand it, either. Satan has certainly fooled them, that's for sure!"

· · · · · · · · · · · ·

Teri's time away from the studies and daily grind at school has given her soul a much-needed boost. It's been a time of rest and relaxation. Leaving the house early for a morning retreat to the gazebo has once again given her the quiet time she needs to meditate and listen to the Lord.

With the spring warmth and the aroma of blossoms surrounding her, her spirit is in tune with the Lord's. She has learned through the years she can spend precious time in the Lord's presence and walk away with a peace she doesn't even understand and is very grateful for. She knows that she knows she has had yet another encounter with her heavenly Father as she walks slowly along the brick path her mother and father laid. The sound of birds singing is an added joy to her morning. Hearing the "chirp, chirp" of a cardinal, looking toward the birdfeeder, she sees the brilliant red bird pecking at the seed. Scampering around the foot of the feeder pole are two gray squirrels scavenging for fallen seed.

A new song whistles through the trees, and looking up, Teri sees a mockingbird whistling happily a chorus of several tunes. Walking under the wisteria-laden arbor and seeing the welcoming bench placed on the side of the path, she thinks, *This is just too beautiful to leave right now.* Sitting down and kicking off her sandals, *Lord, I think I heard you right. I'll have Mom pray with me to confirm what you said. Thank you, Lord, for your faithfulness."* Watching the squirrels, now chasing each other in circles up a tree trunk, *I need to call Chris and see if she can go to Tybee Island with us. I better do that now.* Sliding her feet back into her sandals, she walks quickly, following the brick path to the back door.

"Hi, Mom."

"Hi, honey. Did you have a nice walk? I saw you sitting in the gazebo. Is everything all right?"

"Yes. I just needed some time with the Lord. I need to call Chris to see if she's able to go to Tybee with us, and after that, if you have time, I'd like to talk to you."

Looking a bit worried, she says, "Teri, are you sure everything is okay?"

"Yes, Mom. I just need you to pray with me about something."

"Oh! Of course I will. Go make your call."

Going to her bedroom and picking up the cordless phone, Teri sits in the big armchair and dials Chris's office number.

"Hello, Ms. Wilson's office. Can I help you?"

"Hi, Ginny. It's Teri. Is Chris in?"

"Oh hi, Teri. I heard you were home. I'll bet you're relieved to have school behind you. Do you know what you'll do now? Do you have a job lined up?"

"I'm not sure what the Lord wants me to do, so I haven't inquired about jobs yet. I am definitely enjoying my free time though." Twisting sideways in the chair and throwing her legs across the armrest, she asks, "Is Chris available? I need to talk to her for a minute."

"You're in luck—she just walked in." Teri can hear Ginny, "Teri is on line one. It's good to talk to you, Teri. Maybe we can meet for lunch sometime."

"That sounds great. Thanks."

Chris lays her briefcase on her desk and punches the button for line one. "Hi, Teri, what's up?"

"How are you, too?"

Laughing, she says, "I'm sorry. I just have a lot on my mind right now."

Twisting back around, Teri snuggles down in the big chair, getting more comfortable. "Do you have time to talk?"

"Not really, but is it important?"

"Yes and no."

"Come on, Teri. Is it or not?" Chris asks impatiently.

"I'm sorry, Chris. It sounds like this is a bad time. How about we meet for lunch at that little café around the corner?"

"That sounds great, but I'll be in court until noon, then we reconvene at one thirty. Will that be enough time? I wish you'd tell me what this is about."

"It's nothing important enough that it can't wait."

"Okay. I'll see you at noon."

Teri hangs up and scoots her way out of the armchair and goes back downstairs. Margaret is sitting at the kitchen table drinking a cup of coffee. As Teri enters, she looks up. "Will Chris be able to go with you?"

"I don't know. We weren't able to talk, but we're meeting for lunch at noon, and I'll ask her then."

"Sit down, and let's talk about what's on your mind. Would you like a cup of coffee? It's still hot."

Teri takes a seat across from her mother. "No thanks."

"This sounds serious. What's going through that pretty head of yours?"

Teri smiles as she scoots her chair a little closer to the table. Her mother is always so complimentary. "I've been thinking about what the Lord might want me to do career-wise. When I was in the gazebo, I was praying, and I think I know what He wants me to do. I'd like confirmation, so I thought we could pray together."

Margaret sets her coffee cup to the side and reaches across the table, indicating for Teri to join hands with her. "Then let's pray."

When the prayer ends, Teri is sure now what the Lord wants her to do. Margaret watches Teri's expression. She seems to be deep in thought. Glancing up and seeing her mother watching her, she says, "I know what He wants me to do, Mom. He wants me to go into counseling."

"That's wonderful! What type of counseling will you do, marriage or children?"

"I'll just have to look around. I know it won't be marriage counseling." Laughing, she says, "Who will listen to someone who has never been married?"

"You do have a point."

"I need to go change clothes and get into Atlanta to meet Chris. As you know, we never know how bad the traffic will be!"

Margaret takes her cup to the dishwasher. "Then you need get up there and change your clothes, or you'll be late."

Teri climbs the stairs to her bedroom. "Yes, ma'am."

· · · · · · · · · · · ·

Driving south on Georgia 400, surprisingly the traffic is light. Listening to the inspirational music on the car radio, Teri hums along with the songs. *This time has re-*

ally helped me. I have been so busy that I didn't realize how tired I was. Finding a parking space near the courthouse is almost impossible. Finally she's able to park in a small parking lot; after paying the attendant and taking her parking stub, she walks the short distance toward the courthouse. Just as she turns the corner to go to the café, she sees Chris coming.

Giving each other a quick hug, she says, "You look tired Chris."

"I'm okay. I've just been burning the midnight oil as usual."

Entering the café and taking a seat, they place their orders. "What kind of case are you working on? I hope it's not like that mob one!"

Laughing, knowing Teri is referring to the Mr. Doe trial, she says, "No, Teri, and I keep telling you they weren't the mafia."

Laughing, she says, "I know, I know. But it usually gets a laugh out of you, and right now you look like you need one. Are you okay?"

"I'm okay. This is a pretty simple case, but it always bothers me when the elderly are hurt by some nutcase."

"What happened?"

"An elderly man was robbed at gunpoint. You know how that goes."

"I know. I don't know what this world is coming to. "

Picking up her iced tea, Chris asks, "So what did you want to talk about?"

Teri, pouring blue cheese dressing around the top of

her salad, "I wanted to see if you'll be able to take time off to go to Tybee Island with us?"

"I remember you saying something about it. When are you going?"

Taking a sip of her tea, she says, "We were going next week, but Mary Lou said the hotel we want is booked. It's that really nice one right on the beach."

"So when are you planning to go? Wasn't there someone else going too?"

"Yes, Sally is going, and we'd really like for you to come too, Chris. You haven't had a vacation in a very long time. You need to take time away."

Smiling as she lays her fork down and pats her mouth with the napkin, she says, "I could certainly use one, but you didn't answer. When are you going?"

"Oh, Mary Lou was able to get two adjoining beachfront rooms for the week of June fifth. We'll stay five days. It will take most of a day to drive down and then another to come back. That will give the three of you time to rest up for work."

"I do have two weeks of vacation time coming. I'll have to check my calendar and see what's on the docket and get back with you. Plus it's up to the boss."

"How soon do you think you'll know? I need to let Mary Lou and Sally know."

"I'll let you know tonight. I better get back. I left my briefcase at the office."

. . . .

Pulling into the circle driveway, Teri sees Margaret on

her knees, with her spade in hand, knee-length, dirty shorts, a sun top and sunhat on, digging a hole.

"You look like you're having fun," Teri says, laughing as she walks over to her mother.

Grinning and looking up, Margaret places her hand above her eyes to shade them. "I am having a wonderful time. You know how I like to play in the dirt. How was lunch? Is Chris able to go with you?"

Squatting down, careful not to get dirt on her slacks, she says, "She's going to have to check her calendar, and she'll call me tonight."

"I hope she can go. That girl needs the rest!"

Standing back up, she says, "I know, Mom. She looks really tired. I told her that, too. I better go change clothes before you get dirt all over me."

"I'll be in soon. There's ice tea in the fridge if you want some."

"Thanks."

Teri runs into the house when she hears the phone ringing.

"Hello? Hi, Chris. Did you win your case?"

"It's not over yet. We'll probably finish tomorrow. It sure isn't looking good for the defendant but it never does when I'm going after them!"

"You got that right, my sister, the bulldog! Have you had time to check out your schedule for going to Tybee?"

"Yes. I have a couple of trials those two weeks, but the boss approved my two-week vacation as long as I can get someone to cover for me. I talked to Jeff and Dan, and they're more than willing. They're only short little trials that will only take a few days to wrap up. One might take a week, but Dan said that was fine with him. Both said they can work mine in with theirs."

"So does that mean you're going with us?"

"Absolutely. I can't wait to throw my tired, old body in the Atlantic Ocean!" Laughing, she continues, "So what are the plans?"

Teri gives her mother a thumbs-up sign, letting her know Chris is going. "I talked to Sally last night, and she and I are going to meet at Mary Lou's house and leave our cars there."

"That sounds good."

"Mary Lou has a minivan, and we thought that would be more comfortable for the four of us. That is, if you were able to come."

"Oh, I'm going, little sister. I can hardly wait!"

"I'll call Mary Lou and tell her. We can just swing by your place and pick you up since we'll be coming through Atlanta."

"Okay. I have to run. Jack is stopping by."

"Oh? I didn't know you were seeing him."

"I'm not *seeing* him! He has some information for the trial I have next week."

"Sure he does."

"Bye, Teri." Chris hangs up the phone.

Margaret has overheard part of their conversation. "Who is Chris seeing?"

"Detective Gordon, but she says he's just coming over to give her some information for her upcoming trial. I think it's more than that."

"Really? I remember he worked with her some on the Mr. Doe case. I didn't know she was interested in him."

"I kind of hope she is, and it's more than just stopping by to drop off a file or something. Personally, I think Chris needs to date and get her nose out of briefs."

"I agree. Like I've said many times, she works too hard!"

Chapter 4

Mary Lou is a paralegal for a firm in Gainesville, and Sally is a nurse at a large medical center in Gainesville. Phone calls have been made back and forth between Chris, Teri, Mary Lou, and Sally. The excitement is escalating the closer the time to leave for Tybee Island draws near.

Mary Lou has a two-week vacation. Sally only has a week due to tight schedules at the hospital. She has had to divide up her two weeks whereas Chris and Teri have two weeks.

Driving into Mary Lou's driveway, Mary Lou and Sally are putting suitcases in the back of the van.

Stepping out of her car, Teri sees four suitcases sitting at the back of the van. "Sally, is that *all* your stuff?"

Laughing, she says, "No, some of it is Mary Lou's!"

Holding out a small paper bag with the top folded down, "Well, I'm glad I only brought a small bag."

Both ladies look at Teri. "What are you talking about? Where's your suitcase?"

Trying to keep from laughing, Teri points to her paper bag. "Right here!"

Looking at each other as though Teri has lost her mind, Sally exclaims, "That's all you're taking?"

"Sure! I have toothpaste, toothbrush, and my bathing suit. What else do I need?"

Shaking her head, Mary Lou says, "Woman! Get your suitcases, and let's go get Chris!"

Laughing, Sally gives Teri a hug. "You had me going for a minute."

Once their things are loaded, they leave to pick up Chris and head toward Savannah. Helping Chris carry her beach umbrella, picnic basket, and suitcase down to the car and loading them, spirits are high. The drive starts out with laughter and teasing. Chris soon leans her head back against the backrest and falls soundly asleep.

Looking over at her, Teri feels compassion for her sister. "Chris is asleep. Can we whisper so as not to wake her? She has been on the fast train for way too long."

Glancing in the rearview mirror, Mary Lou smiles. "You're right. She definitely needs the rest."

Sally lowers her voice as she turns in her seat to look back at Chris and Teri. "Teri, wasn't she supposed to have another big case coming up?"

"She said they were just little cases and no big deal."

"I heard there's a big murder case coming up again—the one that's been in the newspaper so much. Do you think she'll be prosecuting that one?"

"I don't know. She loves her job, but to be honest, I wish she wouldn't take those big cases. They scare me, but she says they don't scare her." Shrugging, she says, "As long as she's happy."

Mary Lou asks, "Is she dating anyone, or does she spend all her time preparing for these cases?"

Teri doesn't know it and neither do the others that Chris has awakened. Curious about this conversation, she is pretending to be asleep.

"I don't know for sure. I know she works like a dog and needs to have fun. She says she isn't dating, but I think she's seeing a detective."

Chris bites her lip to keep from speaking out as she continues to listen.

Teri continues. "He's a detective that worked with her on that big case where the attorney and girlfriend were in on a murder. I've only met him once, and he seemed like a really nice man. He's one handsome man, that's for sure!"

Everyone laughs, except Chris.

"I wish I could find someone like that," Mary Lou interjects. "It seems if you're in law enforcement or attorneys or connected with the law, somehow it scares men off. What I see most of the time at the firm is deadbeat dads, accident reports, and divorces. Not much pickings there."

"Well, I have the pick of the crop girls," Sally states. "And you can't have him! Tom is just about the perfect husband. He loves the kids, is a great father, and well, I do have to pick up his clothes," she says, laughing, "but he's learning."

Turning in her seat again, Sally asks, "Do you think Chris really is dating this detective?"

"I think she might be sweet on him."

Chris shoots straight up in the seat. "I am not!"

"Oops, I thought you were sound asleep, Chris."

"Obviously! I don't appreciate you talking behind my back, Teri Ann!"

The atmosphere is tense, and all the women are quiet for a moment.

"I'm sorry, Chris. I was just saying what I think. You don't need to get upset."

Trying to ease the sudden tension, Mary Lou says, "Should we stop in Savannah and eat at the place the pirates ate before going on into Tybee?"

"I don't think I've been there," Sally adds. "I think I've heard of it. Is that the place where they say the pirates would dock their boats and eat?"

Glancing at Sally, Mary Lou says, "Yes, it is. It's a really neat place to eat. The waiters dress like pirates, and the ladies dress like maidens. It's fun but classy, too."

Chris yawns. "How about we save that for a night when we're not so tired. We're almost there, and I'm ready to stretch out on the beach. What do the rest of you think?"

Shaking their heads in affirmation, Sally says, "That sounds like a good idea. I think we're all tired."

Placing an inspirational CD into the CD player, they begin to sing along with the songs.

Chris leans over and whispers to Teri, "I'm sorry I came down on you so hard. I'm so exhausted that I just jump on anything."

Teri reaches over and places her hand on Chris's knee. "I shouldn't have said anything. I'm sorry. It's none of my business if you're seeing someone or not. Please forgive me."

"I am seeing Jack. I've been seeing him for five or six months now. We just went to Lanier last weekend, and it was really fun. Jack has a really nice speed boat, and I almost killed myself water skiing. I haven't said anything about our dates because I didn't want Mother to know, and I know you would tell her. Plus, I don't want it broadcast throughout the courthouse."

"I knew it! Why don't you want Mother to know? She'd be happy for you."

"You know Mom. She'll start planning for grandkids, and I just don't want her thinking anything serious is going on."

"Is it serious?"

"Kind of. I'm not sure. Can we talk about this later?"

"What's going on back there? What's the big secret that you're whispering about?" Mary Lou asks.

Laughing and leaning away from Teri, Chris answers, "We were planning to throw you in the ocean, but now you know so we can't."

• • • • • • • • • • •

Savannah has a century-old atmosphere with many antebellum mansions, cobbled streets, and horse-drawn carriages for the tourists to tour the town in, and is famous for the Spanish moss hanging from the large oak trees. The Savannah River flows through town. Taking the exit off the expressway, they turn into town and slowly drive past shops that line the cobblestone street: a candle shop, a shop that sells brass items, and a T-shirt souvenir shop. Small businesses and art galleries line the cobblestone walkway along the Savannah River. The day is warm, and many stroll by the shops, some licking ice-cream cones and others with soft drinks.

Reaching the street that leads to Tybee Island, Mary Lou asks, "Is there anything anyone wants to do while we're here? Does anyone want to stop and shop or walk River Street?"

All answer no.

"What about stretching our legs and walking around Forsyth Park?"

Chris leans out the window and points toward the front of the van. "Onward and forward, Captain. I smell the beach on the horizon."

Laughing, Mary Lou guns the engine a tiny bit. "Aye, aye, mate. Onward we go."

The drive to Tybee Island is a short twenty miles. The narrow two-lane highway crosses over the ocean inlet. When a hurricane or other severe weather arrives, the only road onto and off of the island is totally underwater. Cars will line in one direction filling both lanes for the full twenty miles, trying to leave the island. Fort Pulaski, with its cannonball holes in the outside walls and some cannonballs still visibly embedded in the wall, sits off to the left. It's obvious, even in passing, that this fort was engaged in one or more sieges at one time many years ago. Traveling on, the Tybee Island lighthouse, the oldest and tallest in Georgia, stands tall.

The lighthouse, from 1773, would guide mariners

from afar into the Savannah River. Its black-and-white tower with rotating signal light on top is now a tourist attraction. The stairs that were used by the lighthouse keeper are now used for tourists to climb to see out over the island. The small gift shop offers souvenirs as keepsakes.

The main street is lined with gift shops, a few restaurants, a church, and beach shops on one side of the street, while hotels and older beachfront homes line the other side. The waves of the ocean can be heard, and the smell of salt air is refreshing. Seagulls squaw as they dip and dive.

"Look, everyone! There's our hotel!" Sally points to the hotel.

"I wish we had bicycles," Chris says.

"We're close to the grocery store, hardware store, pizza place, and everything, but it would be fun to ride bikes around the island," Mary Lou interjects as she turns into the hotel parking lot.

"That would be fun, but we can walk to any of the shops. Some of the restaurants we might want to drive to," Teri says as she looks out the side window.

Having checked in at the registration desk, they carry their bags, umbrellas, and picnic baskets to their third-floor rooms. Swinging the door open, Chris and Teri set their belongings on the floor.

Chris leans the beach umbrella against the back wall of the closet. The adjoining door is between the closet and a desk with a chair; a TV and a small refrigerator line the wall. Two queen-size beds are separated by a stand with a telephone, lamp, and television guide. A round table with four chairs is in the corner near the sliding glass doors. Teri and Chris stand between the suitcases they've set down and stare across the room, through the sliding glass doors, and across a balcony facing the ocean with two beach chairs and a small table.

The sun glistens on the dark blue water as the waves slap the white, sandy beach. "Oh look, Teri! It's absolutely beautiful!" Teri sets the picnic basket down that she's still holding. Walking to the sliding glass doors, opening it and the screen door and stepping out onto the balcony, Chris inhales the salt air deep into her lungs while leaning against the rail. "Thank you so much for inviting me, Teri. I think I've died and gone to heaven."

Teri steps to the rail and, placing her hands on it, she glances at Chris. "I'm so glad you could come. Even though I haven't been working like the others and you, I needed this, too."

Sally and Mary Lou are sharing the other room together. The only difference in the rooms is the color of the bedspreads. Chris and Teri's is tan with gold swirls and Mary Lou and Sally's is blue with cream swirls.

Mary Lou knocks on the adjoining door. "Chris? Teri? Are you decent?" Mary Lou asks while twisting the door knob.

"Come on in. We're on the balcony," Teri shouts over the sound of waves rolling in.

The two walk across the room to join Chris and Teri on the balcony. "Don't you just *love* this?" Sally asks. "I can't wait to get in that water! I hope it isn't still really cold."

Chris looks at Sally as though she's crazy. "You're kidding! It's been in the eighties and nineties. There's no way that water will be too cold!"

Mary Lou places her arm around Sally's shoulder and says in a sympathetic voice, "Honey, don't you worry. If it's too cold, we won't make you go in. Just stick your little toes in." Winking at Chris behind Sally's back, she says, "We'll just push you in!" Laughing, she moves to the side and sits on one of the balcony chairs.

Glancing back into the room, Chris sees their suitcases, beach umbrella, and picnic basket still sitting in the doorway. "I think we need to unpack."

Teri, looking at her watch, says, "You're right, but is anyone hungry? It's six o'clock, and I'm starving. We can do that when we get back."

Mary Lou stands up. "I think you're right. We haven't unpacked either, and I'm hungry too. They have a really nice restaurant here in the hotel, or we can go someplace else."

Teri turns from the railing. "There's a nice little restaurant down the street. It's nothing fancy, but they have good food. What about going there?" All agree, and as Mary Lou and Sally return to their room, Mary Lou waves good-bye. "We'll meet you in fifteen minutes."

Walking the three blocks to the restaurant, everyone is feeling the effects from the long drive. Entering the small restaurant, several people have already gathered for the evening meal. Glasses clink; children are busy with coloring books and crayons; and soft music plays in the background. A waitress approaches and leads them to a table with a checked tablecloth and a small candle in its hurricane vase. A menu is set before them.

"I'll be back in a minute with your water and to take your order," the waitress says and walks away.

When the waitress returns with waters for the table, they all place their order—Mary Lou gets the scallops, Teri orders the shrimp, Chris chooses the grilled tilapia, and Sally settles on fried catfish.

Writing their order on a pad, "And to drink?" the waitress asks.

In unison they all answer, "Sweet tea."

· · · · · · · · · · · ·

Having finished their meal and returned to the hotel, Chris announces while holding her hands over her stomach, "I'm stuffed! I'm glad we walked there and back."

They all agree.

Entering her and Teri's room, with hands still holding her stomach, "I hate to say it, girls, but we need to unpack. And then, I don't know about you, but I'm taking a shower and hitting the sack."

Mary Lou answers, "Now that's a plan! We need to do the same." She and Sally turn to leave the room.

Sally stops. "I'm so glad all of us could come. We're going to have so much fun. See you in the morning." She closes the adjoining door.

Chris removes a few items from her suitcase and says to Teri, "Jack and I went to Stone Mountain Saturday. I can't believe we climbed that mountain! I didn't realize how out of shape I'm getting. Too many court rooms and late nights I guess."

"You've seen him a few times now. I'm glad you're taking time to have some fun."

"We're trying to get together more often but it's hard to do with our schedules. I need to take a shower."

"Okay."

. . . .

Meeting at the beach, all four are excited about their first day of relaxation. Beach umbrellas are unfolded and popped open, protecting them from the sun's rays. Sally's ice chest, filled with bottles of water, sits on the corner of the beach blanket that is spread out on the sand. As folded lounge chairs are opened and positioned, Mary Lou rubs sunscreen across her arms. The waves gently kiss the sandy beach then retreat only to return once again. Small sandpiper birds scamper about, pecking at unseen prey, as waves retreat, leaving their foamy edge.

Reaching into the bag of potato chips, Teri pulls out several chips to offer to the seagulls screeching above. Several have gathered nearby, pushing and shoving each other to get the first of the tasty morsels Chris and Mary Lou are tossing out onto the sand. Holding her chip high in the air, Teri laughs as one seagull dives and snatches the chip from her fingers.

Throwing more crumpled chips onto the sand, Sally laughs. "They're hungry little suckers, aren't they?"

Mary Lou smiles. "They have their potato-chip antenna up."

Reaching into the ice chest, Sally takes a bottle of water. "Does anyone want water? It's starting to get hot out here."

Refusing the water, the others continue to feed the birds. Sally stands. "Who's going to beat me to the water?" she asks and runs toward the water's edge. The others are close behind.

The day is spent relaxing, swimming, feeding the birds, and slathering sun lotion on each other's backs. A lunch break is taken at the nearby fast-food stand.

Stretching, Teri looks over at the other three stretched out on their lounge chairs sound asleep. Smiling, she thinks, *This is exactly what we each needed"* Standing, careful not to wake the others, she approaches the water's edge. Wading out until the cold water reaches her chest, she turns her back to the expanse of the deep-blue sea.

Lowering herself slowly deeper into the water, she ducks her head beneath the surface. The salt burns her eyes. Pushing off the bottom, she pops to the surface, and brushing hair out of her face, she doesn't see the large wave sneaking up behind her. Suddenly the wave crashes over her head, leaving her floundering in the water. Coughing, swiping at her face, and clearing her eyes, she laughs joyfully. *Oh, Lord, I love this!* Another wave slaps the back of her head. Laughing again, *Thank you, God. I needed that.*

Seeing a little girl with her small bucket and shovel on shore, Teri wades through the water as it circles about her feet, trying to pull her back in. Stepping out of the water and walking over to the little girl, who is busy building her sand castle at the water's edge, she says, "Hi. My name is Teri. What's yours?"

Glancing up, she answers, "Carlie."

"That's a pretty name. How old are you?"

Carlie holds up three fingers on one hand as she pats the side of the castle with the other. Smiling, Teri can see the deep concentration the child has on building her castle just right.

"That sure is a beautiful castle you are building. Do you need some help?"

Without a glance and very emphatically, Carlie says, "No!"

Laughing, Teri looks over at Carlie's mother, who is lounging on a chase lounge nearby, and winks. "Okay, Carlie." Standing from her kneeling position, "Maybe we'll see each other again. Have fun building your castle. Bye."

Intent on her castle-building, Carlie dumps another small shovel of damp sand on the edge of her master-piece. Without glancing up, she says, "Bye, Miss Teri."

· · · · · · · · · · · · ·

The mornings before the Georgia sun gets too hot for sunbathing are spent on the beach and playing in the ocean waves. The afternoons are spent visiting the many tourist shops that are displaying flip-flops, swimming suits, lotions, sea shells, and air mattresses as well as vari-ous sundries. Walking along the streets, the girls pass

homes built on stilts along the water's edge, a pier jaunt-
ing out over the water, and several art galleries. In making
plans for where to eat each night the girls have decided
to choose a wide variety of establishments. They're on a
dinner cruise tonight. As the boat takes them along the
Savannah River and along the riverfront shops, a meal is
set before them. A combination of seafood with brown
rice, steamed asparagus, white wine, coffee, and assort-
ed drinks are offered. A host points out various homes
owned by the rich and famous and gives some history of
various points. The evening is spent in a relaxed atmosphere with others from various parts of the country.

Another night is spent on a mystery cruise. A murder
is described during their meal, but the "whodunit" is left
out, and the patrons are to discover the culprit. As part of
their investigation, they are to look for evidence around
the boat. The cruise lasts two-and-one-half hours, and
they sail down the Savannah River and out into the
deeper ocean waters. Chris, Teri, Mary Lou, and Sally
are huddled together discussing the possible culprit.

Chris, being the prosecuting attorney, has an advantage over the others since investigating crimes and trying
them is her profession. The others lean on her for details
to look for. Like Sherlock Holmes, couples crouch down,
peeking around corners and jump when startled by another couple peeking around the same corner when they
come face-to-face. The evening is spent enjoying solving
the mystery. All gather in the lounge to discuss the "case"
and to see if anyone is correct in their discovery. Several
name various culprits.

Teri raises her hand, anxious to give her answer, like a child in the schoolroom. "We know who it is!"

The host of the party smiles and asks, "Really? And who do you think did this dastardly deed?"

Chris begins chuckling, and Mary Lou and Sally smother laughter. Teri jumps up out of her seat and dramatically points at the host, shouting, "You did it!"

Everyone bursts into laughter, and the host bows before them. "You caught me. How did you know?" Teri then explains their evidence.

"I told you she's the drama queen." Chris laughs as they return to the car.

Sally places her hand on Teri's shoulder, laughing. "You really let him know that you knew he was the killer. That was fun."

• • • • • • • • • • • •

As the sun is about to set each evening, the four meander along the water's edge picking up seashells. Stopping, Chris points toward the sunset. "Just look at that! It is so beautiful. It takes my breath away."

The women gaze at God's great creative beauty. No one speaks, and the only sound is the gentle waves caressing the beach and a few murmured voices from couples strolling past them. Even the seagulls are quiet.

Only the Lord hears the silent prayers the four have lifted up to Him as they watch the golds, oranges, pinks, and yellows fade into the horizon. The lights from homes along the shore begin turning on, giving light along the beach. Several couples stroll while others do their evening brisk-walking. The fragrance of meat cooking on barbecue grills is picked up as a breeze carries the aroma. As night begins to settle in, the four turn from the pier they have reached and head back to the hotel. Many of the couples have left, and Chris, Mary Lou, Teri, and Sally have the beach to themselves.

Strolling along, Chris and Teri walk together while Mary Lou and Sally follow a short distance behind. Chris sighs. "I hate leaving and getting back to the grind."

Teri bends to pick up a seashell. Handing it to Chris, she says, "I know what you mean. I need to start looking for a job."

"Have you decided what you want to do?"

"I prayed about it, and then Mom and I prayed together. She confirmed what I thought the Lord was telling me to do."

"Which is?"

"He wants me to go into counseling."

"How do you feel about that? Is that something you want to do?"

Teri picks up another sea shell, fingering it. "Yes. It was on the top of my list."

"I thought you were seriously thinking about teaching."

"I was, kind of. I just didn't know which direction to go. Now that I know, I need to start putting out feelers and some résumés."

Sally and Mary Lou have caught up to them, and walking beside them, Mary Lou says, "I sure hate thinking about going back. This is just too good to be true. I can't believe tomorrow night is our last night."

All agree as they walk across the sand to the hotel entrance.

Waking up early the next morning and planning to spend the entire day on the beach, Teri pulls the drapes open and steps out onto the balcony. Looking out over the great expanse of water, she bows her head and speaks with the Lord, thanking Him for the many blessings He has provided on this trip. Chris wakes up, and seeing Teri on the balcony, she joins her. A breeze rustles their hair and ruffles their pajama legs. A few drops of rain splash on their slippers.

"Oh no, not today. It can't rain on our last day!" Chris exclaims.

Teri holds her hand out over the railing; the rain drops are larger and more frequent. "It sure looks like that's what is going to happen."

Groaning, Chris turns back to the room. "Do you want some tea? You still have a couple of bags left. I'll make you a cup before I make coffee in the pot?"

Teri looks over her shoulder. "That would be nice. It's chilly with the rain, and a good cup of hot tea would lift my spirits." There's a knock on the adjoining door.

"Is everyone up and ready to play?" Mary Lou asks while opening the door slightly.

Chris places the tea bag into the cup of hot water while handing it to Teri. "Yes. Come on in. Would you like some coffee? It's almost finished brewing."

Looking out at the balcony, Sally groans loudly.

"Nuts! It's raining! There goes our beach time today, and it's our last day!"

Mary Lou walks out onto the balcony, sniffing the fresh scent of rain. "It will stop soon, and we'll still be able to go play."

"And in the meantime, why don't we just relax and enjoy being together?" Chris says as she hands each a hot cup of freshly brewed coffee.

Sitting cross-legged on their beds, Chris and Teri are still in pajamas. Mary Lou and Sally have robes over nightgowns. The conversation becomes storytelling about experiences each has had on their respective jobs. Teri, having no job, per se, begins by telling about a professor she had in one of her classes.

"This man looked exactly like the mad professor you see in the movies. In fact, I think they used him to make the picture."

"What'd he look like other than the wild hair?" Sally asks.

"He had these really thick glasses, and when he wrote on the blackboard, his nose was right up against it, and at times, his nose would even smear the writing. I really felt sorry for him. The poor man can't help being the way he is."

"Was he a good instructor?" Mary Lou asks as she sets her coffee cup on the table next to her.

"He was wonderful. It was a little hard to understand him because he had a strong accent. But he was very good. I learned a lot from him."

The room becomes silent as they all seem to be deep

in their own thoughts. Suddenly Sally bursts out laughing. Everyone looks at her, waiting for her to tell them why she's laughing. "I just thought of an incident at the hospital." Walking over to Teri's bed and sitting down on the end of it, she can't stop laughing.

"Tell us!" Mary Lou exclaims.

Taking control of her laughter, Sally begins, "A man comes in for a simple colonoscopy. His wife is with him, and they're an older couple, in their seventies." Once again she begins laughing as she flops back on Teri's bed.

"Come on, Sally!" Chris exclaims, anxious to hear the rest.

Sally swipes at the tears from laughing as she rises back up to a sitting position. "We had him put on the infamous tie-in-the-back gown, and he comes in with only his socks on and the gown." Sally struggles to keep from laughing again as she continues her story. "I had him lay on the table and was taking his blood pressure and, you know, the regular stuff." Taking a sip of her coffee, she continues. "I asked him if he had false teeth, and he said, 'No. Why?'" Again she bursts out laughing.

Chris is getting impatient, and Teri and Mary Lou are laughing only because Sally is laughing. Chris reaches across to the other bed and gently hits Sally on the arm. "Will you get on with it? What happened?"

Sally once again swipes at the tears. "I said, 'Sometimes during the procedure, a tooth can be chipped. We just have to take all precautions so that doesn't happen.' Trying to control bursting out laughing again, she continues, "That man's eyes got as big as saucers. He flew up to a sitting position and looked at me and said, 'You're going to put a tube up me down there, and you're afraid you might chip my teeth? The hell you say!' and he jumped off the table, flew out the door with the gown flapping, his butt shining, and his wife running after him hollering, 'Fred, wait! Stop, Fred!'"

Hysterical laughter fills the room. Ribs hurting and tears staining their cheeks, the stories continue.

The rain has stopped, but the atmosphere has changed amongst the group to a tired, somber, we-don't-want-to-leave air. Chris and Teri have decided to stay in and do some packing. Mary Lou and Sally decide to do the same, agreeing to meet later in the afternoon.

Laying a pair of slacks aside, Chris sits down on the end of the bed. "Teri, what do you think of Jack?"

Teri lays a blouse across the chair. "Jack?"

"Yeah, Jack. Jack Gordon, the detective I've been seeing."

"Oh, that Jack. I really don't know him, Chris. I've only met him once."

"What do you think Mom will do if I invite him over for dinner when we're all there?"

Teri sits down on the edge of her bed. "Chris, I think Mom would be very happy. This sounds like it's really getting serious."

"I guess so. Teri, I'm almost afraid to get too serious. What if he wants kids?"

Moving over to sit next to Chris, she takes her hand in hers. "Have you asked him about that, if he wants kids?"

"Not really. If he brings it up, I change the subject."

"Why? Don't you want children?"

Chris looks at Teri. "Seriously? No. I'm too old, too busy, and too set in my ways for kids. I don't want to give up my career to raise kids. I'm not like you and Mom. I'm not saying I don't like kids. I just don't want any."

Teri hesitates before answering. "Chris, it's okay. Not everyone wants to be a mother, and some don't belong being a mother!"

A knock on the adjoining door interrupts them. "Can I come in?" Sally asks.

Walking back toward her bed, Teri answers, "Sure, come on in."

Entering the room Sally looks at Teri then Chris. Hesitantly, she asks, "Am I interrupting something important?"

Chris picks up a pair of shorts. "No. We were just talking. What have you and Mary Lou been doing?"

• • • • • • • • • • • •

The day seems to drag by. By dinnertime, they have agreed to have room service rather than find a restaurant close by. As they eat their meal, there isn't much conversation. Teri breaks the silence.

"How about we all walk the beach this evening? We can't just sit here and watch the clock until it's time to leave."

Chris agrees, and then Mary Lou and Sally nod in agreement.

Walking slowly along the beach and awed by the sunset, Chris and Teri talk softly.

Teri says, "Chris, you asked about Jack. I think you need to talk to him and tell him how you feel before this goes any further."

Glancing at Teri, she says, "I guess you're right. We're going to spend a day in Helen when I get back. When the timing is right I think we may have to have a sit-down-and-talk session."

"Do you like him that much, Chris?"

Tears fill Chris's eyes. "Yes, Teri. I think I've fallen in love with him." Hesitating and giving a nervous little laugh, Chris stoops to pick up a sea shell then says, "Whatever that is. I'm just not sure since I haven't been in love before."

"You said you've been to the lake with him as well as the theatre, dinners, and several other places. Is it that you aren't sure about Jack or that you're afraid to make that commitment?

"I trust Jack. It isn't that. I guess, because I've seen so many unhappy marriages that I'm afraid to commit to a life-long relationship. How do I know if this is really love?"

"Let your heart speak and pray about it. The Lord will work it out if that's what He has in mind for you."

. . . .

Mary Lou and Sally are some distance behind Teri and Chris when Teri stops suddenly.

Chris stops beside her. "What's wrong?"

Teri shades her eyes and points down the beach. "Chris, do you see that? Something is glistening down there on the beach."

"I can't make out what it is either, but there is something there. Let's go check it out."

Walking quickly toward the object, each keep trying to make out what it is. Suddenly, as they near the object, Chris grabs Teri's arm, stopping her. "We better be careful, Teri. We don't know what it is."

Teri grins, removing her arm from Chris's grip. "My sister, the suspicious detective."

Walking more slowly and trying to make out what the object is, Chris holds Teri back. "We need to be careful, Teri! We have no idea what we're approaching! It could be a gun for all you know!"

"Oh come on, Chris. Now who's the drama queen?"

Laughing, Teri moves forward and recognizes what the object is. Running the rest of the way, she stoops to pick it up. The neck and cap of the foggy, blue bottle is all that sticks out from the dark, wet sand covering it. Teri kneels down, digging with her bare hands, and extracts the bottle. Chris runs to her side and stops suddenly as Teri holds up a bottle. Wiping the sand off, she sees that inside there's a piece of paper. "Chris, look. There's a note inside!"

Chris reaches for the bottle. "I wonder what it says." As they examine the bottle carefully, Mary Lou and Sally join them. Mary Lou sees the bottle.

"Hey, a real message in a bottle. I wonder where it's from."

Teri answers, "I do too, but let's wait and try to open it back in the room."

Sally bends forward to look at it more closely. "The paper looks old from what I can see of it. Come on, let's get back. It's getting too dark to see anything anyway."

Entering Chris and Teri's room, Teri holds her treasure to her chest. Chris, laughing, says, "Are you going to share your treasure or keep it all to yourself?"

Teri sets the bottle on the table. Mary Lou walks over to examine it. "I'll bet some kid threw it out there and is waiting to see if anyone finds it."

Sally shakes her head. "I don't think so, Mary Lou. It looks old to me and, look, the cap is even rusted."

Chris picks the bottle up and carefully examines it. "It does look old. I wonder where in the world it came from. Let's see if we can open it without breaking it."

. . . .

Moving the room-service trays aside, they gather around the table as Chris tries to unscrew the cap. Grunting and twisting, it finally comes loose, but the bottle flies out of her hands. Teri screams as it sails through the air and plops onto the bed. Sighs of relief fill the room. Teri gently picks up the bottle and places it ever so gently on the table. All stand back looking at it as though it's a foreign object that has just dropped out of the sky.

Looking around, Chris picks up a knife from one of the dirty plates. "We can see if we can pull the note out with this."

"Please be careful, Chris. I don't want my bottle broken," Teri pleads.

"I'll be careful, Teri. I don't want to break it either."

Chris tries and tries to wiggle the loosely rolled note from the bottle with no success. Exasperated, she sets the knife down. "I don't think we're going to get it out without breaking the bottle, Teri."

"No! Try again," Teri desperately commands.

Another thirty minutes pass when suddenly the note falls out of the mouth of the bottle. Everyone says "Hallelujah" as Teri picks up the note.

The graying paper is fragile, and very gingerly, Teri unrolls it. Laying it gently on the table and holding the ends down so they can read it, Teri sucks in her breath. The writing is faded and difficult to read. Teri leans close. "Sally, can you move that lamp a little closer?"

Sally scoots the lamp where the light is brightest on the mysterious paper. All four are leaning over the table as though they are examining a very small, strange bug. Teri begins to read, "'I've been lost but now I'm found. Please call," and a number is given. Teri looks up, puzzled. "It's dated 2008."

Mary Lou stands up. "Well let's call the number!"

Teri looks at her. "I think it's a foreign country. I don't recognize anything like our area codes."

Chris leans forward, examining the note. "It is a foreign number. I don't know what country, but we can give it a shot."

Teri excitedly grabs the phone and hands it to Chris. "Here, Chris, you call."

"It's your bottle and your note. I think you should make the call."

The other two chime in. "Yes, Teri, you make the call."

Nervously, Teri dials for the hotel operator. "Can you please connect me to this number?" She gives the operator the number.

"Ma'am, that's a foreign country. Are you sure you want to call from the hotel phone?" the operator asks.

Teri looks at the others. "Do you know what country?"

The operator takes a moment then answers, "I think its England, but I'm not real sure. You don't know who you're calling?" the operator says, rather astonished.

Teri laughs and explains the situation.

Turning to the others as she hangs up the phone, "Does anyone have free long distance to England on their cell phone?"

"England!" all three exclaim at the same time.

"That's where the operator said she thinks this number is from."

Sally says, "Wait a minute," and runs through the adjoining doors, returning with her cell phone. "Hubby can just pay the bill. We need to call!" Laughing, she hands the phone to Teri, and Teri dials the number.

Excited, she sits down on the edge of the bed as the phone on the other end rings. Chris, Mary Lou, and Sally are standing, holding their breath. Teri slowly closes the phone and lays it on the bed. Looking up at the others, tears have formed in her eyes.

Throwing her hands in the air, Chris can't stand the suspense. "For crying out loud, Teri, what?"

Teri looks sadly at the others. "This number has been disconnected."

Suddenly everyone plops down on a chair or a bed. The excitement is replaced by a silent room filled with disappointment.

Chapter 5

Chris faces murder, mayhem, deception, and lies daily. Her zeal for truth remains strong even under strong opposition. Wearing a dark blue skirt and a powder-blue blouse with a gold rope chain glittering at her neckline, Chris stands before the jury, and without speaking, she looks at each juror. In her mind, she's sizing them up. A young man with a shaggy haircut and blue jeans sits slouched in his chair, chewing gum. An elderly woman that looks like a little Mrs. Clause stares at Chris then shyly smiles. Chris has read each form the juror's filled out so she knows that two women have children the same ages as the two small victims. One middle-aged man yawns while another has a pen and notebook, ready to take notes. Seven women and five men fill the jury box, with one male alternate. Chris considers who has paid close attention to the proceedings, such as which seem bored and if there were any tears. All are important when making her summation.

Standing before the jurors, Chris begins her summation. "Ladies and gentleman, you have seen evidence that cannot be refuted. You have heard witnesses who saw the defendant in the area at the time of the murder." As she walks, Chris points to a poster-sized photo, set on an easel, of a small boy smiling with freckles dotting his nose and cheeks, and blazing-red hair. Chris emphasizes, "Jamie, only six years old, is dead!"

Stepping toward another poster-sized photo on its easel next to the one of Jamie, Chris stands beside it. "And what about Annie? She was only five years old, and now she's dead, too." Annie's bright smile and long, reddish-brown hair, thrown forward on her shoulders in pigtails with red bows tied neatly at the ends, smiles back at the jurors.

Her brilliant, sparkling eyes seem to search each face in the jury box, reminding them of her innocence.

Chris walks closer to the jury box and continues, "There is no question these two beautiful children were abducted and brutally murdered by—" pointing to the defendant "—Mr. Comstack!"

The defendant sits picking at his dirty fingernails then reaches his hairy arm up to scratch the back of his straggly, dirty hair. Unshaven and dressed in the typical prison garb, he seems unconcerned.

Walking over to the defense table and strategically standing where Mr. Comstack can clearly be seen by the jury, Chris, with much disdain in her voice, says, "This man, this child killer, snuffed out Jamie and Annie as though they were less than animals!"

The defendant never glances up.

Chris continues. "They will never finish school. They will never play in the pond near their home again, be able to ride their bikes, never marry or have children of their own. Why?" Chris stabs her index finger toward the defendant. "Because he murdered them!"

Slowly scanning the faces of the jurors, she sees the two mothers and Mrs. Clause wiping tears from their eyes. The slouching young man with the chewing gum looks as though he wishes he could have his cell phone so he can be texting his friends, and another yawn escapes the man in the center back row. The others seem attentive.

Walking back to the jury box slowly, so as to allow her words to impact the jurors, Chris follows along the railing, continuing to look at each juror. "There is ironclad evidence." She snaps her index finger up so all can see. "Number one: absolute, one hundred percent-positive DNA." As she slowly moves, she snaps another finger up. "Number two. His knife, with his fingerprints on it, was found in the bushes near Jamie and Annie's mutilated bodies."

Taking a breath and adding another finger, she says, "Number three: his bloody footprints and blood-stained shirt. Number four: the children's hair and blood found in the trunk of his car." Turning, Chris walks back toward the center of the jury box and stands near the two mothers. Leaning forward with her hands on the railing, Chris emphatically says, "Number five: Jamie and Annie's bloody and shredded underwear were found in his apartment. He kept them as souvenirs!" Stepping back slowly to give them time to chew on her last words, she walks to the photos of the children. "Ladies and gentlemen, give

Jamie and Annie the justice they deserve." Looking at the jurors and pointing to the defendant, she says, "Find this man guilty! Thank you." Chris turns, and her high heels click on the floor as she returns to her table.

After Judge Walker instructs the jury, they file out to begin their deliberations. The defendant is escorted out of the room, and Chris begins placing papers in her briefcase and gathering bags of evidence. A hand softly touches her shoulder and, turning, she sees Detective Gordon looking down at her.

"Wanna go to lunch?" the detective asks.

Slowly shaking her head, she says, "Jack, I don't think I could swallow a bite of food right now." She picks up her briefcase. "How about some three-day-old coffee in the lawyers' lounge?"

Jack can see this trial has really gotten to Chris. Her usual joy-filled smile is gone, and her makeup doesn't completely hide the dark circles under her eyes. It seems it's touched something deep within her. "Sure," he replies. "Lead me on."

Chris is silent as she sips her coffee, and Jack isn't sure what to say. Finally, so as to break the silence, Jack asks, "How about we go to the lake this weekend? I'll fill up the boat, and we'll speed across the water and let the bugs splatter our teeth."

Chris smiles a weary smile while setting her cup down. Before she can answer, her cell phone rings. Answering it, the only word she speaks is, "Okay." Hanging up, she stands. "The jury is back." Looking at her watch, she says, "That was fast! They've only been in there thirty minutes."

Jack escorts her back to the courtroom, and as she takes her position at the prosecutors' table, Jack takes a seat in the spectators' section.

When the judge enters and all have been seated, he looks at the bailiff. "Bring in the jury."

Watching the faces of the jurors as they file in, Chris can't tell what the verdict might be. *Please, Lord, your justice be done. Don't allow this monster to go free. Amen.*

The foreman stands, handing the verdict paper to the bailiff who in turn hands it to the judge. Judge Walker unfolds it, glances at it, and hands it back to the bailiff to return to the foreman. "How do you find?" Judge Walker asks.

The foreman unfolds the paper as he swallows several times, causing his Adam's apple to prominently bob up and down. "We the jury find Charles Dean Comstack guilty of the first-degree murder of Jamie Lee Cross. We find him guilty of the first-degree murder of Annie Margaret Cross." He then announces "guilty" to each charge on the list of charges brought against the defendant, and the list is long: guilty of kidnapping, guilty of sexual assault, and guilty of assault on a minor. Guilty, guilty, guilty.

The defendant, standing beside his lawyer, has no expression on his face as he stares down at the floor. From the jury box, a woman sniffs back tears. Blinking several times in rapid succession, Chris is determined not to allow the tears that are threatening to flow show. *Thank you, Jesus.*

Sobs are heard behind her as Jamie and Annie's parents cry with relief. Friends and family gather around Chris, thanking her. The mother, with tears streaming down her cheeks, grabs Chris, hugging her so tightly that Chris has trouble breathing.

"Thank you so much, Miss Wilson."

Gently pushing her away, she says, "You're very welcome."

"We can't thank you enough," the father says as he shakes Chris's hand.

• • • • • • • • • • • •

Driving slowly out of the courthouse parking lot, Detective Gordon reaches across the seat and lays his hand on Chris's knee. Like taking the cork out of a tightly closed bottle, Chris bursts into tears. Detective Gordon removes his hand, placing it back on the steering wheel, and guides the car to a quiet side street and parks next to the curb. Jack thinks Chris is reacting to the verdict so he asks, "Would you like to talk about it?"

"Jack, we need to talk. Will you please just take me home?" she says as she wipes away her tears.

Looking at her for a second, Jack reaches for the ignition key, starts the car, and pulls away from the curb without speaking.

• • • • • • • • • • • •

"Would you like a cup of coffee?" Chris asks as Jack takes a seat in the recliner.

"No, thanks. Do you have something cold?"

After walking to the refrigerator, Chris opens it, leaning over to see what she has available. "I have some lemonade, ice tea, and Dr Pepper."

"Lemonade will be fine."

After pouring his lemonade, she pours herself ice tea. Jack is a little uncomfortable not knowing what Chris wants to talk about. His fear is that this is good-bye, and the diamond ring in his pocket will have to be returned to the store.

Chris sips her tea. "I don't know where to start," she says softly.

Jack takes a deep breath. "Is this like a Dear John letter, Chris?"

"No!" Chris exclaims.

"Then would you like to tell me what this is all about?"

Placing her feet underneath her as she positions herself on the couch, Chris is hesitant before speaking. "I need to know where we're going in our relationship."

Walking over to her, Jack sits down beside her. "I think you know, Chris."

"I really care for you, Jack, and I need to know if you want kids, are you a Christian, and how you feel about me continuing to work. I love my job, and what if—"

"Whooo." Jack laughs.

Chris takes a breath, looking at him seriously. "I need to know, Jack."

"I know you do, and I'll tell you anything you want to know."

"We've never talked about your faith. Are you a follower of Christ, a Christian? Chris asks shyly.

"Yes. I was saved and baptized when I turned twenty-one." Smiling he adds, "I was a slow learner."

"What about kids?"

"I love kids!" Scooting closer to her, he says, "I think we should have at least fifteen."

Chris can't help but burst out laughing and thinks, *We?* "You can't be serious!"

Jack can tell she caught the "we." He leans closer to her and lightly runs his finger along the nape of her neck and whispers near her ear, "What about you? Do you want kids?"

With Jack so close, Chris fans her face and says, "It's getting awfully hot in here. Ah what? Oh, that's right, kids? Yes and no."

Jack starts to ask her why but lets it slide for now. As he sits back up straight, he says, "I know we haven't talked about a lot of things, and I guess we should have. It's kind of hard to talk with bugs splattered on your teeth. What else do you want to know?"

"How long do you have before you retire?"

"I plan to retire when I'm fifty-five. We're allowed to do that and I have a good retirement plan."

"Then what? I know you don't like to golf."

"Oh, I don't intend to spend my golden years fishing or golfing. I want to travel. There's a lot of places I've always wanted to see and have never gotten to."

"Like where?"

"Well, I've never been to England or Israel or Hawaii."

"You want to go to Israel!?"

"Sure. Don't you?"

"I've never thought about it."

The discussion lasts well into the night. Chris finally has all the answers to her many questions and stands. Walking Jack to the door, Chris looks up at him. "About the lake this weekend . . . I'd like to go home for the weekend. Would you like to come to dinner Saturday night at Mom and Dad's?"

Smiling, Jack looks down at her. "Sure. I'd love to meet your parents. From what you've told me about them, they sound great."

Jack has left the diamond ring in its small velvet box in his pocket. *I don't think this is the right time,* he thought during their talk.

• • • • • • • • • • • •

Driving slowly down the shaded driveway, Chris sees Teri and her mother sitting on the front porch rocking in the rocking chairs with glasses of drink in their hands. Teri jumps up when she sees Chris's car and stands at the top of the stairs grinning. Chris parks as Margaret joins Teri. The weather has been hot, so Chris is in blue-jean shorts and a Braves T-shirt. Teri is dressed the same but wears a Falcons T-shirt, where Margaret has knee-length pants on and a bright yellow, short-sleeved shirt. The evening has cooled down, and Chris had hoped to arrive earlier, but the Friday work traffic on Georgia 400 is the usual "parking lot."

Gathered around the table having dinner, Chris asks, "Mom, is it okay with you if Detective Gordon comes to dinner tomorrow night?"

Teri smiles as she covers her mouth with her napkin.

Chris looks at Teri with a silent warning: "Don't you say a word!" Teri just smiles back with knowing showing in her eyes. Margaret smiles brightly and answers, "Of course not! I would love to meet him. Wouldn't you, Clay?"

Clay nods his head as he chews and then swallows his food.

Margaret is trying hard not to show the excitement bubbling up within her.

Chris glances at Teri then her mother. *She's already planning baby blankets, cribs, and counting how many.* "Will six o'clock be okay, or maybe he could come earlier and we'll have time to visit?" Chris asks.

Teri can't wait to get her two cents in. "I think he should come in the morning, and then we'll have all day to get acquainted. What do you think, Chris?"

Chris knows Teri is being sly in her question, but wanting to let Teri know she better keep quiet, she says, "I think around four would be time enough to get *acquainted,* as you so eagerly put it."

Teri laughs as she picks up her fork.

Clay leans forward with his elbows on the table and addresses Chris. "Is this a serious relationship, Chris, or just friends?"

Teri and Margaret can't wait to hear Chris's answer. Margaret holds her breath anxiously for the answer. Chris has never lied to her parents and hesitates while looking at each of them; she clears her throat.

Margaret is about to wet her pants in anticipation and finally taking a breath, "Well, honey?"

Chris looks at Teri, who is mouthing the words: "Tell them!"

Clay patiently waits for an answer. He already suspects by Chris's hesitating and seeming to be uncomfortable with the question that it's serious. Not just friendship.

Chris finally answers. "We've been dating for some time now."

"But you've never mentioned it! Why have you kept this such a secret?" Margaret asks.

"Mom, I don't want to hurt your feelings but I knew you would start planning for babies, cribs, and baby clothes. I just wasn't ready for that. To answer your question, Dad, yes, it's serious. I love him, and I think he loves me."

Margaret jumps up and down in her seat. "Oh, how wonderful!"

Teri bursts out laughing.

• • • • • • • • • • • •

When Chris hears a car coming up the driveway, she nervously steps out onto the porch. She knows it's Jack because they agreed he should come about four o'clock.

He's seldom late, and when he stops the car, she walks out to greet him.

Wearing tan slacks, a short-sleeve green shirt, and loafers, Jack doesn't seem a bit nervous. Where others may feel threatened by meeting the parents of one they love, Jack is quite relaxed. He has decided, and has no doubt in his mind, that he will be asking Chris to marry him tonight.

After cool drinks have been served, everyone retires to the porch, and Chris and Jack sit together on the porch swing. Laughter and joking around, the group enjoys the afternoon. Margaret stands. "I guess I better get in there and prepare the rest of dinner."

Teri stands to join her mother. "I'll help you, Mom."

Chris looks at Jack as he smiles and stands. "Why don't we all meet in the kitchen and make a real project out of this?" Jack says. Margaret looks a little surprised. "That sounds nice. There isn't that much to do, really."

Everyone follows her into the kitchen, and naturally she dons her apron. Lifting an apron to place on Jack, she stands on tiptoes but can't reach high enough to put the apron strap over his head. Laughing, he takes it from Margaret and slips it on. Looking down at the imprinted words, *Kiss the cook*, he looks at Chris with a secret smile and winks. Chris can't help but laugh as she ties the ties behind his back.

"I'll make the salad," Jack says as he reaches for the head of lettuce Margaret has set on the counter.

"Mom, do you want these rolls in the oven yet?" Teri asks.

The kitchen is buzzing with activity while the family is laughing and teasing each other. Jack is no exception.

Meatloaf, gravy, mashed potatoes, buttery rolls, steamed asparagus, corn on the cob, and tossed salad are eagerly devoured as everyone enjoys the time together.

As the women clean up the dishes, placing them in the dishwasher and washing the pots and pans by hand, Chris can see her father and Jack through the kitchen window sitting on the back patio talking. *I sure hope Dad isn't grilling Jack like some teenage boy about to take his daughter on their first date.* It doesn't seem that way when she sees them laughing. *At least they seem to like each other.* With the dishes cleared, Chris steps out onto the patio. "Okay, you two, what's going on out here?"

Laughing, Clay replies, "We're plotting."

"What are you plotting?" Chris asks as she takes a seat.

"We're going to steal Teri's car and go for a joyride." Clay laughs as he winks at Jack.

Jack looks at Chris. "Wanna go for a walk?"

Chris smiles. "Sure. You haven't seen all the beautiful gardens Mom and Dad have made."

Clay grins while standing up. "You kids go ahead. I'll see what the other two are up to."

Jack and Chris begin following the path. "Did your Mom and Dad lay these bricks?"

"Yes. They bought a book that had different designs and how to do them, and they did it all themselves."

"Wow. That had to be quite an undertaking."

Laughing, she says, "You don't know my mother.

Once she sets her mind to something, she won't quit until it's done."

"I wondered who you got that from. It's beautiful. How long did it take them to do all of it?"

"I'm not sure. With Dad working, Mom would do what she could, like lay out the bricks in the pattern. When Dad was home, they'd work together."

Stopping at the arbor, Jack reaches up and pulls a cluster of flowers down, breaking one off and handing it to Chris. "Did they build this arbor, too?"

"They sure did. Most everything you see here they did themselves. Mom loves gardens, flowers, trees, you name it. She takes great pride in her yards."

"I can see that."

Chris takes Jack's hand and leads him to the gazebo. "Teri and I used to spend hours in this gazebo as kids. Even now I always find it very peaceful." Taking seats, they chat about cases they've worked together and various trips each have taken. When there's a lull in the conversation, Jack quietly slips his hand in his pocket. Before arriving at Chris's parents' home, he took the ring out of the box and slipped it into his pants pocket.

Chris has turned her head, looking at a deer standing in the clearing close to the trees. "Oh, Jack, look," she whispers as she turns to face him, only to find him on one knee, grinning at her. "What are—" she starts as he reaches for her hand.

"Christine Marie Wilson, you have made my life miserable!"

Chris looks shocked but says nothing.

Jack continues. "I am absolutely miserable when I'm not with you. I love you more than life itself and—" Suddenly he jumps up and yells, "Ouch!" Looking down, he sees a yellow jacket has stung him through his slacks. Swatting the bee aside, he laughs. As he rubs his leg where the bee stung him he says, "Woman, will you marry me!?"

Throwing her arms around his neck, she yells, "Yes, yes, yes."

Suddenly cheers fill the air from the back porch. Chris's voice has carried to the patio where her parents and Teri sit talking quietly, until they hear the happy "yes, yes, yes," coming from the gazebo.

When they return to the house, Margaret can't wait to greet them. "Ohhh, I'm just so happy!" she exclaims as she throws her arms around Chris's neck.

Chris struggles to get free. "Mom, you're choking me!"

Margaret lets go suddenly, and everyone can see tears have formed in her eyes.

Teri laughs. "Okay, Mom, stop counting the grand-kids."

Clay shakes Jack's hand and, grinning like a Cheshire cat. "Good job!"

Laughing, Jack blushes a little, which is rare for him. Chris exhibits the beautiful, sparkling marquise diamond resting on her left hand's ring finger as Margaret and Teri hold her hand, inspecting the diamond.

Teri has tears in her eyes as she hugs Chris and whispers, "I'm so glad you and Jack talked. I know you did, or you wouldn't have brought him home."

Chris whispers back, "Can we talk later?"

Teri lets go of Chris. "Sure." She wipes the tears from her eyes.

Chris smiles and turns to Jack. "You have made me, *and* my mother, very happy today, Jack Gordon."

Leaning over, Jack gently kisses Chris. Margaret is about to pass out with excitement as Teri cheers and Clay claps. Chris knows exactly what her mother is thinking: grandkids!

Walking back into the kitchen, Margaret speaks over her shoulder to the others following her in, "Would anyone like some banana pudding?"

"You bet," Jack answers. "Banana pudding is my favorite."

Margaret smiles broadly as she sets saucers on the kitchen counter. Jack walks over to her. "I really appreciate your wonderful meal tonight. It was very good. Thank you."

Margaret turns to face him. Looking up at him, her eyes fill with tears. "I am so happy for you and Chris. I know you'll be very happy together." Wiping at her eyes, she turns back to scoop the delicious banana pudding onto the plates.

Sitting around the table eating the dessert, Clay looks at Jack. "How long have you been in law enforcement, Jack?"

After swallowing his food, Jack replies, "Sixteen years. I've been a detective for ten of those."

"You must have made detective pretty fast. Isn't that quick for moving up the ladder like that?"

Jack laughs. "I don't know if you'd call it moving up the ladder, but yes. I've always been pretty ambitious."

"There's nothing wrong with that."

Looking at Chris, Clay asks, "Do you plan to keep prosecuting the bad guys, Chris?"

Chris glances at Jack then back at her father. "Sure. I love my job and plan to keep right on doing it."

Margaret is listening carefully and trying not to be too pushy as she asks Chris, "When do you think you'll get married?"

Chris grins. She can see the wheels turning in her mother's head. "Mom, we just got engaged an hour ago!"

"I know, I know."

Teri interjects, "What kind of trials do you have coming up? Jack, do you help her with a lot of them?"

Chris answers first. "I have one I'm working on now that will start next week. It's a robbery case and looks like it's pretty much a slam dunk." Chris glances at Jack, as though to say, "Your turn."

Jack lays his fork down. "I work on some with her, but usually it's the big cases. Murder and stuff like that."

Chris smiles broadly and says, "I have my own detective who investigates most of my cases." Reaching over, she squeezes Jack's arm and smiles up into his face. "I guess I'll have to fire him now."

Jack grins, looking down at her with love in his eyes.

As the sun sets, Jack and Chris walk slowly out to his car. Jack turns to her and leans against the door while taking both of her hands in his. "You have a wonderful family. I see why you want to come home as often as you do. I really enjoyed meeting them."

Chris smiles while secretly not wanting him to leave just yet. "They are very special to me. We've always been close. I'm glad you like them, and I know Mom and Dad like you."

"I sure hope you can cook like your mother! That was really good."

Chris feigns being insulted and steps back from him. "Of course I can! She taught me! Chris grins and admits, "Well, maybe not quite as good."

Laughing, Jack reaches out and pulls her up against him and, lowering his head, their lips touch. "Good night, my almost-as-good-a-cook-as-your-mother," Jack says as he pulls her closer into a passionate good-night kiss.

• • • • • • • • • • • •

"Girls, are you ready for church?" Margaret yells up to Chris and Teri in their bedrooms. Chris steps out onto the top step, smiling down at her mother.

"Yes, Mom. I didn't sleep last night, so I'm up and ready to go. I don't know about Teri though." With that she turns toward Teri's room. "Teri? Are you coming?"

A faint, "I don't think so. You go ahead" is muffled through her bedroom door.

Chris steps back up into the hallway and approaches Teri's door, knocking lightly. "Teri, can I come in?"

"Yes, come on."

Opening Teri's bedroom door, Chris steps into the

bedroom. Looking toward the bed, she sees Teri bundled under her blankets. Her tear-stained face is difficult to hide from Chris. "Teri, what's wrong?" Teri begins crying again. "Teri? This isn't like you. What's going on?"

Teri throws the top blankets back but stays covered with the sheet, wiping her eyes with the corner of the sheet. "Chris, I'm happy you and Jack are getting married. But you said you don't want children." She is crying again and speaking through her tears. "It just breaks my heart that you won't know the joy children will bring you."

"Hold on, and let me tell Mom we're not going to church. She's waiting downstairs."

"No, you go ahead. I'm just feeling sorry for myself."

"Sorry for yourself? Why?"

Throwing her hands up and covering her face as she begins sobbing, she says, "Because I'll never have nieces or nephews to love!"

Chris tries to keep from laughing but doesn't have much success. "Oh. So that's it. I'll be back in a minute."

Walking downstairs, she finds her mother wiping the kitchen counter. "Mom, Teri and I won't be going to church this morning."

Margaret turns. "Why? I thought you were ready."

"I am, but Teri isn't up to par this morning, and I thought I'd stay with her."

"Oh dear, is she sick? I better go check on her."

"No, Mom, it isn't that. She and I need to talk, and this is the best time."

Margaret lays the dishrag down and looks a bit puzzled. "Okay, if you say so. Are you sure she isn't sick?"

"She isn't sick, Mom. She just needs to work some things out. You go on to church. We'll be fine."

"Okay."

Margaret and Clay leave for church as Chris climbs the stairs. Knocking lightly, she hears Teri say, "Come in."

Walking back to Teri's bed, Chris smiles. "The coast is clear. We can talk now."

Teri scoots up and leans back against her pillows; she wipes the last of the tears from her cheeks. "I'm sorry, Chris. I'm being selfish and silly."

"No, you aren't. If that's what you're feeling, then there's nothing wrong with that. God understands, and I do, too."

"Thanks."

"Seriously, Teri, you have a right to want kids around to love. You'll have your own, and you'll probably have a couple of mine."

Teri's eyes fly wide open, and she begins stuttering. "But you . . . you . . . you said you didn't want kids!"

Chris smiles. "I know."

Teri throws her feet over the edge of the bed and, jumping to her feet, she runs to the dresser.

Chris watches her, puzzled. "What are you doing?"

Teri turns with a pad and pencil in her hand, grinning. "I want to document what you just said just in case I wake up and it was only a dream."

Laughing, Chris stands. "Put that away, you silly goose, and come sit down. I have a lot to tell you."

Teri does as she's told and sits next to Chris on the bed. "So speak. I can't wait to hear this."

"Jack and I had a long conversation the other night. I had a lot of questions for him and, praise God, he was so patient with me."

Teri smiles and says nothing.

Chris takes a deep breath. "We both had questions, and one that he asked me was why I didn't want kids. It took me by surprise."

Softly Teri asks, "Why don't you want kids, Chris?"

Standing up and walking to the window and looking out over the acreage, Chris takes a long minute before answering. Teri sits quietly, knowing Chris needs time to think about her answer. Almost in a whisper, Chris starts to answer Teri and Jack's question. "I have seen so much pain parents have gone through."

Teri interrupts. "Chris, I can't hear you."

Stepping to the side and sitting down on the big armchair next to the window, Chris begins again. "I have seen so much pain parents have gone through in raising children."

"But—"

Chris cuts her off. "Let me finish, Teri."

"Sorry."

"You know I prosecute a lot of people for a lot of different crimes. Some of those are crimes against children. Like the case I just had with the five- and six-year-olds."

"I know that had to be very hard," Teri softly says.

"It may be one of the hardest cases I've had in a very long time." Looking at Teri, she says, "You can't even imagine what people will do to kids! I don't know how God can watch it, much less allow it!" Chris says sternly.

Teri studies her for a moment. "I don't either, but I don't think anyone does, Chris. We just have to accept that He knows what is going on."

Chris quickly turns her head toward the window to hide the tears welling up in her eyes.

"Don't forget, Chris, the bad people still have to answer to God. Even if they are found not guilty, even though they are guilty, God will pass His verdict, and His judgment is final."

Chris wipes a tear that has spilled over.

Teri walks over to her and puts her arms around Chris from behind her. She knows it's difficult for Chris to show "weakness," as Chris puts it at times.

"Chris? Is that what you're afraid of? If you have children and love them that someone will hurt them?"

Chris is now sobbing. "Yes! I may not be able to protect them from slime like Comstack."

Teri holds her tighter and allows her to cry. *Now I understand why she's been so adamant about not having children. Lord God, please help Chris. She's scared and hurting.*

Chris's tears slow, and she wipes her eyes with her sleeve. "I'm sorry. I don't know what came over me."

As Teri loosens her hug on Chris, she says, "Tell me what you and Jack have decided. That is, if you want to share that with me."

Chris gives a short little laugh and turns her swollen eyes and tear-stained face to Teri. "We want kids, and we're going to trust God to keep them safe."

Teri suddenly starts dancing and running around the room yelling, "Yes! Yes! Yes!"

Chris bursts out laughing.

Teri runs to her and hugs her again. This time Teri cries. Her tears are tears of joy. "Thank you, Lord, thank you." Teri cries.

"Do you want to hear the rest, or are you going to blubber all over me?" Chris asks through her laugher. Teri sits down on the floor, leaning back against the foot of her bed, and Chris begins telling her parts of the conversation she and Jack had. "He's a Christian and, Teri, he has strong faith."

"That's good," Teri replies.

"He said he can retire in another few years, and he'd like to do some traveling. You know, like to the Caribbean, England, places he's never been."

"How do you feel about that?"

"Oh, it's fine with me. I think it would be fun."

"What about your work, Chris?"

Chris smiles. "When he retires, so will I. Do you really think I'm going to let that handsome husband of mine loose in Hawaii or wherever?"

Teri laughingly replies, "I guess not. Speaking of Hawaii, do you know where you'll go for your honeymoon?"

Chris bursts out laughing. "No, Mom, I don't."

Without realizing how long they have been talking, each is surprised when they hear footsteps on the stairs. "Chris? Teri? Are you up here?" Margaret asks.

"We're in here, Mom," Teri replies.

Margaret opens the door and smiles as she sees Teri

sitting on the floor and Chris in the chair. "Is everything okay?" Margaret asks cautiously.

Teri stands up and walks over to Margaret. "Mom, I'm sorry. I just needed to talk to Chris about some things that were upsetting me."

"Is everything okay now? Do you need my help?"

Chris smiles, knowing that's her mother's gentle way of asking, "Okay, what did you talk about?" Teri smiles, hugs her mother, and says, "We're fine, Mom. Everything is okay now."

"I'll be fixing lunch pretty soon," Margaret replies and proceeds downstairs.

Teri looks at Chris and asks, "Are you going to tell Mom of this decision about having children?"

"I don't think we need to say anything. I don't think she knows otherwise."

"You may be right." Laughing, Teri walks toward the door. "If she knew otherwise, she would bug you until the day you die!"

"You got that right!" Chris follows her downstairs.

Chapter 6

. . . .

The trip to Tybee Island renewed the women's spirits and seemed to instill a peace that each has carried into their workplaces. Teri has decided she needs to get serious about starting a career.

Teri and her parents are sitting at the kitchen table having a conversation when Clay picks up the now-cherished blue bottle with the note inside then sets it back on the table. "That's still a mystery as to who wrote that note, isn't it?"

Teri runs her finger along the bottle edge. "Yes. I wish we could have found out who wrote the note and where it was dropped into the sea."

Margaret smiles. "Well, it doesn't look like that's ever going to happen since that phone number has been disconnected."

Clay leans over, looking at the bottle more closely. "We may be able to find out who had that phone number before it was disconnected."

Jerking her hand back, Teri excitedly asks, "Do you really think we can do that?"

~~~~~~~

"Well, I think I still have some clout." Clay laughs as he begins to stand.

"Wait, Dad. I think that would be great, but I wanted to talk to you and Mom."

Sitting back down at the kitchen table, Clay moves his breakfast plate to the side.

"This sounds sort of important."

Margaret has walked to the coffee pot, pouring them each another cup of coffee. Teri waits until she has returned and sits down. "I think I need to start putting out some feelers for jobs. I can't play forever."

Margaret glances at Clay. "Where will you start looking?"

Teri can tell this is going to be a touchy subject. "I'm not sure, but talking to a few people, there's several positions open."

Clay takes a sip of coffee. "Where? Are they around here, the Atlanta area?"

Teri knows her answer will not be easily accepted by her mother and looks down at her plate. "Some are, but there's one in California I'd like to check into."

Shocked, Margaret replies, "California! No, no, Teri, you can't go that far from home. We'll never see you."

Smiling, Teri looks up and takes her mother's hand. "Mom, I'm just going to check it out. I didn't say I will take it."

With tears forming in her eyes, Margaret slides her hand away. "Teri, please try for something here. I couldn't stand having you so far away."

Clay looks at Teri then at Margaret. "Honey, they

have to leave the nest sometime. She's just going to check into it."

Teri begins clearing the dishes as Clay and Margaret finish their cups of coffee. Carrying the plates into the kitchen and setting them on the counter, *I really would like to see California. I think it would be exciting. Mom really is going to put up a fight if I decide to go to California.*

"Teri?" Clay puts his hand on her shoulder.

Startled, Teri spins around quickly, almost dropping a plate. "Oh, Dad. I didn't hear you come in."

Glancing over his shoulder, he sees Margaret walking toward the stairs. "Teri, if you are led to go to California, then you go where the Lord wants you to go, and if it's California, then your mother and I will just have to accept it."

Placing the plate in the dishwasher, Teri turns back to her father. "Dad, I really would like to go to California, but if that isn't where I'm supposed to go, then I won't."

"I know, honey. You do what you need to do."

"Thanks, Dad. I will."

Margaret did not go upstairs as expected and has heard their conversation. *Lord, please don't send her to California. That's just too far away, and we'll never get to see her. I'm sure you have something closer to home.* Quietly she climbs the stairs.

Leaving the kitchen, Teri slowly walks, deep in thought, on the brick path leading to the gazebo. "Teri, telephone. It's Chris," Margaret yells.

Teri stops and turns back toward the house. "Okay, Mom."

As she enters the house, Teri can hear Margaret talking on the phone. "Here's Teri. I'll talk to you later." She hands the phone to Teri.

"Hi, Chris."

"Hi, Teri, are you busy?"

"No. I was headed to the gazebo when Mom hollered you were on the phone."

"Is everything okay? You usually go to the gazebo for some heavy thinking."

"I do have some things on my mind. So how are you doing? How's Jack?"

"We're fine. Can we get together? If you can come over to the apartment after I get off work, I'll stop and get us something to eat."

Teri can tell by Chris's tone of voice that she wants to talk about something. "I assume you mean tonight, and yes, that would be great."

Chris sighs quietly. "What about six thirty? That will give me time to stop and get Chinese or something. I'll be leaving a little early today."

Now Teri knows something is going on. Chris *never* leaves early. "Can I bring anything?"

"No, I'll pick up everything. I have to run. I'll see you tonight."

I wonder what's so heavy on her mind. I hope everything is okay with her and Jack.

• • • • • • • • • • • •

Having completed their Chinese food, Chris carries the empty boxes to the trash can. *Chris really has something on her mind, and we need to get to the bottom of it.* Picking up the cup of hot tea, Chris sits back down at the table. Staring out the sliding glass doors, Chris seems deep in thought. This concerns Teri greatly. *Lord, please don't let this be bad news.*

"Chris? Is there something you want to talk about?"

After walking to the sliding glass doors, Chris stands silent for a moment. "I'm not sure I want to get married."

"Why?" Teri asks, shocked.

"I'm just not sure I want to give up my freedom."

Teri walks to Chris's side. "Chris, what are you talking about? You can still work. Jack said so."

"I know he did, but that's what they say *before* the I dos. Then all of a sudden, they want a baby factory for a wife."

"Chris, you can't be serious! Has Jack given any indication of that?"

"No. But you never know until it's too late."

"I think you're getting cold feet. Have you set a date yet?"

"September fifteenth and, Teri, we don't want a big wedding, so if you say anything to Mom, you better make it clear about that!"

Laughing, Teri reaches over to touch Chris's hand. "Ohhh, Mother will have a hissy over that! Besides, it's your place to tell her not mine."

The conversation continues as they each share what has been happening since their time together at home.

"So you have decided to start inquiring about jobs?" Chris asks.

"Yes, but I don't think Mom is going to be happy."

"Why's that?"

Watching Chris to see what reaction she will give at the news, "There's a great job opening in California that I know I can get if I apply."

"That's great! What is it?"

The rest of the evening is spent discussing the pros and cons of the job and living so far away. Teri is excited that Chris thinks it's a wonderful opportunity and that she's encouraging her to apply.

"Chris, please don't tell Mom I'm going to apply. She almost broke down in tears when I even mentioned checking into it."

"How's Dad feel about it? Does he know?"

"He said I should do whatever I feel the Lord is leading me to do. If that means California, then they'll just have to accept it."

Looking at her watch, Chris stretches. "It's almost ten. I don't want to throw you out, but can we do this again? I have to be in the office really early tomorrow morning."

"You aren't throwing me out. Do you feel better now that we've talked?"

"Yes. Thank you for getting my head screwed back on straight. Now leave and be careful driving home. Tell Mom and Dad I said hello."

• • • • • • • • • • • •

On the flight to Los Angeles, Teri remembers her mother

begging her not to take the Los Angeles position. "Aren't there other jobs close to home?" Margaret tearfully asks.

"Yes, Mom. There are several, but this is where I'm supposed to go. Plus, I want to."

Clay interrupts her, "But, Margaret, she needs to go where she's led. She can still fly home. It isn't that far."

"Yeah, Mom, I can still come home."

I should have told Mom I applied for the job sooner and that I got it. I knew she'd be upset. I'll just try to go home as often as possible. Leaning back and closing her eyes, Teri takes a short nap.

A bump on her elbow wakes her. "Oh, I'm sorry. I didn't mean to wake you." The gentleman in the seat next to her apologizes.

Raising her seat back to its full upright position, "It's okay. I was just dozing."

The man turns offering his hand. "I'm Larry. Larry Martin."

Teri shakes his hand as she says, "I'm Teri Wilson."

Hesitantly releasing her hand, "Are you going to be staying in LA or going on to someplace exotic?" Larry asks as he smiles broadly.

"I have a new job in LA, and I'll be starting in two weeks. I'm coming out early to find an apartment and settle in a little before I start."

"Oh, where's your new job?"

"It's a large counseling center. I'll be one of the counselors."

"My, you don't look like a shrink."

"I'm not." Teri says through her laughter.

"Who will you be counseling?"

Teri glances out the window and back at Larry. "Mostly young people, some adults. I'm not totally sure yet."

"Hmm."

Larry says nothing for a few minutes as Teri returns her attention to the clouds.

Larry interrupts her thoughts. "There's a large counseling center just outside of LA, going north on Highway 101. I guess you aren't familiar with it. It's close to the water and quite successful in their programs."

"What's the name of it?"

She's as beautiful as her picture. Smiling at his thoughts, he sets his drink on the small drop-leaf table and gives her the name of it and watches closely her reaction.

Teri's mouth drops open and in utter surprise. "That's where I'll be working!"

Larry loves her reaction. *I know. I hired you.* "Really!" *I should tell her. She'll find out soon enough.*

Before he can say anything, Teri asks, "Are you familiar with the place?"

I really should tell her. "I've had some dealings there. Yes, I'm acquainted with it."

Teri is excited now to be able to talk to someone who is acquainted with where she will be working. "Tell me about it. What's it like?"

The remainder of the flight is spent in conversation about the center, the general area, tourist spots in LA, and a little about themselves and their interests. As the plane wheels touch down on the runway, Teri is so excited, she can hardly stand it.

Waiting to deplane, Larry asks, "So where are you staying until you find an apartment?"

"A hotel, I guess. I don't know anyone here," she replies rather cautiously.

Being a psychiatrist, Larry recognizes her sudden discomfort. He waits a minute before speaking. "I see some concern on your face. Believe me, I'm not one of those guys you've probably heard about out here."

Teri sighs.

Larry continues. "I have a sister. She's single and a Christian. You said you're a Christian, and she has four bedrooms. She uses one as an office. Let me call her, and maybe she'll enjoy a roommate until you find an apartment."

Teri hesitates, not sure what to do. "I'm not sure. She doesn't know me, and I wouldn't want to put her out."

"Well, I can ask her, and if she says no, then nothing lost."

Teri hesitantly asks, "Are you sure?" as the line slowly moves toward the plane exit.

"Yes, I'm sure." Larry stops for a moment to pull their bags from the overhead compartment before continuing. "I'll call her while we wait for our baggage."

Teri moves forward a few steps, waiting for the man ahead of her to retrieve his bag from the overhead rack. At the baggage claim area, Larry stands far enough away so Teri can't hear his conversation as he talks with his sister.

Watching for her bags to appear on the carousel, Teri sees one and reaches down to grab it as it slides in front of her. Larry's arm reaches around her and grabs the suitcase and sets it down beside her. He then grabs her other ones and his own. "It's all set. She said she'd love to have you and to bring you right over."

• • • • • • • • • • • •

As they place their suitcases in the trunk of his convertible, the uneasy feeling Teri has had doesn't totally subside. Larry darts around to her side of the car and opens the door for her. Sliding in, Teri still isn't positive this is what she should do. *What if he's an axe killer, and his sister is his helper?*

"Do you mind if I put the top down?" Larry asks as he slides behind the steering wheel.

Teri quickly replies, "That would be great!" *If I need to, I can jump out.* He does and then slowly pulls out of the parking lot.

Thankfully it isn't yet time for the horn blowing, hand gestures, and bumper-to-bumper LA traffic. As they pass housing tracts and businesses, the freeway leads north out of town. Teri says little as they speed down the freeway. Her interest isn't so much on sightseeing right now even though she's admiring the palm trees . *It's awfully generous of him to offer this. We only met a few hours ago. Lord? Lord, what am I getting into? Am I doing the right thing?*

Teri turns her attention back to Larry and asks, "What does your sister do?"

He glances at Teri then back at the road. "She's a head nurse at the center. She works in the medical hospital of the center."

"I don't remember them mentioning a hospital."

Larry slows the car, preparing to exit onto the ramp. "It's connected to the center yet separate. Any emergencies or medical needs are taken care of there."

Teri breathes deeply as the sea breeze whips around her short hair. "Ohhh, that smells so clean and fresh. We must be near the ocean."

Making a right turn onto a narrow side street, Larry points ahead. "There it is."

Beach homes line the sandy beach. Some look like small cottages with decks jutting out over the sand and stairs leading onto the beach. Others are larger and more modern-style with patios. The glistening water stretches as far as the eye can see. Teri sucks in a breath and is quiet as she watches a few children playing at the water's edge.

Larry pulls his car into a short driveway, stops, leaving the engine running, and watches Teri as joy, awe, and excitement dances across her face. Smiling broadly, Teri exclaims, "This is absolutely beautiful! I can't believe I'll be living in such a beautiful place."

"Come on; let's go meet my sister. She's expecting us."

Following along a stone sidewalk, Teri suddenly stops, stretching her arms out wide and breathing deeply, with her head thrown back. "I can't get enough of the sea air. This is so different than home. I love the ocean."

Larry pushes back a hanging basket with bright red bougainvillea cascading down the side out of the way. Before he can ring the doorbell, the door flies open, and a slender woman, dressed in shorts and a halter top, squeals and grabs Larry into a hug.

"You're not very excited to see us, are you? Michelle, this is Teri Wilson. Teri, this is my sister, Michelle Bellum." Teri reaches out her hand to shake Michelle's.

"Oh, don't be so formal." Michelle laughs and pulls Teri into a hug.

I think I like her already. She's certainly not shy, Teri thinks.

"Come on in, you two. I can make us some sandwiches if you're hungry. How was your flight, Teri? I'll bet you're exhausted. Did my brother bore you to death?"

"Whooo, slow down, sister." Larry laughs. "You'll wear her out more with your nonstop questions."

Teri stands in a small living room with a large couch facing sliding glass doors. A recliner, armchair, and coffee table claim most of the center of the room. "This is beautiful," Teri says, looking at large ceramic seagulls hanging on the wall above a short settee. A small kitchen sits off to the left with a breakfast bar and four straight-back stools nestled up against it. A kitchen table is next to large windows looking out over the beach.

"May I step outside?" Teri asks as she walks toward the sliding glass doors. A large covered patio, several wicker chairs, a settee, and several potted plants stretch along the back of the house, greeting the sand and water that seem to come right to the door.

Opening the refrigerator, Larry asks, "What do you have to drink, 'Chel? Any iced tea?"

"It's in the pitcher behind the milk. Teri, would you like some iced tea?"

Teri glances, unable to draw her eyes away from the ocean outside the sliding glass doors. "That would be nice. Thank you."

"Chel, do you want some?"

"I'll take a Dr Pepper."

Joining Teri and Larry on the patio, Michelle hands her a glass of tea. "Thank you" and breathes in deeply again.

"Michelle, I don't think I'll ever get used to this sea air, but I'm sure going to try." Lifting her glass and taking a large drink, Teri chokes. Trying hard not to spit the tea out or make a face and embarrass herself, she swallows slowly and wipes her mouth with a napkin. Not succeeding to hide the face she's made, Larry bursts out laughing loudly.

Setting her glass onto the glass patio table, Teri turns back toward the water, trying to hide her embarrassment. Larry walks over to her. "Are you okay?"

"Michelle, she's from Georgia! They drink *sweet* tea."

Michelle rushes over to her. "I'm so sorry! I didn't mean to try to kill you!" Bursting out laughing, Teri reaches for her tea when Michelle takes it. "I'll add some sugar if that's okay."

"Since you're still alive after my goof, I'll show you the house." As Michelle leads the way, she points out a bedroom on the left with a bathroom across the hall. "This is my office," she says, pointing to another room just past the bathroom. Peeking in, Teri can see nursing diplomas and specific training certificates covering a large portion of one wall. Three file cabinets are lined side by side along another wall, and a large L-shaped computer desk, with a computer, printer, fax machine, and scanner hugs one corner of the room with a large swivel chair pushed against it. Folders are neatly stacked on one end of the desk, and seeing an eight-by-ten picture facing the chair, Teri assumes it's of her and Larry.

Michelle leads her to the end of the hall. "This is my room." A panoramic view of ocean waves gently caressing the white sandy beach and the sea breeze softly rustling the sheer curtains invites Teri into Michelle's bedroom. There is a large king-size bed, king-size dresser with two attached mirrors, a cedar armoire, chest of drawers, and a nightstand on each side of the bed.

To the right of the entrance to Michelle's bedroom, a door opens into another bedroom. "This will be your room. It has its own bathroom." Teri enters the room, and it's a bit smaller than her bedroom at home, but Teri likes it. Large windows with sheer curtains rustle in the breeze. The blinds are pulled up and the view of the ocean is spectacular. An armchair is in the corner next to the window. A queen-size bed, chest of drawers, and dresser take up much of the space. A decorative ceiling fan slowly spins in the center of the room.

"I love this! It's beautiful. Are you sure you want me to have this room?" Teri turns back to look out the window before she says, "Michelle, are you sure about this? I mean taking me in. You don't even know me."

Michelle places her hand gently on Teri's arm. "Yes,

I'm sure. I get lonely here sometimes, and I would love to have you stay. You never know, we may even become the best of friends."

"Thank you so much."

Larry has retrieved Teri's luggage from the trunk of his car, leaving it near the door. "Michelle, I better get going. I know Teri is probably tired. She's still on Georgia time. I know I'm tired and need to get some rest."

Michelle gives him a hug, and Teri walks down the stone walkway with him. "Larry, I don't know how to thank you. Your sister is wonderful, and I love her home."

"I knew you would. I think the two of you might have some things in common from what you told me on the plane."

"I'm sure we'll become good friends in no time."

Larry slides into the car. "Take care, Teri. I'll see you soon." He backs the car out onto the street.

Chapter 7

The first couple of days with Michelle, Teri spends unpacking, walking the beach, and trying to get acquainted with the area. She doesn't want to be more of a burden than she already feels she is, so she plans to rent a car. Sitting on the patio watching the sunset with Teri, Michelle asks, "What are your plans? Are you going to get an apartment? How are you getting your car?"

"I'm going to rent a car until my friends drive mine out. They're going to bring it here and then fly home. I'm going to get a map and watch the papers for apartments that are available."

"This is a big town and easy to get lost. Would you like for me to help you locate these places?"

"I'll be fine. I certainly don't want to be more of a burden than I already am."

"Teri, you're no burden. I enjoy you being here, and if you want to use my car when I'm at work, you're welcome to. You can take me to work, and Larry can bring me home."

"I really appreciate all you're doing for me already. I

won't impose any more than I have. I'll be okay. I'll holler if I get so lost that I can't find my way home."

Michelle replies sternly, "You're not imposing!" Jumping up from her chair, she stomps into the house.

Surprised at Michelle's reaction, Teri whispers, "Thank you," and walks toward the water. Stepping into the shallow water's edge, Teri gazes out at the orange, red, and yellow hues reflecting on the now calm sea. *Only God can do this. It's beautiful!* Sitting down on the sand, she hugs her knees to her chest and prays. Stomping the wet sand from her feet, she approaches the screened patio doors.

"Michelle, are you busy?"

Michelle walks to the screen doors. "No."

"Would you mind if we sit out here and talk for a few minutes?"

"Sure. Do we need some drinks?"

"You go ahead. I'm fine." While Michelle gets a Dr. Pepper, Teri gazes out at the sea, deep in thought. Not hearing Michelle return, Teri is startled when she hears Michelle's chair scrape the cement patio as she sits down.

Looking up at Teri, as Teri walks to her chair and sits down, Michelle says, "You look worried. Is something wrong? Can I help?"

Teri isn't sure she should go into her concerns so she hesitates before speaking. "I'm worried about work, not having my car, and I haven't found an apartment. I don't know what I'm going to do." Michelle watches her as she continues. "Do you know of any apartments for rent or maybe someone at the center who is looking for a roommate?" Tears well up in Teri's eyes. "Maybe I was wrong and this isn't where the Lord wants me. Maybe I just wanted to get away to see more of the world than just Georgia."

Watching Teri, Michelle sees the anguish on her face. "Have you prayed about this?"

"Yes, constantly! I'm getting no answers, and it's frustrating."

"Usually that means God wants you to wait on Him."

"But I start work Monday. That's the day after tomorrow!"

"I know, Teri. I see no problem there."

"You don't understand. I can't rent the car forever. I'm running out of money, so I can't afford much, and I can't continue to live here and impose on you!" Realizing she has slipped and said more than she intended to, Teri stands.

"Please sit down, Teri. We need to discuss some things."

Teri stares down at Michelle. *Oh, God, is this where she tells me they are axe murders?* Quietly taking her seat, she says nothing. *God, what do I do?*

Michelle looks over at her while holding her drink. "I know you've been worried. I haven't helped in that department either."

"What do—"

"Just hear me out," Michelle interrupts.

"I know I've acted kind of strange lately, and you've probably thought it's because I'm angry at you. It's not!"

Teri remains silent, not knowing what to say.

Michelle continues. "Larry and I have been having some disagreements." Trying to reassure Teri, she smiles. "You know how siblings are. I've been praying, too."

Teri's curiosity is about to get the best of her, but she waits for Michelle to finish.

Michelle stands and, staring out over the water, she continues without looking at Teri. "I'd like for you to stay here. We can be roommates. You pay your half, and I'll pay mine."

"I can't do that!" *She doesn't even like me anymore.*

Michelle turns back to face Teri. "Why not? We're close to the center, we get along well, and we pretty much like the same things."

Teri's flabbergasted and not sure what to say. "But you don't need a roommate. You only took me in because I had no place to go and as a favor to Larry."

"That's not true. After Larry told me about you on the phone, I 'took you in,' as you call it, because I was looking for a roommate! I wanted a roommate that's a Christian and someone I thought could be a friend as well as a roommate. Larry thought I'd like you, and that's why he suggested you stay with me. When he called from the airport, he was excited. He knew enough about you that he thought we could room together."

Teri stares at her in disbelief. Michelle continues, "I *did not* take you in like some lost puppy that would starve to death without my help!"

"Are you absolutely sure about this? I don't want it to be a decision made out of pity because of my circumstances."

Michelle understands but wants to make it perfectly clear that is not why she has asked her to room with her. "You're not a lost puppy, and I'm not your rescuer! Yes, I am absolutely sure."

"I think I'd like to pray about this before giving you an answer. I think I'll go for a walk. Thank you for the offer."

Rising early the next morning, Teri dons her bathing suit and walks toward the water with her towel, sunblock, and a bottle of water. Standing at the edge of the water and gazing out across the sea, *Lord, your work is amazingly beautiful. No one else could create such beauty. You have truly blessed me with this place. Lord, should I stay here with Michelle as her roommate? I need your guidance.*

Without going in for a swim, Teri begins walking slowly toward the house. Teri steps onto the patio. The sliding glass doors are open, so Teri can hear Michelle on the phone.

"Larry, she's going to find out! Now you tell her or I will!"

Quickly turning, Teri drops her towel, lotion, and water bottle onto the lounge chair and races back down to the water. Sitting down in the sand, tears form. *Lord, what have I gotten myself into? Lord, you have to help me. What do I do? What does she mean, 'she'll find out soon enough?'"*

Teri hesitates, returning to the house, when she sees Michelle continuing to pace the living room floor as she speaks into the phone. Slowly wading through the warm sand, she sees Michelle standing at the sliding glass doors looking out. *Lord, help me!* Teri tries to smile as she steps onto the patio, but before she reaches the sliding glass door, Michelle abruptly turns and disappears down the hall. Not understanding, Teri enters and slowly closes her bedroom door quietly behind her. *This is all just too confusing. I think I need to get an apartment. Lord, again, what do I do?*

• • • • • • • • • • • •

Rising much earlier than Michelle, Teri is about to step out the door with her keys, map, and newspaper in hand.

Michelle suddenly appears in the kitchen. "You're up early."

Teri stops with her hand on the door knob. "Yes. Good morning. I'm still on Georgia time."

"I made some coffee if you'd like some."

"So where are you off to this early?"

"I found some apartments in the newspaper, and I thought I'd check them out."

Michelle assumes Teri has made her decision about rooming with her. Her tone of voice relays her disappointment and disapproval when she says, "Oh," and walks toward the hall.

• • • • • • • • • • • •

The LA traffic is horrendous. Most of Teri's driving is sitting in bumper-to-bumper traffic, going nowhere. If there is movement, it's at a snail's pace. Some of the people are hanging out their window trying to see what the holdup is; others sit quietly drinking their coffee; and one woman Teri notices is looking in her visor mirror, applying her makeup. All four lanes are stopped or barely inching along. In deep thought, Teri is startled when a horn blasts behind her. *Okay, okay. I'll hurry up to go ten feet!* Finally able to exit the freeway, Teri sighs. "Thank God!" she says loudly.

The four apartments she plans to see are fairly close in proximity, so she'll not have to get back on the freeway until she's ready to go home. Ringing the manager's office bell at the first apartment, she learns it was rented last night. Disappointed, she goes to the second one on her list. After climbing four flights of stairs to reach the apartment, she's shocked to see it's barely the size of a studio apartment. *Good grief, it even has a wall bed! No way!*

"Thank you, but this is too small for my needs," she says to the manager.

She then descends the four flights of stairs. Stopping for breakfast, she continues to the third complex only to realize it's much too far from the center to commute. Plus, she would have to drive the horrible traffic even more. Reaching the fourth complex, she slowly passes by it as she looks at the unkempt building and overgrown weeds and grass.

Returning home, while unlocking the door, she hears the living room phone ringing and runs to answer it. "Hello."

"Hi, Teri. It's Sally."

"Hi, Sally! It's so good to hear from you. You won't

believe what's been going on." She then begins telling Sally about how disappointed she is about the apartment situation. Suddenly the dam breaks and all the pent-up emotions pour out.

"Sally, I don't know what to do. Michelle has asked me to be her roommate. The traffic is horrible, my money is running out, and the Lord isn't telling me what I need to do. Sally, I'm just not sure this is where I belong. It's so different from Georgia."

Sally listens patiently as Teri continues nonstop. Suddenly Teri realizes she hasn't allowed Sally to talk. "Oh my gosh. I'm so sorry. I've talked your ear off and haven't let you get a word in edgewise. How is everyone?"

"Everyone at church misses you and asks about you. Your mom and dad said they talk to you every few days or so. Your mom is worried about you, of course."

"I know. The thing is I've only been here two weeks, and I'm already homesick."

"It's too early for you to be homesick. You'll be fine once you get settled in and start your new job. We'll get your car out to you in a week or so, and that will help."

"When do you think you'll be able to bring it? Is Mary Lou still able to come with you?"

"Yes, she's coming. We plan to come in about a week, if that works for you.

"That's fine."

"Trust the Lord, Teri. He'll see you through all of this. You know He is our strength."

"I know, but it's just hard to do at times. How long do you think it will take you to get here?"

"I'm not sure, but we'll only be able to stay three or four days at the most before we fly home. Sally laughs and then continues, "Unless we decide to call our bosses and tell them we're stuck in snow and can't make it home for another few days. That way we can really sightsee."

"It doesn't snow here, you silly goose! Oh, Sally, it's so good to hear your voice. I miss you and can't wait for you and Mary Lou to get here.

. . . .

"I have really enjoyed your being here, and hopefully we can be good friends." Michelle says as she and Teri stroll along the beach.

Smiling, Teri stops for just a moment then continues to walk slowly. "I've been so confused. I need to confess something to you before we make the final decision as to my living with you. Is that okay?"

"Of course."

Looking down at the sand, Teri is a little embarrassed. "I hope you don't think I'm crazy, and I really hope you don't take offense to what I need to tell you."

"Take offense? Why would I be offended?"

Maybe I shouldn't tell her. I wouldn't want someone telling me I thought they were axe murderers.

Teri stares at the ground for a minute then blurts out, "I thought you and Larry were axe murders, and you planned to kill me!"

At first shocked, Michelle only stares at Teri then bursts out laughing. She can be heard all along the beach. "You what?!" Laughing even harder, she plops down on the sand, holding her ribs. When she looks up, tears are streaming down her face.

Teri is so embarrassed, she turns her back to Michelle. *Dear Lord, I should have kept my mouth shut. Now she'll really think I'm awful.*

Teri turns to face the house. *I wish I could just disappear into the sand.*

Michelle gasps for air while wiping her eyes and trying to stop laughing, realizing Teri is embarrassed. Finally able to stand, Michelle asks Teri, "Would you turn around please?"

Teri slowly turns, looking down at the sand. "I am so ashamed!"

Michelle reaches out, touching Teri's hand. "I don't know where you ever got that idea. Teri, listen to me." Michelle struggles to keep from laughing as she says, "We don't even own an axe!" She falls back onto the sand laughing.

Teri, feeling very hurt now by Michelle's reaction to her confession she places her hands on her hips as anger swells up in her suddenly. "I'm so glad you think this is so funny!" she says and stomps back to the house.

Teri is so angry she grabs her bedroom phone and calls Chris. "Hi, Teri. What's up?"

"Chris I am so mad right now I just need to blow off some steam!"

"Okay. What has you in such a dither?"

Teri paces around her bedroom as she tells Chris about how Michelle reacted to her confession. "Chris she just laughed! You could hear her all over the beach!"

"What did you expect her to do?"

"I don't know! I sure didn't expect her to fall in the sand in hysterical laughter!"

"Come on, Teri. It couldn't have been that bad."

"It was! Do you know what she said when I told her I thought they were axe murderers?"

"No."

"She thought it was so funny and said, 'We don't even own an axe' and then fell in the sand laughing! Can you believe that!?"

Chris can't help but laugh. "I'm sorry. I don't mean to laugh, but it is kind of funny."

"Christine Marie, are you taking her side? A little sympathy would help here!"

"I'm sorry. I know you're upset." Chris decides to change the subject hoping Teri will calm down. "I talked to Mom last night and she asked about you."

"How is she?"

The conversation continues and when Teri hangs up, she decides to take a long hot bath.

• • • • • • • • • • • •

Teri starts her new job this morning and has awakened much earlier than she has been. Excited and a bit nervous, she holds one outfit after another in front of her as she stands before the full-length mirror. *Lord, what am I going to wear? This my first day, and I want to make a good impression.* Holding up a light cream dress with light tan stripes reaching down to the waist and meeting a narrow belt that separates the solid cream skirt from the bodice, she looks closely at herself in the mirror. The short sleeves, scooped neckline, and snug-fitting bodice make her appear more slender than she already is. *With my tan heels, I think this will do.*

Michelle knocks at her door. "Are you decent?" she asks as she cracks the door open slightly.

"Yes, come on in."

Michelle steps around the door as Teri smoothes the dress down over her body. Turning slowly in a circle, she asks, "Do you think this is okay?"

"I think it's beautiful, and everyone will be envious."

Teri slips on her high heels. "I'm ready if you are."

Teri is quiet as Michelle maneuvers her way through traffic. Michelle pulls up to the front of the building near the entrance. "I'll let you out here then park in the employee's parking lot."

Teri looks nervously at Michelle. "I appreciate that. I'm really nervous."

Michelle places her hand on Teri's shoulder. "You'll be fine. Larry will be here, and you've already met him." Teri is so nervous that she doesn't realize what Michelle has just said about Larry being here.

As Teri opens the car door, Michelle leans toward her, pointing at the front doors of the building. "The elevators are on the right side just inside the lobby. Go to the fourth floor, and the third door on the left is Larry's. He'll take you where you need to go. Good luck."

Walking slowly down the long hall, reading each nameplate on the doors, Teri stands in front of the third door on the left. Printed on the glass is "Executive Director—Larry Martin." Confused, Teri stands, looking at the name. *Wait a minute! He said he's just acquainted with the center!* Looking back down the hall, back at the door, and down the hall again, *I don't believe this! He deliberately deceived me!* Pushing the door open and entering, a secretary looks up from her computer.

"Can I help you?"

Teri is angry at Larry's deception, yet she smiles. "Yes, I'm here to see Mr. Martin."

"Your name?"

"Teri Wilson."

"Oh, yes. Larry said you will be joining us. Welcome."

"Thank you." *Lord, I need your calm right now.*

The secretary speaks into an intercom, "Miss Wilson is here to see you."

"Oh good! Send her in."

Larry is walking around the corner of his large desk as Teri enters. Files are stacked on the corner with a computer, pen holder, and nameplate. Large windows take up most of the wall behind his desk. Teri can see shimmering blue water a short distance away. A bookcase takes up one portion of a wall, with a large picture of a mountain scene hanging near it. On the other wall is a huge picture of the ocean with a surfer skimming along under the crest of a wave.

"Good morning!" Larry enthusiastically greets Teri.

"Good morning."

"I'm sorry I haven't been able to visit you while you've been at Michelle's. It's been kind of hectic around here. Please take a seat." He walks back around his desk and sits in his big leather chair facing her. Teri can see an open file with her five-by-seven picture stapled to it.

"We have a little catching up to do. How do you like California now that you've spent a little time here?" Larry casually asks.

Teri doesn't want small talk. She wants to get right to the point. "You said you are *acquainted* with the center. You didn't say you're the executive director!" Looking past him she can see seagulls hovering above the water. "May I be frank with you?"

"Of course, is something wrong?"

"Yes. I believed you on the plane when you straight-out said you were acquainted with the center. You deliberately deceived me!"

Calmly, Larry says, "I don't advertise my position in general conversations."

"Did you know this is where I was starting my new job *before* I told you?"

"Yes, I hired you."

"So the entire conversation on the plane was all just fun and games with you! You knew all along everything about me from the application!"

Embarrassed, Larry steps around his desk and sits on the corner of the desk facing her. "Teri, I'm so sorry. I was going to tell you."

Teri is not used to confronting someone in Larry's position, but her anger won't be squelched with a simple "I'm sorry." "You've made a fool out of me!"

"Teri, please sit down, and let's talk about this."

Teri slowly takes her seat. *There's no excuse for what he did!* "I'm listening."

"Would you like a cup of coffee, something to drink?"

Teri won't be dissuaded. "No thank you."

Instead of returning to his chair behind his desk, Larry stays in the more relaxed position, hoping to ease the tension. He can see Teri is really upset. "I'll tell you whatever you want to know. We need to be upfront with each other if we're going to work together. This isn't a very good start, but I think we can clear things up."

"How did you manage to sit next to me? I'm sure that wasn't accidental!"

Larry can't help but smile. "I saw you at the ticket counter getting your seat assignment. I assumed you were on the same flight as me, so I asked if I could change my seat to sit next to you. I wanted to get to know you a little better is all."

"So you and Michelle didn't have this all planned out ahead of time?"

"Where in the world did you get that idea? Of course not!"

So they aren't axe murders. "Oh."

"Teri, I'm so sorry. I wanted to tell you, but every time I started to, we got involved in the conversation at hand. I had absolutely no intention of deceiving you, and I'm really sorry I have led you to believe I have."

"That's no excuse, but I forgive you. I do have to say, though, that if lying is a regular practice around here, then I am afraid I won't be able to work here." Teri picks up her bag and stands, ready to leave the office.

Shocked, Larry walks over to her. "Deception is not a habit I engage in. Again, I'm sorry I didn't tell you. We need you here, and I hope this will not deter you from becoming one of our valued counselors."

Teri looks him right in the eye and hesitates before answering. "I would like to join your staff. I didn't fly out here for nothing." Teri sits back down, placing her bag on the floor beside her. "So where do we go from here?"

Larry relaxes. "We need to talk about which area you would be best suited for. By the way, Michelle called last night and said you have decided to be her roommate. I think that's great. She's been looking for one."

So she didn't lie about that. "I prayed about it, and I feel the Lord wants me to, so, yes. My friends are driving my car out next week from Atlanta, so I'll have transportation and not have to impose on her any more than I already have."

"That's a long drive."

"It is a long drive. I don't know how long it will take to drive across the country, but they're really excited about it. I'm hoping they can stay more than a few days. They really want to 'rub elbows with the movie stars,' as they call it. Plus I really miss them and want to spend as much time with them as I possibly can."

Larry walks around his desk and sits back down in his big leather chair. He leans back with his arms behind his head, happy that she has become more relaxed and calmer.

"Good luck finding celebrities. They usually stay

pretty hidden or disguised. The vultures usually follow them wherever they go. That has to be a pain!"

"Tell me about my job."

Larry tells her about the center, the purposes, goals, treatment programs, and where he thinks she will do the most good. "I see you're interested in the children's program."

"I love kids, but I'm not sure my training is sufficient for that area."

Larry closes the file. "We have a training program here. The education you have and a few months of training should be quite sufficient for you to work with the children. There are other counselors on the unit, and they'll help in whatever ways you'll need. We also have a psychiatrist assigned to each unit. Our children's program is for kids four years old and up to about ten. Then they are transferred to the pre-teen program. Many leave before that happens. We have exemplary programs here. We're quite proud of the success we have."

After fully discussing what is to be expected, such as the training and various programs, Larry looks at his watch. "Are you getting hungry? It's lunchtime, and as you've probably heard, my stomach is growling."

"I'm a little hungry. Is there a cafeteria here?"

"Oh now, Miss Wilson, you don't think I'd subject you to cafeteria food on your first day, do you?"

"I don't know, would you?"

Larry presses a button on his intercom. "We're going to lunch now, Cindy." He looks back at Teri. "Absolutely not!"

• • • • • • • • • • • •

The first week at work, Teri is taken on a tour of the center and is introduced to Claire, who will be her training instructor. "Larry has said you are particularly interested in working with the younger kids," Claire says as they walk down a long hall.

"Yes, I am. I really love kids, and hopefully I can be of help to some. I can't imagine little ones being treated as these have."

"Oh, you have no idea what parents can do to their children!"

Entering the children's unit, young girls and boys are playing with toys while sitting on a soft, gray carpet. Bugs Bunny, Snoopy, Pooh Bear, and other cartoon characters are painted on the walls. Two counselors are speaking with two of the children. They look to be four or five years old. Leaning over the shoulder of one little girl, the counselor speaks softly. "That is really good," she says as the little girl walks her doll toward a large, plastic dollhouse. One side of the dollhouse is open, and the various rooms are visible. She points to one of the rooms in the dollhouse. "What room is that?" the counselor asks the little girl.

Suddenly the child scoots away and throws her doll down.

"We can talk later," the counselor says and walks away.

Tears come to Teri's eyes. Seeing the fear on the child's face, Teri can't imagine what this child is afraid of. Claire touches her arm.

"She'll be okay. I know it tears your heart out, but part of your training is to help you be able to help without breaking down yourself." Claire's cell phone rings. "Excuse me." She says to Teri and takes a few steps down the hall. Teri hears her say, "Okay." Returning to Teri, she says, "Larry would like us to come to his office."

. . . .

Larry is sitting at his desk as Claire and Teri enter. "How's it going?"

Teri hasn't seen him since her first day at the center but is sure Michelle has told him about her confession. Claire answers, "She's doing wonderfully. We'll start her official training next week. In the meantime, I want to introduce her to a few of the children and let them get acquainted a little before she starts working with them."

Larry knows they just left the children's unit and turns his attention to Teri. "What do you think, Teri? Do you still want to work with these very hurt children?"

Larry isn't about to bring up the "axe murderers" confession in front of Claire. He can tell Teri probably suspects Michelle told him. Teri looks at him, determined not to show her embarrassment about the confession.

"I'm willing, all right. I can't imagine what these kids have gone through. Maybe I can help them with some training."

"I'm sure you'll do fine. I need to talk with Teri, if you don't mind, Claire. We have a few things we need to discuss. Thanks for taking her under your wing." Larry then turns his attention back to Teri. "Claire's the best. You're in good hands."

"Thank you," Claire says and leaves the office.

Larry suggests, "Why don't you sit down, Teri."

Teri does. *Oh, Lord, here it comes! He's going to laugh at me for thinking he's an axe murderer.* Larry sits for a long moment studying her. Teri lowers her head for a moment.

"Michelle told me about your confession to her."

Teri raises her head and looks directly at him. "I'm sorry," she starts.

Larry raises his hand, stopping her. "I'm not here to ridicule you. I want you to know I completely understand. Sometimes Michelle isn't the most sensitive person in the world, and I apologize for her inconsiderate reaction to your confession."

Teri says nothing as he continues.

"I'm glad you told her. That had to be quite scary for you. We only spoke for a couple of hours on the plane. I'll bet you were praying like crazy."

"I did a lot! But I wasn't getting any answers, and by the time we got to your car, I couldn't very well say no."

"Are you more at ease now that you've told her and have agreed to live with her?" All the while, Larry is watching her closely.

"I'm not sure I should have told her but, yes, I feel peace about moving in permanently."

"Good. How about having lunch with me?"

Teri feels greatly relieved that Larry has not ridiculed her. "Only if you promise no cafeteria food. Been there, done that."

During their lunch, Teri asks, "How did you become such a bigwig?"

"Well, it's kind of a long story. Are you sure you want to be bored?"

Teri nods her head yes as she takes a bite of her baked fish.

"When I was a senior in high school, one of the teachers brought the class here. He felt we needed the experience of seeing hurting people. It was one of the best things that happened for me."

"How's that?"

"I was so taken with the center and what they seemed to be doing for these people that I became a volunteer."

"Wow. It must have impressed you."

"Just before graduation, they offered me a paid position, and I took it."

"What about college? How did you work all that in?"

"They were great. They let me set my own schedule around my classes, and to make a long story short, the 'higher ups' seemed to take notice and started advancing me."

"So you started at the bottom and worked your way to where you are now."

"Only by the grace of God!"

"What about college? What was your major?"

"I majored in psychology, and then decided I wanted to be a psychiatrist. My minor was business administration."

"You really had a long haul with college and then medical school."

Larry signals the server for the check and says, "It was a lot of hard work, but it's been very gratifying, to say the least."

Teri can't help but be impressed and admires all his hard work and success. "I only hope I can do half as much as you have."

On the drive back to the center, Teri turns to him from looking out over the ocean. The top is down on the convertible, and the wind is blowing her hair, causing her to brush back the hair blowing in her face. "Thank you for not laughing at me. I felt so badly about telling Michelle such an awful thing and that I could even think such a thing!"

Grinning and wanting to tease her, Larry decides not to. "That isn't something that should be laughed about. Having those thoughts, not knowing us, had to be terrifying for you. Larry glances at her and then back to the road. "Plus, Michelle told me about how badly she treated you while we were arguing about who should tell you about my position."

"Well it's behind us now, and I'm sure Michelle and I will be the best of friends." Finally able to laugh a little about it, she grins. "Just don't bring any axes to work with you!"

Bursting out laughing, Larry pulls the car into his parking space.

• • • • • • • • • • • •

Reaching for the telephone, Teri is awakened from a sound sleep. "Hello," she answers groggily.

"Oh, Teri, I'm so sorry. I woke you up, didn't I? It's Mary Lou. I can call back later. Go back to sleep."

"Oh, hi. What time is it?" she says while yawning.

"I'm so sorry. Its ten o'clock here."

"I need to get up anyway. Michelle and I are going to church this morning, so you did me a favor. How is everyone?"

"They're fine. I talked to your mom, and boy does she want you back home!"

"I know. I hesitate to call her anymore. I know that sounds awful, but she just cries and begs me to come home."

"I'm so sorry. That has to be tough for you."

"It is, but that isn't why you called. What's up?"

"Sally and I are planning to leave Saturday to bring your car to you." Excited, Mary Lou squeals, "I can't wait! There's so much to see on the way out there, then we get to rub elbows with the movie stars and shop along Rodeo Drive in Hollywood, no less!"

"I'm sorry you'll be so bored." Teri laughs as she scoots up in the bed.

"Yeah, me too. Have you found an apartment yet?"

"No."

"What are you going to do?"

"Michelle and I had a long talk, and she's asked me to room with her."

"Have you decided? Sally told me you were praying about it."

"Michelle said she hasn't been mad at me and that it's stuff she and Larry are going through. Apparently it's one of those sibling things."

"Are you going to take her up on her offer?"

"I just have a peace about it. I don't understand it, but I sense the Lord wants me to stay with her, so, yes. I'm going to be her roommate."

"Then that settles it. Are you going to have the rest of your stuff shipped out there, or do you want us to bring it? We can always tow your car behind a U-Haul truck."

"There isn't much there. If you would bring the rest of my clothes and the picture on my dresser, I'd appreciate it."

"Sure. What picture?"

"It's the one of Chris and I standing beside the gazebo when it was first built. Mom and Dad are hanging over the railing acting funny. I forgot it, and I'd really like to have it."

"Okay. I'll call you Saturday morning before we leave. We better make that Friday night. We're leaving really early."

"I can't wait to see you, and I'll be praying for traveling mercies."

"I need to go. I'm on my break at work. Hang in there. I'll call you before we leave. Bye. Take care."

· · · · · · · · · · · ·

Teri jumps out of bed, excited about her first visit to a church in California. Just as she steps toward the shower, her phone rings.

"Hi, Chris. Is everything okay? You don't usually call me on a Sunday morning."

"Everything is fine. I just thought I'd call and see how things are going in Southern California."

"I'm fine. Michelle and I are going to church this morning. I'm excited to visit a new church. This is the first time I've gone since I've been here."

"That's great. I went last week. I'm thinking about visiting the new church here. That one that was being built is finished, and I hear the pastor is really good."

"I remember it being worked on. They sure finished it fast. Let me know what you think of it when you go. I hate to cut this short, but can I call you later? I was just getting into the shower and my bare fanny is getting cold."

"Okay. I'll talk to you later. Have fun at church."

"Okay bye."

• • • • • • • • • • • •

Teri is used to wearing "dress-up clothes" to her church at home, she dons a dress with short, puffed sleeves and a flowing skirt. Slipping her high heels on and picking up her Bible, she walks out into the hall, ready to leave. Michelle almost bumps into her.

"My, don't you look nice!"

"Thank you. Is this all right?"

"Well, you are a bit overdressed."

"I am?"

"You're in California now. We're much more casual."

"Oh dear, what would you suggest I wear?"

"You can wear jeans, or if you're more comfortable in a dress, then how about a light summer dress?"

"I don't think I'd be comfortable in jeans. What are you going to wear?"

Michelle points to her slacks. "Just what I have on, my slacks and blouse."

Teri runs toward her room and says over her shoulder, "I can do that."

. . . .

Pulling into the small parking lot, Teri is impressed with the small church. The front is decorated with stone. The long walkway leads them to two heavy, wooden doors. A cross is intricately carved on each. Stepping inside, air-conditioning greets them.

"This is nice," Teri says as she looks to the front of the sanctuary.

Michelle taps her on the shoulder. "Is this okay with you?" she asks, pointing to a row of seats.

"Oh, sure, wherever you want to sit is fine with me."

Others begin filing in and taking seats. Teri says nothing but is shocked to see some of the women wearing knee-length shorts and T-shirts. A few of the ladies are wearing spaghetti-strapped sundresses. *The older women in my church back home would faint dead away if women came dressed like that.*

Michelle looks at her and grins. "Is this too much of a shock for a Southern girl?"

"I was just noticing some of the apparel being worn and the reaction it would get in my church at home."

"You're kidding. Southern women can't be that close-minded."

"Most aren't, but the older women have grown up with dressing up for church. They think it is a must."

The drummer steps behind his drums while two guitar players place the guitar straps over their heads. One young man lifts a trumpet off its stand and gently blows into it. Three young, jean-clad women stand to the side, ready to lead the singing, and an elderly woman, dressed in slacks and blouse, takes her seat at the piano, flipping open the music. While the pastor walks to the podium, Michelle leans toward Teri.

"That's Pastor Johnson. I really like his preaching."

Teri just nods. Pastor Johnson appears to be in his mid-forties. He's a handsome man with dark, wavy hair and flashing brown eyes. His smile is intoxicating. Wearing light tan slacks and a pale green shirt, he greets the congregation. "Good morning."

The congregation echoes back, "Good morning."

"I'd like to start with prayer," he says, and everyone bows their head. His prayer is nothing like Pastor Mike's. Teri is expecting a long, drawn-out prayer and is surprised when Pastor Johnson says, "Amen."

Suddenly a guitar note blares through the speakers, lifting the roof off, and everyone stands to sing. The congregation is clapping, dancing at their seats, and their voices ring out. Teri loves every minute of it.

When everyone is seated, Pastor Johnson begins his sermon. "What's the matter with us as a church?" Looking out over the congregation, "What are we doing as a church? Are we sitting on our duffs and letting the world go to hell?"

Teri gasps.

The pastor continues. "If we as a church don't start getting some backbone and standing up for what we believe, that's exactly what is going to happen!"

Michelle glances at Teri and almost bursts out laughing. Teri's eyes are as big as saucers, and her mouth is hanging open. Michelle whispers to Teri, "Close your mouth. You'll catch flies."

Teri glances at her but ignores her comment. As Pastor Johnson continues, Teri is riveted to his words.

· · · · · · · · · · · ·

Leaving the sanctuary, Teri is deep in thought about the sermon.

Michelle asks, "What do you think? Did you like the sermon?"

Teri doesn't answer until they've walked outside. "That was incredible!"

Michelle laughs. "I'll take that as a yes."

As the two drive home, Teri's enthusiasm bubbles over. "I loved that sermon! Your pastor sure doesn't pull any punches, does he?"

Before Michelle can answer, Teri goes on and on about various points the pastor made. The sound of seagulls and the aroma of hibiscus and sea air are prevalent as Michelle pulls slowly into the driveway. She leaves the car idling as she sits quietly while Teri finally winds down. "Teri, I'm so sorry you didn't like the service." Michelle says through her laughter.

Turning the ignition off and stepping out of the car, she laughs all the way to the front door.

Chapter 8

Sally and Mary Lou are excited as they throw the last suitcase in the backseat. The trunk is full with suitcases filled with Teri's clothes. They've started very early, hoping to get the miles covered as quickly as possible. Not fully realizing just how long of a trip it is, they talk non-stop as they begin their journey. By dusk they are tired and stop for the night.

Each day the miles fly beneath their wheels. By the third day, the excitement has been transformed into wanting to get this trip over with and being able to have some fun. Like tunnel vision, California is at the end of the tunnel.

As they slowly turn into the beach house driveway, Teri is already waving, laughing, and crying tears of joy. *Oh thank you, God. They're here.*

Mary Lou leans her head onto the steering wheel without turning the engine off. Teri runs to the driver's side of the car and throws open the door. Leaning in, she excitedly hugs Mary Lou's shoulders. "I'm so excited you're finally here!"

Mary Lou continues to lean on the steering wheel

without responding to Teri's hug. Glancing over the back of the seat, Teri can see Sally leaning her head back on the head rest with her eyes closed. Teri looks at Sally and then Mary Lou and is confused by their actions—or lack of actions. "Come on, you two. I want you to meet Michelle."

Sally slowly reaches across for the ignition keys and turns the ignition off. Teri backs away a few steps. "What's wrong?" she asks, not speaking to any particular one.

Sally struggles to get out of the car and slowly maneuvers her way to the driver's side, holding onto the car for support. She leans over carefully and kisses the top of the car and whispers, "You did good." Turning toward Teri, she tries to smile.

Teri is now really concerned for her friends. *Something has happened!* "Sally, are you two okay? Has something happened?"

Sally says nothing as she leans against the car. Mary Lou lifts her head slowly off the steering wheel, revealing tear-stained cheeks.

"Oh my gosh, something has happened!" Teri exclaims. Just as Teri reaches for Mary Lou to help her out of the car, Sally slowly starts sliding down the side of the car to the ground.

Michelle is just walking to the end of the walkway when Teri screams, "Help me, Michelle," and runs to try to catch Sally.

"Come on. Come on in," Michelle gently says as she helps Mary Lou out of the car. Teri has wrapped her arm around Sally's waist, trying to keep her from completely falling to the ground.

Lord, help us! Teri pleads as she slowly starts walking Sally toward the house. Michelle has already been able to walk Mary Lou into the house. When Teri and Sally enter, Teri sees Mary Lou stretched out on the couch and Michelle placing a cold rag on Mary Lou's forehead. "Put Sally over here." Michelle says as she points to the other couch.

Michelle quickly glances over their bodies for wounds or broken bones and checking their pulse, she calmly states, "I don't see anything broken or anything." Turning to Teri, "I think they're just completely exhausted. We'll let them rest while I get their room ready."

"Thank you" is all Teri replies as she sits on the floor between the two.

Nightfall has arrived, and both women have been helped into the guest room. Neither has said more than two words, whispering "thank you" as they lay side by side on the king-size bed. Teri is almost frantic with worry. "Michelle, what do you think it is? I've seen exhaustion before but never like this! It's almost like they're in shock on top of being exhausted."

"I've been thinking the same thing. Something happened, but we need to let them sleep, and in the morning, when they're more rested, then they can tell us."

"Are they going to be okay?"

"I think so. I'm going to bed. Teri, don't worry. They'll be okay once they get some rest. Good night."

Still looking at the hallway, Teri whispers, "Good

night. Thank you for your help." She tip toes to her bedroom and calls Chris.

"Hi, Teri. Did Sally and Mary Lou make it okay?"

"Chris, something happened. We don't know what."

"What are you talking about. They're there, aren't they?"

"Yes. They just got here a while ago, and it's like they're in shock."

"Shock! from what?"

"That's just it. We have no idea. They haven't even spoken!"

"Have you called nine one one?"

"No. Michelle is a nurse and checked them over and nothing's broken or anything like that. She thinks it's shock, too. We put them to bed and they're asleep."

"I hope they're okay. Let me know what happens and I will say a prayer for them."

"Thanks and I will let you know when we find out anything. Bye."

. . . .

Mary Lou and Sally are still asleep when the doorbell rings early the next morning.

"Michelle? Are you expecting anyone this early?" Teri asks as she sets her cup of hot tea on the table.

"No. I'll go see who it is."

Pulling the sheer curtain back that covers the full-length window on the door, two men in suits hold up their badge to show her. Opening the door, Michelle asks curiously, "Can I help you?"

"I'm Detective John Wells, and this is Detective Art Morgan."

Still holding the door open, Michelle looks at Detective Wells and then Detective Morgan. Before she can say anything, Detective Wells glances past her then asks, "Is there a Mary Lou Reynolds and a Sally Pierce staying here?"

Michelle cautiously answers, "Yes."

"We'd like to talk to them." Teri has walked up.

"Ma'am, if you don't mind, we'd like to come in and ask them some questions," Detective Morgan says as he deliberately looks past Michelle and at Teri.

"Are you Ms. Morgan or Mrs. Pierce?"

Teri, shocked at seeing detectives standing at their door, replies, "No. They're still asleep."

Detective Wells glances at his partner then asks, "Would you mind waking them up? We need to ask them some questions. May we come in?"

Both women move to the side, allowing the detectives to enter.

Michelle asks, "Can this wait? They just arrived last night, and they're absolutely exhausted."

"No, ma'am," Detective Wells states as he walks to the center of the living room.

Both women want to question the detectives about what is going on, but instead Michelle says, "Please sit down. Would you like a cup of coffee? We just made a fresh pot," Michelle offers.

"That would be nice," Detective Morgan replies as he and Detective Wells take a seat on the couch.

Teri gently knocks on the guest room door, and when there is no answer, she quietly opens it. Both women are sound asleep. She leans over and gently touches Sally on the shoulder. "Sally, Mary Lou, wake up." Neither stirs. She hesitates before saying louder, "Sally, wake up!"

Mary Lou stirs as Sally groans.

"You need to get up. Two detectives want to talk to you." Sally lifts herself onto one elbow, yawning. "What?"

Teri repeats what she said, and Mary Lou yawns. "Did you say detectives?" she asks.

"Yes. You need to get up. They're waiting and want to talk to you."

Teri returns to the living room and, sitting down on a stool at the breakfast bar, tells the detectives, "They'll be out in a minute."

Mary Lou, in gown and robe, enters the living room with Sally following behind her. The detectives stand and introduce themselves again. "If you don't mind, we'd like to ask you some questions about what happened yester-day." Detective Morgan says."

Sally nods, and Mary Lou starts toward the kitchen. "Can we get a cup of coffee first?" Mary Lou asks.

"Sure," Detective Wells answers as they sit back down.

Detective Morgan asks Mary Lou and Sally, "Would you mind starting from the beginning and telling us exactly what happened?"

Trying to hide a yawn without success, Sally then takes a sip of her coffee. Stifling another yawn, she begins. "We left early because we wanted to get an early start."

"Where were you when you first saw the car?" Detective Wells asks.

Teri and Michelle are listening closely.

"We were just about to Beaumont," Mary Lou answers.

"Were they in front of you or behind you?" Detective Morgan asks.

"In front of us," Mary Lou answers then takes a drink of her coffee.

"Go on."

"The car was slowing down. We were near some woods that lined the road. We were in a no-passing zone so I had to slow down, too."

Both detectives watch Sally and Mary Lou's body language and expressions as they continue talking.

Sally scoots a tad closer to Mary Lou on the settee. The detectives notice she's anxious. Her hands begin to shake a little.

Detective Morgan smiles. "You're doing fine. What happened next?"

Mary Lou glances at Sally. "They pulled off to the side of the road near the trees, but not all the way, so we had to practically stop. There was a car coming from the opposite direction."

Setting his empty coffee cup on the coffee table, Detective Wells asks, "Did you by chance get a license number?"

"Now why would we do that? There wasn't anything

really out of the ordinary. They just pulled off the road!" Mary Lou snaps, upset.

"It's okay, Ms. Reynolds. Can you remember any numbers or letters? Was it California plates?"

"I don't think so."

Sally suddenly says, "I do! It was a California license plate, and I remember seeing a seven. There was a 'J' and a 'F.' I don't remember anything else about the plate."

"A seven, J, and F," the detective repeats and writes it on the small notepad he has in his hand.

"What happened next?" the detective asks.

Michelle stands up. "Would you like more coffee?"

Detective Morgan replies, "No, thank you, I'm fine."

Detective Wells holds out his cup. "I'd like a little more if you don't mind."

While Michelle is refilling his cup, Sally moves another inch toward Mary Lou. Mary Lou sits up a little straighter and tries to move closer to the armrest, feeling crowded by Sally.

"I was driving," Mary Lou states. "When the oncoming car passed, I pulled around them, and when I looked in the rearview mirror, they had opened the trunk and pulled something out. I thought it was odd."

"How far ahead of them were you?" Detective Morgan asks.

"Not very far at all. I was still going slowly. We had barely passed them. I hadn't sped up yet."

Sally is almost sitting on top of Mary Lou now. The detectives notice that as the story continues, Sally moves closer and closer to Mary Lou.

"Did you see their faces? What happened next?"

"No, but I saw one of the men. There were two, watching us. That's when I started getting a little scared. Sally, will you give me some room!?"

Sally scoots back over to her side of the settee.

"Go on."

"I started speeding up and praying."

Sally is wringing her hands as they begin shaking more than before, adding to Mary Lou's statement. "I turned and looked out the back window when Mary Lou told me what they were doing. That's when I saw them carry what looked like a body and lay it beside the road next to the woods." She scoots back up against Mary Lou.

Michelle gasps, and Teri's eyes are as big as saucers as she covers her mouth with her hand and gasps.

The detectives glance at each other. As she elbows Sally in the ribs, agitated, Mary Lou speaks up, "When Sally told me she thought they just dumped a body, I took off like a bat out of hell! Excuse my language."

Detective Morgan notices Sally's almost in tears. "You're doing great, Ms. Reynolds. Do you need to take a short break? We know this is difficult." "Please," Mary Lou replies and stands up, walking toward the hall.

Michelle and Teri seem to be glued to their seats. They're so shocked that they don't even speak. The detectives walk to the sliding glass doors, opening them; they step outside. Teri can hear them talking but can't make out what they're saying.

Returning to their seats, Detective Wells begins.

"How far did you get before you realized they were chasing you?"

Teri almost falls off her stool.

"They must have tried to hide the body in the woods, if that's what it was, because we were almost to Redlands by then. I confess I was *flying* down Highway 10!"

Once again, Sally continues to slide closer with each dramatic event. Detective Wells hides a chuckle when he sees Mary Lou glare at Sally as she elbows her in the ribs again.

"Suddenly they were behind us, and that's when they shot at us." Mary Lou continues. "I'm so sorry about your car, Teri." I was so scared, and Sally was screaming, 'Go faster!' I just romped on it! The angels couldn't even keep up with us!" Both detectives can't help but laugh.

Mary Lou continues, "The traffic was heavy as we got close to Redlands, and so I was able to put some cars between us, and they must have been afraid to shoot anymore. I guess they thought someone might call the cops." Taking a deep, jagged breath, she continues, "As soon as I could, I pulled into a busy store, and we ran inside. That's when we called the police. They must not have seen us because they passed the store and kept going."

Sally is visibly shaking now, and Mary Lou puts her arm around her shoulder to comfort her. Mary Lou is hiding her nervousness, or trying to, but both detectives are fully aware.

Teri bursts out, "Oh my gosh! I can't believe you had that happen! No wonder you were in shock when you got here! Was it a body? Did they really put a dead body beside the road?" She asks the detectives.

The detectives look at each other and then Detective Wells stands. "Yes, ma'am. That's why we're here."

All Michelle can say is, "Oh my gosh!"

"You gave the police this number. How long are you going to be in town?" Detective Wells asks.

"*We're getting the hell out of here right now!*" Sally thinks.

Mary Lou replies, "We're flying out Sunday night. We're taking the red-eye back to Atlanta."

"Thank you, ladies. I think we have everything we need," Detective Morgan says.

Mary Lou follows them to the door, and the detectives stop just outside the door.

"In case we have more questions, give us your Georgia phone numbers," Detective Morgan says as he holds his pen to the notepad.

She does.

"We'll be in touch if we have more questions."

Mary Lou nods and watches them walk to their black sedan and pull away.

Michelle and Teri are flabbergasted. "Can I get you another cup of coffee? Would you like some breakfast? How can we help you?" Teri is talking so fast that she isn't even taking a breath in between her questions.

Michelle hands each a fresh cup of coffee, and they all walk to the kitchen table. For several minutes, no one speaks. All are deep in their own thoughts. Of course there are a million questions, and when Teri starts to ask,

Michelle looks at her and shakes her head no. Puzzled, Teri stops.

Mary Lou stands and, speaking to no one in particular, says, "I'm going back to bed. I hope you don't mind." She walks away.

Sally gives a weak smile. "I think I'll join her."

• • • • • • • • • • • •

"I just can't believe someone really shot at them!" Teri says as she and Michelle walk slowly along the beach.

"You saw the bullet hole in your trunk lid. It's a miracle they didn't hit the gas tank."

"It's a miracle they didn't hit one of them! Do you think they'll catch the guys?"

"Probably, they have a partial license-plate number, and that's a big help right there."

"I keep thinking how scared they must have been! I don't think I would have even been able to drive if someone was shooting at me," Teri says.

"Oh, I think I could drive. I might look like I've been shot out of a cannon, but that car would be moving!" Michelle laughs.

"I just hope they're going to be okay. What a rotten way to start their vacation."

"I wonder if they're awake yet. Let's head back to the house." Michelle turns and starts back in the direction they came from.

As they near the house, they see Sally and Mary Lou sitting on the patio with cups of coffee in their hands.

Mary Lou is yawning, and Sally is staring out at the ocean.

"Good afternoon," Michelle says as she walks toward the women. "Are you hungry? We can fix you some sandwiches or something."

"No thanks," Mary Lou answers as she turns to Sally. "Are you hungry?"

"No, I don't think so. I think I'd like to go for a walk."

Teri immediately offers to go with her.

"Are you okay, Sally?" Teri asks. "I mean, you have to still be shaken up about everything."

Without answering right away, Sally stops. "You know, Teri, I've never been so scared in my life! All I could think of was not ever seeing my husband and kids again." Tears well up in her eyes.

Teri grabs her in a hug. "I'm so glad you're okay. I can't imagine going through what you did. What if those guys find out you're from Atlanta? They may come after you there."

"I don't think they'll come all the way to Atlanta to find us when we didn't actually see them kill the woman. That's a relief."

"It was a woman! How do you know it was a woman?"

"Detective Wells called. That's what woke us up. He had a couple more questions, and I asked him."

"Why would someone want to kill her?"

Sally wants to change the subject. "I don't know. Can we talk about something else?"

• • • • • • • • • • • •

Michelle hasn't asked Mary Lou anything about what happened. *If she wants to talk about it, she will bring it up.* Mary Lou sits, quietly staring out at the ocean.

"This is good for the soul. How long have you lived here?" Mary Lou asks Michelle.

"I've been here about ten years now. I used to live around Phoenix, but Larry offered me a job at the center, and I couldn't say no. Plus he was here, and that makes it nice. We've always been fairly close."

"Where are your parents? Do they live close by?"

Lowering her head, Michelle shakes her head no. "They were both killed by a drunk driver. Larry looked after me like a father after that."

Mary Lou nods and asks, "How old were you?"

"He was twenty-one, and I was eighteen."

"I'm so sorry."

"Thank you. It's been a long time ago, but at times I still miss them terribly. Larry helps me through those times."

"Teri told me he's a psychiatrist. Boy, could I use one about now!"

Michelle studies her for a long moment then gently says, "Mary Lou, you and Sally have been terribly traumatized. Larry would be more than happy to come over and talk with you and help you through this."

"Oh, I couldn't do that. We'll be fine." The mist in her eyes says differently.

"I want to call him and ask him to come to dinner tomorrow night, if that's okay. You two really need to talk to someone besides Teri and me."

"Let me ask Sally how she feels about it. To be honest, I really would like to talk to someone, but I thought I'd wait until I get home."

"I'll call him anyway. If Sally doesn't feel comfortable talking to him, then you and he can talk."

"That's awfully nice of you. Thank you."

"I see Teri and Sally. Why don't you join them, and I'll call Larry and then join all of you."

• • • • • • • • • • • •

Larry has agreed to come to dinner after Michelle tells him what happened. The rest of the day is spent relaxing on the beach, wading out in the water, and getting acquainted with Teri's friends. That night Michelle hears moaning coming from the guest room where the women are asleep. She has expected some sort of repercussions, from one of them at least. Suddenly she hears Sally scream, "Go faster!" Jumping out of bed and racing to the bedroom, she doesn't knock. Mary Lou is hugging Sally, softly telling her it's okay. They're safe now.

• • • • • • • • • • • •

The barbecue is simmering, and placing thick rib-eye steaks on the grill, Michelle can hear the others laughing in the living room. Upon entering, Larry is telling them some of his experiences with celebrities. From the laughter, one would never know how traumatized these two women really are. After dinner Larry suggests they all go out on the patio and watch the sunset. Michelle has told Teri why he's there.

"Why don't you three go, and Teri and I will clean up. We'll be out in a little while."

It's almost nine o'clock when Larry comes in. Sally and Mary Lou stay outside and are talking softly.

"Larry? Are they going to be okay?" Teri whispers.

"Yes, they'll be fine. I suggested they see someone a few times, at least, when they get home."

"Good!" Michelle says.

Larry looks at Teri with a knowing smile. "If they can 'go rub elbows with the movie stars,' that will help."

Teri laughs. "I'll see to it. Can you give us some suggestions as to some of the places they can go?"

"Sure. Do you have a pencil and paper?" Teri quickly gets them and returns to the table. "There's Universal Studios. They can go to some of the sets and participate in some of the game shows if any are being filmed."

"Oh, that would be wonderful!" Teri exclaims. "They'll love that!"

Continuing his list as he speaks, "Then there's Grauman's Chinese Theatre and the stars walk of fame. That's where all the stars' handprints are in the cement walkway."

"Oh, I've heard of that!" Teri says, excited.

"That's a big attraction for tourists. Then there's Disneyland, Knott's Berry Farm. Malibu Pier is a good place to go. That's where stars can be found pretty often and Venice Beach."

"What's there?" Teri asks.

"That's where all the people ride skateboards and skate along the walkway, some with weird haircuts and women with shorts that barely cover their bottoms and swimsuit tops. It's quite an experience."

"What movie stars are in the stars at that place you mentioned?" Teri asks.

Michelle has gone to her room. Mary Lou and Sally are still on the patio.

Larry leans back in his chair and, placing his hands behind his head, laughs. "Oh, there's plenty of them!"

Mary Lou and Sally step through the sliding glass doors. "Plenty of what?" Sally asks.

"Movie stars." Larry replies.

Excited, Teri leans her elbows on the table. "Like who?"

Mary Lou and Sally plop down in the other chairs, with their eyes sparkling. "Yeah, like who?" Mary Lou excitedly asks.

Larry begins naming some. "Lana Turner, Harrison Ford, Cher, Sophia Loren, Marilyn Monroe."

All three women are so excited, they can hardly stand it. Sally jumps up. "What about Elizabeth Taylor? Is she there?"

"Yes, she's there and a bunch more."

"Name some more," Mary Lou says.

"Marlon Brando, John Wayne, Kris Kristofferson, Humphrey Bogart—"

"Oh, my husband loves Humphrey Bogart! He's going to die of envy when I tell him!" Sally squeals.

"That sounds like the hot spot you ladies want to

hit," Larry states as he stands up. "As much fun as this has been, I do have to go to work in the morning. Teri, would you walk me out to the car?"

Teri is worried. *What is everyone going to think when they find out he was here? I sure don't want any gossip.* She stands up, hesitating for a moment. "Sure."

Mary Lou and Sally stand. "Thank you so much, Larry," Mary Lou says. "It's been a pleasure meeting you, and I'll do what you said."

Sally chimes in, "Me, too. Thank you."

Teri and Larry walk to the door. "You're welcome. Maybe we'll get to visit again before you leave. Tell Michelle I said good night."

Standing beside his car, Teri is curious as to why he asked her to walk him out.

"I asked you to come out with me, Teri, because I wanted to tell you that your friends will be fine. I'd like for you to take tomorrow off and go with them."

"But—"

"Don't argue. It's only one day, and it's a Friday. They'll be leaving Sunday. You want to visit with them before they leave, don't you?"

"Of course!" She takes a step back then says, "Larry, I don't want any favors. I've heard about office gossip, and I don't want to be the subject of it."

"I understand, but you have to realize you live with my sister. That stops any gossip right there, which we take care of in a heartbeat! You don't have to worry about it. Take tomorrow off and enjoy your friends, and come back to work Monday. It's that simple."

"Thank you. I do want to spend as much time with them as I can. I really miss them."

"I'm sure you do. I'll see you Monday."

"Thank you. Good night."

• • • • • • • • • • • •

The next three days are spent touring. The girls are loaded down with cameras, water bottles, shopping bags, and a tablet for autographs, excitement fills the air. The three women take pictures of each other kneeling down next to their favorite movie star's star, having a stranger taking a picture of the three of them together at Venice Beach, and at the Malibu Pier, they've cornered at least four movie stars for autographs and pictures. Shopping along Rodeo Drive is yet another experience they won't forget. By Sunday, they are exhausted. Mary Lou won't admit she's had a couple of nightmares, and Sally has only awakened the household once screaming.

Standing near the security checkpoint at the Los Angeles International Airport, all three women are in tears as they hug and say good-bye. Teri already feels homesickness seeping in. "Please, please, please don't say anything to Mom about what happened. She will come out here herself and drag me back home!"

Both women emphatically say in unison, "We won't!" Suddenly Sally's cell phone rings. "Hello."

"This is Detective Morgan. Is this Mrs. Pierce?"

"Yes."

"Mrs. Pierce, I'm sorry to call so late, but I just wanted to let you know we caught the men you saw on the road coming out here. Are you still in LA?"

"Yes, but we're just getting ready to board our flight back to Atlanta."

"Can you stay another day or two longer? We might need you to identify them."

"But we didn't see their faces! We don't know what they look like!"

The detective is silent for a moment. "Okay, if we need you, I'll call you. Have a safe trip."

Mary Lou and Teri are listening and when Sally flips her cell phone closed. "Who was that and what was that all about?" Mary Lou asks.

"That was Detective Morgan. He said they caught the guys that dumped the body and wanted us to stay another couple of days.

"Praise God!" Teri says.

"From what you said he must have agreed to let us go home." Mary Lou says as she takes hold of the handle to her carry-on bag.

"He said he'd call if they need us."

Sally and Mary Lou step in line to go through security.

Teri watches her friends as they place their bags on the security conveyer belt and exit on the other side. Not being allowed to go to the gate area with them, Teri has to wave good-bye as they pull their carry-on baggage down the long concourse.

Teri hasn't called Chris yet to tell her what happened so when she arrives home she immediately calls her.

Chapter 9

Wedding plans are in high gear as the September fifteenth wedding date nears for Chris and Jack. Margaret and Chris are at odds a good bit of the time over the planning. Margaret wants the big church wedding with all the trimmings and many guests. Chris wants a small, private wedding in the church she grew up in.

Margaret has her legal pad on the table in front of her, listing the names of all the guests she wants to send invitations to. "Chris, it's only going to be a hundred and fifty to two hundred people. That's considered a small wedding."

Reaching across the table and sliding the legal pad in front of her, Chris looks at her mother. "Mom, look at this! I have no idea who ninety percent of these people are! No! I want a *small* wedding. No more than fifty people at the very most."

"But, Chris, these are our friends and colleagues."

"*Your* friends, *your* colleagues!"

"Honey, don't be that way. You're my firstborn, and I only want it to be a wonderful, memorable day for you. You only get married once."

Frustrated at trying to make her mother understand, Chris shoves the notepad aside and stands. "Mom, this is *my* wedding! I know you want to make it the best, and it will be. But it will be the best *small* wedding around."

"Chris, please. What about the cake, your dress, flowers? Are you going to skimp on them, too?"

Now infuriated, Chris says nothing as she stomps to her bedroom. Margaret sits staring at the list and finally leaves, walking along the stone path amongst her gardens. Sitting down on the cement bench along the path, she begins praying. She isn't asking God to grant her the wish for a big wedding but asking Him to bring peace and harmony between her and Chris. "Lord, may Your will be done. Amen."

Chris is also praying, asking for forgiveness for being so harsh with her mother, and adds, "Lord, am I wrong to not want a big wedding like Mom wants?"

. . . .

Teri's phone rings

"Hi, Chris."

"Have you got a minute?"

"Sure. You sound upset. What's going on?"

"Now don't go freaking out on me! Dad has had a *very, very* mild heart attack.

Teri plops down on her armchair by the window. "*God, please let him be okay.* Please tell me he's okay, Chris."

"He's okay, the doctor said it was very, very mild and gave him a blood thinner."

"Are you sure he's okay? Do I need to move back home?"

"There's no reason why you need to come home."

"How is Mom taking this?"

"You know Mom. She's imagining all sorts of things. The main one is that he'll have a major heart attack and she'll be left totally alone, with no one."

"But she has us."

"I know, and that's what I keep telling her, but she argues. Teri, she's not going to be satisfied until one or both of us are living in the house or right next door."

"Chris, we can't do that! Doesn't she understand that?"

"Right now she's eaten up with fear, and I think that's a large part of her diving headlong into planning a big wedding. It makes her feel needed and keeps her mind off the other stuff."

"So what can I do?"

"Nothing. Continue to do what you planned. Teri, we can't enable her in her fears. If you come home, that's exactly what she wants. The next step is she'll have you moving in with her. She's already tried that with me."

"No! You're kidding. You're getting married. Surely she doesn't expect you and Jack to live with her! I'm so sorry, Chris. I feel I should be there to help."

"You're fine right where you are. I'll keep you updated, so don't worry, Teri. Dad is fine. We don't need you at home. We have lives, you know."

Once Teri calms a little she asks, "How are the wedding plans coming along?"

"Mom is still determined to make this wedding a big flippin' deal."

"I'm sorry, Chris, but we knew she would."

"I know, but it's gotten old fast! I'm ready to elope and forget the whole thing."

"Come on, Chris. It isn't that bad, is it?"

"I'm seriously considering the drive-thru wedding window that's next to the drive-thru divorce window in Las Vegas. If not that, there's also an Elvis Presley chapel, and I have always liked Elvis."

"You're kidding!"

"Nope. Teri, you should see the list of people she wants to invite! I don't know ninety percent of those people!"

"Do you think it will help if I talk to her?"

"I don't think anyone can get through to her except maybe Dad. I'm going to talk to him tonight."

"What's Jack saying about all of this?"

Chris can't help but laugh. "He's staying as far away as possible. He agrees with me, but he said he's not starting the mother-in-law bit any sooner than he has to." Sitting down on the edge of her bed instead of pacing, Chris is calming down. "So are you coming home for Labor Day weekend?"

Teri hesitates before answering. "No. Being the new kid on the block at work, I can't take that many days. Labor Day weekend is only three days, and I'd only get to stay a day or two with having to fly back and forth."

"Mom's not going to be happy about that. You know how much she wants you home."

"I know. She never lets me forget when I call, but I can't take extra time off for that and then four or five days for your wedding."

"I understand. I just hope Mom does."

· · · · · · · · · · · ·

Larry has agreed to go to church with Michelle and Teri, but when he arrives, Teri is down on the beach near the water. Standing at the sliding glass doors, he sees her sitting on the sand, hugging her knees and staring out at the water. Michelle walks up beside him.

"She's really upset, Larry. I don't think she slept a wink last night. I heard her up, and before I could come to see what's wrong, she had already left. She's been there since dawn."

Larry glances at Michelle and then back at Teri with a concerned look. "What's happened?"

"Her sister called. Her dad had a mild heart attack."

"Why don't you go on to church, and I'll go talk to her."

"I thought that's what you would say. Her mother really wants her to move back home and is putting heavy duty pressure on her."

With great concern, Larry slides the door open and steps out onto the patio.

"She'll get through this, 'Chel." He stoops and removes his shoes and socks.

Sitting down in the sand next to Teri, he says nothing but is aware of tears streaming down her face. Minutes pass, and finally Teri softly says, "I think I need to move back home."

"Michelle just told me."

More long silent moments pass, and then Teri suddenly sobs. "I don't want to move home! What kind of a daughter does that make me?!"

• • • • • • • • • • • •

Michelle left early in order to attend the Bible study and the worship service. She's surprised when she arrives home to see Larry and Teri still on the beach talking. *I'll leave them alone. I think Teri has needed to talk for a long time.*

Larry returns to the house, and while sitting on a chair putting his shoes and socks back on, Michelle stands behind him. "Is she okay? Is she moving back home?"

"I don't know. It's something she has to decide."

Michelle glances at Teri and then looks directly at Larry as he stands. "You're in love with her, aren't you?"

Larry looks down at her then away. "I've got some paperwork I should get done. I leave for Philly in the morning."

Michelle smiles as he walks to the front door. *Yep, he's in love with her!*

Teri, after talking with Chris several times and her father twice, has decided not to move unless absolutely necessary.

• • • • • • • • • • • •

Margaret has finally conceded to a small wedding, but she and Chris have agreed to make some concessions. Margaret has cut the guest list down to people Chris and Jack know, a few family friends, a few of Chris's colleagues, and some of Jack's friends. The total is now seventy-five people.

Chris has agreed to a large reception if that's what will make her mother happy. It will be held on their lawn just as they did for the anniversary party. That way her mother can invite all that she wants, and they won't have to rent a hall. They've agreed on the flowers and cake, and Margaret is thrilled that Chris has asked her to help her choose a dress. Of course, Margaret wants the long, flowing gown with a long, flowing veil, and Chris wants a less expensive, simple dress.

"Mom, I can't afford an expensive wedding dress. We want to go to the Caribbean for our honeymoon, and we plan to stay a week. That's why I don't want to spend a lot for a dress I'll wear for only an hour."

"You're right, Chris." Margaret admits. "I didn't think about your honeymoon expenses. You know your father is paying for the wedding. He'll also pay for your dress."

"I know, Mom, and I appreciate that very much, but it isn't necessary. I just don't like paying a bunch of money for something I'll never wear again."

"You can always have it for your daughters to wear when they get married." Margaret coyly says.

"Come on, Mom. We have to stop by the grocery store on the way home." *The woman just never gives up!*

• • • • • • • • • • • •

Larry has been traveling to conferences and business meetings, so Teri and Michelle don't see him very often. When he is in town, he and Teri go to dinner, ride bicycles in the park, and take walks along the beach. Teri has pretty well settled into her position as a children's counselor, having completed her training period. She's still working on learning not to break down when talking to a small child that is working through the issues of being abused. One little girl cries as she tells what her daddy did to her, and Teri quickly leaves the room with tears flowing. Claire has stepped in immediately so the little girl doesn't think she's done something wrong.

One ten-year-old boy is being transferred to the preteen unit after going through much therapy. Eighty percent of his body is covered with scars from his drunken father pouring gasoline on him and setting him on fire. Teri can't help but break down. *Why do you allow these things to happen, Lord?*

She also praises God for the progress the children make. Many times when arriving home, she goes directly to her room and sobs for hours. Michelle has learned to let her cry it out. She's very familiar with the pain and suffering these children go through. She's treated many of them in the hospital unit. It isn't an easy job, but they both love what they're doing.

• • • • • • • • • • •

Chris is trying another murder trial. The man on trial has been in court before, and Chris "put him away." He's been out on parole for a month, and this time he's in court for murder. As she's examining a witness, the defendant suddenly jumps out of his chair, yelling, "You lying sack of scum!" Throwing the defendant's table over, he rushes toward the witness stand. The deputy sheriffs, that are standing nearby, rush to stop him. In the scuffle, the man grabs one of the deputy's guns and starts firing.

Screams are heard throughout the room, and people begin running for the doors. The judge has dropped down behind his desk, and the witness hides behind the partition on the witness stand. A deputy tackles the man but not in time to prevent another shot from being fired.

Chris is trying to get under the prosecutors' table to have shelter from flying bullets. As she runs across the room, she feels a sudden impact and falls facedown on the floor. Blood is spilling from her chest, but the defendant has not been completely restrained, so no one dares to try to get to her. Four deputies are wrestling with the man, and one is able to kick the gun out of his hand and out of reach. While the defendant kicks and yells profanities, the deputies are able to handcuff him and jerk him to his feet, shoving him toward the side door.

One of the deputies runs to Chris and, seeing she's unconscious, grabs his radio. He yells into it, "Get an ambulance over here now! The prosecuting attorney has been shot! We're in courtroom ten."

With sirens blaring, Jack can't seem to get to the hospital fast enough. It's only minutes before the news has spread across police radios. Rushing into the emergency room, Jack demands, "Where's Christine Wilson?"

"She's in surgery, sir."

Several other officers gather around Jack. "She'll be okay, Jack. She's tough. Come on and sit down. I'll get you some coffee," his partner says.

Phone calls have been made, and Margaret and Clay speed to the hospital. Margaret is almost hysterical, and as Clay speeds through traffic with emergency flashers blinking, he's praying for his daughter like he's never prayed before.

After several hours, the surgeon appears in the waiting room. Margaret, Clay, and Jack stand before him as friends and officers stand within hearing distance but not crowding the doctor while he speaks to them.

"I think she's going to make it now," the doctor says.

"Now?" Clay whispers. He's barely able to speak for fear of losing his daughter.

Margaret stands, wide-eyed, crying, but silent.

The doctor continues, "We lost her on the table, but were able to bring her back. She's lucky to be alive. The bullet severed a main artery, and had it been an eighth of an inch farther to the right, it would have killed her. It missed her heart by a hair."

Margaret is sobbing, and Clay is holding on to her to keep her from fainting. Jack nervously listens.

"We're taking her to the ICU unit and will watch her closely. If she makes it through the night, she'll be okay." Everyone is stunned, including the group that has gathered. Clay sits Margaret down in the closest chair available as she sobs. Jack can barely stand. His partner stands next to him.

"Jack, she'll make it. Look, these people are already praying for her."

Jack barely hears him through his shock.

• • • • • • • • • • • •

Larry is tossing salad, and Michelle and Teri are cooking the chicken, mashed potatoes, and fresh green beans when the phone rings. It's one of the rare nights that Larry can join them for dinner. Being the closest to the phone, he picks it up.

"Bellum residence."

A shaky voice on the other end says, "Is Teri there? This is Jack."

Larry hears, "Doctor Lee, Doctor Lee, please call the operator," in the background. Larry knows instantly this call is from a hospital.

Teri is laughing about something Michelle has said and turns. Larry is reaching out the phone to her, and she immediately knows something has happened by the expression on his face. Larry stands close to her as Jack explains what happened.

Teri can only cry then finally says, "I'm taking the next flight out," and hands the phone to Larry. Dropping to the floor on her knees, Teri's sobs come from deep within her. Larry is speaking softly on the phone with Jack. When hanging up, he kneels beside Teri, holding her against his chest as he strokes her hair.

Michelle starts to speak, but Larry mouths, "Not now."

As Teri throws clothes in a suitcase, Larry tells Michelle what's happened. "You help her, 'Chel, and I'll get on the phone."

Teri has no idea the center has a corporate jet, so when Larry says he'll take her to the airport, she just nods her head. Larry seldom makes use of the jet, but in emergency situations, he has access to it on a moment's notice. Michelle returns from Teri's room.

"She's almost packed. Are you taking the center's jet?"

"Yes."

"Go with her, Larry. She needs you."

"I'm going. She's not in any shape to make that trip alone. Don't worry. She'll be well taken care of."

Teri is numb, so when Larry guides her up the steps of the corporate jet, she's barely aware it's a private plane. For most of the flight, she's quiet, even though Larry tries to engage her in conversation and reassure her that Chris will be all right.

"Teri, she's in God's hands. He's going to take care of her."

"How do you know that? Maybe He wants to take her home."

"You know God is aware. He is the Almighty Healer, and you have to trust Him. Chris is going to be okay. I sense it."

Teri merely looks at him and turns to stare out the window. Larry doesn't realize that she has been praying the whole time they've been in the air. Larry reaches into his bag and lifts out a small Bible.

"Here. I thought you might like to have this."

"Thank you" is all Teri says as she takes it and turns back to the small window.

As the jet pulls to a stop on the tarmac, a black sedan pulls up to the side of the jet. Jack steps out. Teri looks surprised but hands Jack her suitcase and slides into the backseat. Jack has said nothing to her but shakes hands with Larry, introducing himself. The ride to the hospital, to Teri, seems to take forever. Jack and Larry have been talking softly.

Jack looks in the rearview mirror and says, "Teri, she's doing well. She had some rough spots during the night but came through them. The doctor says she's out of the woods but still in critical condition."

Teri tries to blink the tears back.

• • • • • • • • • • • •

Quietly entering the ICU room, Teri gasps at seeing Chris hooked up to lines that seem to invade every inch of her body. Margaret and Clay are sitting in chairs next to her bed. They jump up and hug her.

Margaret starts crying, and Clay says, "Let's step outside."

He leads them to the lounge just down the hall. Jack has sat down in one of their chairs and stares down at Chris. Larry has checked into a nearby hotel.

"Mom, Dad, you go rest. I'll stay here with Chris. You look like you're ready to drop," Teri says.

"We'll be fine," Margaret says as she starts to sit down.

"Please, Mom. Jack and I are here, and Larry reserved a room for you just down the street. You can rest there."

Looking surprised, even Jack agrees. "Teri's right. We'll be here, and we can call if there's any news. You aren't helping her by getting sick yourselves."

Clay is grateful, and although he hasn't met Larry officially, he feels close to him.

• • • • • • • • • • • •

Meeting in the hotel restaurant for breakfast, Clay, Margaret, Jack, and Larry are gathered around the table engaged in conversation.

Jack looks at his watch. "I need to get back to the hospital. I told Teri I'd be there by nine." Standing and pushing his chair up against the table, he reaches out his hand. "Larry, I can't thank you enough for all you've done. We'll look after Teri, so don't worry about her."

Before Larry can reply, Clay reaches out his hand as he stands to shake Larry's. "We appreciate everything you've done. Thank you."

Margaret looks up at Larry and can't help but see the love and concern in Larry's eyes. "She'll be fine. She's home now." Jack has turned and started to walk away.

"Jack, do you mind if I ride to the hospital with you? I'd like to see Teri before I leave."

"Sure."

• • • • • • • • • • • •

Larry pulls Teri out into the hall and takes her gently by her shoulders.

"Teri, I have to get back to the center. You stay as long as you're needed, and don't worry about anything with work. When you're ready, call me, and I'll fly out and get you."

Teri looks down at the floor.

Larry lifts her chin gently. "I mean it. You take all the time you need. Just keep me posted about how Chris is doing, and we'll be praying for her and you, too."

Glancing back into the room, Teri sees Chris move slightly in the bed. Most of the tubes have been removed over the past couple of days, and the prognosis is good. She looks into Larry's eyes for a long moment.

"I don't know how I could have done this without you. Thank you, Larry, and I'll call every day if necessary. Have a safe trip home, and tell Michelle thank you, too."

Larry wants to lean over and kiss her, but this is not the time or the place, so he says good-bye and walks down the long corridor to the elevators.

• • • • • • • • • • • •

Teri has decided to stay with Chris in her apartment during her recovery. Margaret and Clay call every day, checking to see how Chris is and to speak to her for a few minutes on the phone.

"Chris," Margaret says, "we'll have to postpone the wedding. You're not up to that right now."

"Mom, I'm doing great. I don't want to postpone it. We may have to hold off on the honeymoon for a little while." Chris suddenly sneezes and then continues, "I want that man as my husband just as soon as possible."

Margaret can't help but laugh. "Are you sure? Your dress might fit pretty snug in the bodice. Won't that hurt?"

"For Jack Gordon, I can endure anything."

"Okay, honey, if that's what you want."

. . . .

It's been almost two months since Chris was shot, but Teri is still uncomfortable leaving Chris alone, even though Chris is doing very well.

"Jack is coming over, so get your butt out of here and go visit Mom and Dad," Chris orders. Grinning as she continues, "We need some alone time."

Laughing, Teri puts her hands on her hips. "Chris, you better be careful."

"Oh, silly, we're not going to do *that*! Now go."

Later, Chris is nuzzled close to Jack as they sit on the couch watching *Law and Order* on TV. Looking up at Jack, "You never have told me how you got into law enforcement. How did you?"

Turning the TV volume lower, Jack looks down at her. "Well, my dad was a cop for as long as I can remember. He was answering a call for a burglary in progress, and when he arrived and stepped out of the car, the guy shot him. He died two days later in the hospital."

"Oh, Jack, I'm so sorry. Didn't you tell me your mom died of cancer when you were seventeen?"

"Yes."

"How old were you when your father died?"

"I had just turned twenty-one and was eaten up with anger. I applied for the police academy and got hired."

Jack stares at the TV for a minute then continues, "I was so angry that some scumbag killed my father that I was determined to rid the city of every murderer, drug dealer, prostitute, bank robber, and anyone else I could think of."

"I'm surprised they hired you."

"I think having a father as a cop helped."

"So what happened? You obviously didn't succeed in getting rid of all the criminals."

"A guy who knew my father took me under his wing and got me straightened out. Joe McCarthy really loved my father. They were partners for several years. He's retired now."

"I'm sorry you had to go through all of that."

"Thanks."

· · · · · · · · · · · · ·

While Teri speaks to Larry on the phone, Margaret and Chris are downstairs talking. Margaret still wants Chris to wear the flowing wedding gown. Chris turns to face her mother, knowing her mother might faint at what she's going to say. "Mom, I've decided I want to wear a nice suit. I saw one in the bridal magazine I really like."

Before Chris can say another word, Margaret,

shocked, "Christine Marie Wilson, I will not have you marry in a suit! I am adamant about this! No daughter of mine will wed in a suit! You can choose your wedding *dress,* but I am standing firm on this!"

Chris sighs loudly, knowing her mother will not change her mind. "Okay. But *I* am going to pick the dress, and I don't want any flack about it, Mom."

Feeling satisfied and trying to lighten the tension, Margaret says, "Besides, you'll want your daughters to wear it when they marry. I didn't have the money to buy a beautiful gown when your dad and I married."

Chris looks at her and smiles. "If we have any, what if it's boys, not girls?"

By the time they sit together for lunch, the tension between them has lessened. Margaret looks across the table at Chris. "Chris, I know you've seen so much suffering and pain in those courtrooms. When that little boy and girl were so brutally murdered, I saw a change in you."

Chris looks surprised. *Where did this come from?*

Taking a bite of her salad and then laying her fork down again, Margaret continues, "I know I have probably driven you nuts about my wanting grandchildren."

Oh, Lord, here we go again. Chris says nothing as she lifts her glass of water. "Chris, honey, I know you're afraid to have children."

Shocked, Chris almost chokes on her water.

"I can't say I blame you after all you've seen done to them."

"Mom, where is this going?"

"I want you to know that I can accept it if you and Jack decide not to have children. Yes, it will break my heart, but it's a decision the two of you have to make. I'm not going to be an interfering mother-in-law."

Remaining silent for a long moment before speaking, Chris isn't sure if she should say anything. *If I don't tell her, then she's going to worry herself to death about this. She'll find out soon enough anyway.*

"Mom, Jack and I have talked about all of this. Yes, I was scared to death about having children because I was afraid I couldn't protect them."

"Oh, honey."

"Let me finish, Mom. Jack and I have decided we will have children."

Tears jump up in Margaret's eyes. "Oh."

"Mom, both of us want kids. I was just scared something like what happened to the kids you're referring to would happen to ours. We've decided that when we have kids, we will immediately give them to the Lord, and it's His responsibility to protect them."

Margaret can't sit still for another second and jumps up, knocking her chair over, and runs around the table to Chris. As she grabs Chris in a hug, she almost tips Chris and her chair over. "Oh, I'm so happy."

Chris begins laughing and holding onto the table. "Mom, we're going to hit the floor if you don't let go of me."

As Margaret releases Chris, sobs of joy and tears of happiness flow down Margaret's face.

Teri joins them.

"Are you going to be able to stay for the wedding?" Chris asks Teri.

"Larry is absolutely wonderful about all of this! Even though I've been here three months he said I'm not to worry about work and to call when I'm ready to come home."

Margaret sighs a sigh of relief.

"I knew he would. I think you have yourself a great guy, Teri. I like him." Chris says.

• • • • • • • • • • • •

Chris hasn't completely healed yet from the bullet wound, but she's letting nothing get in the way of marrying Jack. Large white bows grace the end of each line of pews. A large, floor-standing crystal vase, with two dozen brilliant red roses, stand on each side of the stairs leading to the stage inviting the bride and groom. A candelabrum holds three tall, white candles, with a polished wooden cross standing near the back of the stage. Pastor Mike stands facing the guests as Jack, dressed in his rented tuxedo, stands expectantly to the right of the stage. Joe McCarthy stands beside Jack as his best man, and two of Jack's longtime friends stand smiling. Teri, acting as Chris's maid of honor, stands with the three bridesmaids. Teri already has misty eyes as she waits for her sister to walk toward them. The four of them are dressed in knee-length, soft violet dresses. Delicately laced sleeves reach to their elbows and the scoop neck line shows off the diamond necklace Chris gave Teri as her graduation gift.

Margaret is sitting on the front row, holding tightly to a lace hanky. She knows the tears will flow as her firstborn daughter speaks vows to love and honor to her son-in-law-to-be. She and Clay have grown to love Jack as though he is their son. The love, concern, and care he showed Chris during the trying time after the courtroom shooting has been more than impressive. To Margaret, he proved to be a man with great character and an honorable man. Margaret dabs at a tear and gently straightens the A-line skirt of her pale pink dress. Friends of the family, Chris's secretary, a few colleagues, friends, and Larry and Michelle, as well as several detectives that have worked with Jack over the years sit quietly speaking in the pews.

Chris stands in the narthex waiting for her cue to enter. Her white dress has laced, short sleeves and a satin bodice with an overlay of lace; a full skirt comes to her knees. Her brown hair shines as though the sun is kissing it. A shoulder-length veil flows from a rhinestone-and-pearl tiara. Her eyes sparkle, and the joy she feels in her heart can't be described. Clay stands looking down at his daughter.

"You are so beautiful." Leaning down, he kisses her on the cheek. "I am so proud of you, and I love you very much. You know you're still my little girl. You'll always be my little girl. I know you'll be well taken care of. Jack is a wonderful man, and I'm proud to have him as a part of this family."

"Thank you, Dad. I love you, too. I love Jack so much. I know he's a fine man."

As the organ begins to play, Chris takes a deep breath, and she and Clay step into the doorway. Holding her bridal bouquet of peach roses, pink Asiatic lilies, purple dendrobium orchids, and subtle sparkles of rhinestones, she places her arm in the fold of her fathers. Clay looks at her, grinning.

"Let's get you married," he says as they begin the slow walk down the aisle and into her future.

Chapter 10

Chris feels well enough that she and Jack decide to go on their honeymoon now instead of waiting. Jack is able to rearrange their flight schedules and had previously reserved a room in Barbados. When Teri approached her about inviting Larry and Michelle to the wedding, Chris thought it would be wonderful if they could come. After all, Larry made it possible for Teri to be there for her all this time. Teri decided that if they could come then while Chris and Jack are on their honeymoon, they could all fly back to California together. Teri gives Chris a hug, then Jack.

"You have fun. We'll talk when you get back."

Waving good-bye as they walk down the jet way Chris and Jack board their flight to Miami. Teri, Michelle, and Larry board the corporate jet.

The flight is spent chatting about the wedding, all that Chris has gone through, whether she would return to work, and various things that have gone on at the center in Teri's absence. Parking in the driveway of Teri and Michelle's home, Teri raises her arms above her head and, spinning around, she laughs.

"Oh, the smell of the ocean again!" Laughing, they enter the house and begin opening windows and the sliding glass doors. Teri steps out onto the patio and, breathing deeply, she turns to Larry who has just stepped out behind her.

"Larry, thank you again. I'm so grateful to you for giving me all the time I needed. Chris really needed me there with her."

"You're very welcome. I missed you. I *really* missed you. Welcome home," he says as he leans down and brushes her lips with his.

Teri smiles. "I missed you, too."

· · · · · · · · · · · ·

Chris and Jack deplane in Barbados and, being tired from the wedding, the huge reception her mother insisted on, and the hustle and bustle to make their flight to Miami, they choose to stay in for the night. Sitting on the balcony of their hotel the sea breeze soothes their weary bodies.

"This is beautiful," Chris says as Jack leans against the railing. Chris eases back in the lounge chair as melodious sounds of Caribbean music whispers through the palm trees.

Their first day on the island is spent playing in the crystal blue waters, wind surfing, while being careful not to veer too close to the many coral reefs, and taking naps in the sun. That evening is spent at a lobster fest with live local entertainment. The bongo drums and stomping feet of the dancers is intoxicating.

Walking along the stone pathways in the fifty three

acres of flower gardens leaves Chris and Jack in awe of their surroundings. Tropical flowers and plants that they have never heard of or seen seem to engulf them. It's like a jungle of beauty that appears only on postcards. Chris can't help but burst out laughing as green monkeys flit effortlessly through the banana trees chattering and playing. One grabs a banana from another and they chase each other through the trees as though the branches are stepping stones. Another hangs precariously from his long tail and invites Chris to feed him a banana by reaching out to her.

Welchman Hall gully is filled with interesting attractions. Chris and Jack take in all they can. Jack ducks his head as they enter Harrison's Cave.

"I'm glad I don't have claustrophobia," Jack says as he stoops to miss bumping his head on stalagmite on the low ceiling. The tour guide informs them the age of the cave, how it was discovered, and much information about the stalagmites and stalactites that are still present. Chris is in awe, as she gently touches a rough, hewn wall.

The days and nights are filled to the maximum, and on their last day, they decide to go on the Catamaran tour. As the boat skims across the crystal sea Jack leans his head back with his face soaking up the sun.

"Am I dreaming?" he asks Chris.

Chris places her hand on the bill of her hat, with 'Barbados' written across the front. "If you're dreaming then I am, too. Do we really have to go back?"

Jack lowers his head and placing his hand above his eyes for shade, "I'm afraid so, darling." Scooting closer to her he leans over and kisses her lightly. "This sure beats sirens and courtrooms."

Chris closes her eyes and in a dreamy voice says, "You got that right."

• • • • • • • • • • • •

As Teri steps into her office, she sees her phone light is blinking. Setting her briefcase on the floor next to her desk, she punches the button. Clay's voice comes through the speaker. "Hi, honey, it's Dad. Would you give me a call when you come in? Everything is fine. I just want to talk to you for a minute. Love you. Bye."

That's kind of odd. Dad never calls me at work. He didn't sound upset or anything. I wonder what he wants to talk about.

Checking her other messages, Teri removes her light jacket and sits down. Dialing her father's office number, the phone rings several times. Just as Teri is about to hang up, her father answers.

"Hi, Dad. I was about to hang up. Are you busy?"

"No. I just came in from a meeting and grabbed the phone. I've been expecting a call from a client, and Jessie is out to lunch."

"You said you wanted me to call you. Is everything okay? Are you all right? Is Mom okay?"

"Everything is fine, honey. We're all okay. I have some news for you and couldn't wait to tell you."

"News? What kind of news? You sound a little excited."

"Remember the bottle with the message inside that you found when you went to Tybee Island?"

"Sure. What about it?"

"Remember I said I'd see if I could track down the person that had the disconnected phone number?"

"Oh my gosh! Did you find out who sent the message?"

"I sure did."

"Tell me, tell me!"

"The number on the note was an England number. It's taken all this time to track it to the person who wrote the note. He now lives in Australia."

"Oh, this is so exciting! And?"

"Teri, I haven't talked to him. I thought you should do that since it's your bottle. You found it. I'll give you his name and phone number, but it's up to you to call him."

"I'm so excited! Did you tell Chris?"

"No. That's something else I thought you should do."

"Oh, I wish she was here so we could call together."

"Or you could be here so you could call together."

Teri is silent, surprised her father would say that instead of her mother.

"Are you there?" Clay asks, thinking they may have been disconnected.

"Yes. I'm just surprised you said that. Mom's the one who is always asking me to come home or implying it."

"Oh, honey, I'm sorry. I didn't mean it that way. Your mother isn't the only one that misses you, though."

"I know. I miss you, too."

"Do you have pen and paper handy? I'll give you this information, and then I have another meeting to go to."

Writing the information down, her dad's words still bother her. He's never said or implied he wanted her to come home. It isn't as though he doesn't want her to visit, but this soon after being there for three months, she's surprised.

Larry pops his head into her office; he very seldom does that.

"Hi. What are you doing down here in the trenches?" She laughs.

Stepping into her office and taking a seat in front of her desk, he stretches his long legs out, placing his arms behind his head. "I thought you might like to go to lunch with me since I have a few hours free. Are you all tied up?" He already knows she isn't.

Teri quickly looks down at her calendar. "No, as a matter of fact. When do you want to go?"

"We can go now if you can. I thought we'd go to the seafood restaurant we went to once before. You liked that one, didn't you?"

"Oh yes, they really have good fish."

"Then come on. Let's get out of here before someone finds me."

Riding along the freeway on the way to the restaurant, the air has become cool. Teri hugs her jacket closer around her.

"Are you cold?" Larry asks. "I can put the top up."

"Just a little. I'll be okay. I like the fresh air."

"We'll be there in about five minutes. I'll put the top up coming back."

Entering the restaurant, Larry asks for a table next to the window so they have a good view of the ocean. He knows how much Teri loves the water. They've been able to swim a few times while he's visited Michelle and her but not nearly as often as Larry would like.

Waiting for their meal, Larry looks over at Teri. She's admiring the view, and just as she turns to say something to him, he says, "Are you happy here, Teri?"

"Yes! Of course. I love it here. What makes you ask a question like that?"

"I was just wondering. You seem to miss Georgia a lot, and I wondered if you wanted to move back now. Do you?"

As the server places their plates in front of them and refills their water, it gives Teri time to think.

"Larry, this is totally unexpected. I don't have any desire to move back home. If something happened to one of my parents, I might consider it but, no, I don't want to move back to Georgia. I love living here, I love my job, and—" She stops, turning her attention to a seagull hovering near the window.

Larry looks at her intensely. "And?"

I think I've fallen in love with you. "Can we say the blessing before I starve to death?"

They eat in silence for a few minutes then Teri suddenly exclaims, "Oh I forgot to tell you! Remember me telling you and Michelle about the bottle with a message in it that I found on Tybee Island?"

Larry takes a moment to remember. "Oh, yes. You and Chris went with a couple of friends."

"Yes! My dad said he was going to try to see if he could trace the number back to the owner before it was disconnected."

"Okay."

"He did! He called a couple of days ago and told me. I have the information written down, and blast it, I can't find it! I wanted to call Chris and tell her but not until after I talk to the man."

"It's probably on your desk and slipped under some files."

"I looked, but I can't find it, and I'm sure Dad got rid of the information. He'd have no reason to keep it."

Larry knows she has deliberately changed the subject but says nothing. "Did he say anything other than giving you the information, like where the man lives?"

"Oh yes. The man's name is Cruz, and he lives in Australia now."

"Wow, that's a long way from England."

"I have just got to find that number and call. I've been so busy that I actually forgot about it."

Disappointed that the conversation has changed direction, Larry can only reply, "I'm sure you'll find it."

The rest of the meal is spent talking about her concerns about a few of the children, and then they return to the center. Walking into her office, Claire stops her.

"Teri, your sister called and said she needs to talk to you right away. I hope everything is all right. She sounded a little upset."

Teri runs to her phone. "Thanks, Claire," she says as she grabs the phone and starts dialing.

Chris answers as soon as she sees Teri's name on the caller ID. "I'm glad you called, Teri."

"Chris, what's wrong? Claire said you sounded upset."

Chris cautiously answers, "Nothing's really wrong. I was upset because I missed you. You had already left."

"Chris, I know you, and I can tell something's wrong. Did Dad have another heart attack?"

"No, he's fine."

"Mom? Is she okay?"

"Yes, Mom's fine."

"Chris, stop playing games with me! Now tell me what this is all about!"

Chris is silent for a moment then shouts at the top of her lungs, "I'm pregnant!"

Teri has jerked the phone away from her ear then excitedly starts shouting. Suddenly realizing where she is, she quietly says, "Are you sure? Have you told Jack? Does Mom know yet? I'll bet she's ecstatic!"

Chris is laughing and crying at the same time and answers, "Yes, yes, and yes."

Claire peeks around the door into Teri's office to see if everything is okay. Teri is leaned back in her swivel chair, laughing with tears rolling down her cheeks. Claire's puzzled but doesn't want to interrupt, so she ducks back behind the door. Teri covers the mouthpiece on the phone and yells, "Claire, I'm going to be an aunt!"

Laughing, she gives Claire a thumbs-up when Claire appears in the door.

"Congratulations," then Claire goes about her work.

Teri can't help but tell everyone she comes in contact with. Everyone congratulates her but has no idea how happy this news has made her. She's just about come to the conclusion that she'll never have children of her own considering she isn't married yet and really has no hopes of getting married in the near future. She's mentioned this to Michelle a couple of times in their discussions, and Michelle encourages her not to think that way.

"You aren't so old you can't marry and have children. You have plenty of time."

Michelle has asked Larry over for dinner. Thanksgiving is next week. Teri has plans to go home for Thanksgiving, and Larry will be out of town.

Larry walks into the living room and asks, "Is Teri here? I didn't see her car."

Michelle is in the kitchen stirring noodles into a pot of boiling water. "She went to the store for me. We're out of butter."

Looking almost relieved, Larry sits down at the breakfast bar. "Oh."

During dinner the conversation is about the cold weather, office talk, and their plans for Thanksgiving. "We're both going to be out of town, Michelle. What are you going to do for Thanksgiving? Please come home with me. We'd love to have you join us." Teri says.

Michelle looks at Larry and then at Teri. "Thanks,

but I already have plans. I've been invited to dinner with some friends. I won't be alone."

Larry smugly asks, "Is it anybody I know?"

Michelle glares at him. "No."

Teri can't help but notice the smug look on Larry's face and Michelle's irritation. She looks at one, then the other. "Am I missing something here?"

Michelle moans. "I might as well spill the beans. I've been seeing someone. It's nothing serious, so don't start getting any ideas."

Larry laughs, and Teri is surprised. "I didn't know you were dating anyone. You've never said anything."

Michelle begins to clear the plates. "It's no big deal. We've only been dating a couple of months. Can we talk about something else? Why don't you two go for a walk while I clean up?"

Larry stands and stretches. "Good idea. I'm stuffed and need to walk some of this off. Do you want to walk along the beach, Teri?"

"Michelle, I can help if you want."

"No, there isn't much. Take Larry and drown him in the ocean."

"Oh, that isn't very nice, sister." Larry laughs. "You'll need your coat, Teri. It's cold out there."

Walking along the beach, Larry sees a large piece of driftwood. "There's a piece of driftwood. Would you like to sit for a while?"

Teri snuggles her coat tighter around her. Seeing she's cold, Larry puts his arm around her shoulders and pulls her close. As they reach the driftwood, Larry takes her hand and helps her sit down. She's snuggled down in her coat with the collar up around her ears. Her slacks aren't thick enough to keep her legs warm, and she begins to shiver.

"You're freezing out here," Larry says. "Maybe we better go before you're frozen solid."

"Maybe we should."

Instead of standing up to help Teri stand, Larry scoots off the driftwood and kneels before her. "I love you, Teri. I have from the moment I met you. Will you be my wife?"

Reaching into his coat pocket, he brings out a small velvet box. Opening the lid, a brilliant diamond sparkles in the evening light. Teri forgets about the cold and jumps up, knocking him backward as she jumps into his arms.

"Yes," she says, then kisses him passionately while he's lying in the sand and she's on top of him.

• • • • • • • • • • • •

Chris and Jack are sitting on the couch in Margaret's living room. Teri and Larry stand in front of the fireplace as though they are warming up from the cold weather after their short walk through Margaret's gardens. Margaret and Clay are laughing at a joke Chris has told. Larry clears his throat, and Chris nudges Jack in the ribs. Teri has deliberately hid her engagement ring so her mother would not see it. She wants their engagement to be announced "officially."

Chris isn't surprised at what is about to happen. Teri had called Chris and told her all about the proposal.

Tapping his glass lightly, Larry gets the attention of everyone. Margaret is taken totally off guard. Larry and Teri face Margaret and Clay. Larry says, "Teri and I are asking your permission to marry." Before anyone can say anything, he quickly adds, "Well, I guess we're a little late for that. I asked her to marry me, and I'll be darned if she didn't say yes!"

Margaret lets out a scream and flies out of her chair, running to hug each of them. Of course her tears are flowing, and Chris and Jack sit laughing.

"I'm glad I'm not in Mom's path. She would have knocked me over," Chris says.

Clay shakes Larry's hand and hugs Teri. "Welcome to the family, Larry. We are honored to have you."

Now Teri starts crying. Chris and Jack stand and, reaching out to her sister, Chris gives her a big hug and turns to Larry. "You have a family that will hunt you down for the rest of your life if you hurt my sister!"

Larry is shocked and not sure what to say. The intensity in Chris's voice tells everyone she is not kidding.

"Chris!" Margaret scolds. Teri is dumbfounded.

Larry looks at Chris with all sincerity. "Chris, I love your sister more than anything on this earth. I wouldn't hurt her, and if I do, I don't blame you a bit if you hunt me down. I would deserve it."

Now Chris is shocked. She certainly wasn't expecting an answer like that one.

Jack slaps Larry on the back and laughingly says, "Don't let her scare you. She's just overprotective."

Clay starts toward the kitchen. "Is anyone going to eat some of that pumpkin pie, or am I going to get it all?"

The tension has been broken, and excitement is replacing it.

. . . .

Thanksgiving morning is spent finishing up the last-minute preparations for the dinner they have planned. Jack, Clay, and Larry are in the den, and occasionally the women hear a burst of laughter from the three men.

Teri smiles and turns to her mother. "Mom, Larry and I plan to marry around the first of the year."

"That's kind of soon, isn't it? You haven't known each other very long."

"We've spent a good amount of time together, I live with his sister, and people at work have known him for several years."

Concerned, Margaret starts to say something, but Teri holds her hand up to stop her.

"I'm in love with him, Mom. You always said that when the right one comes along, you'll know right down to your toes. Even my toes are tingling."

Margaret can't help but laugh and walks to Teri and gives her a hug. "Will you at least get married here?"

"Larry and I have talked about that. We'd really like to get married in California, but because my family and friends are here, then we'll marry here." Margaret is almost afraid to ask Teri if she'll have a big wedding. After the disagreements she and Chris had over Chris's wedding Margaret doesn't want to hear Teri insist on a small wedding.

She hesitates for several minutes. "Teri, honey," she finally says.

Teri turns from what she's doing.

"Teri, what kind of wedding do you plan to have?"

Teri knows exactly what her mother is thinking and as a way of teasing her she pretends to be thinking. "Hm-mmmm." Margaret holds her breath.

"Oh, I don't know, Mom. I thought I'd have a big one. You know, maybe three or four hundred people."

"Yes!" Margaret yells and runs over to hug Teri.

Teri is laughing as Chris comes through the door. "What's so funny?"

Margaret is dancing around the kitchen swinging a dish rag like it's a banner. "Teri? What has Mom been drinking?"

"I just told her Larry and I want a big wedding."

"You do!?"

"Sure. You were happy having a small wedding, and I want a big one. Like Mom told you, 'you only get married once.'"

• • • • • • • • • • • • •

The next two days, Chris and Jack and Larry and Teri tour some of the various sights. Even though Larry has been to Atlanta many times, he has never spent time outside of meetings and conferences before flying back to California. This is a rare treat for him. Riding the sky lift at Stone Mountain and looking out over the city, riding the train around the mountain, Larry is fully enjoying their outing. Of course, Teri has been here many times, but she hasn't enjoyed it nearly as much as she is with Larry.

Arriving back at Jack and Chris's home, Teri takes Chris aside.

"I'm sorry, Chris. I didn't mean to imply your wedding wasn't great or anything like that when we were in the kitchen. I hope it didn't come across that way"

"It didn't. Don't worry about it. Mom has been chomping at the bit for a big wedding and, actually, I'm glad you want one. That makes Mom so happy."

"I couldn't help but laugh when she started dancing all over the kitchen."

"So have you set a date yet?"

"We've decided on March fifteenth. That gives us a little time to plan, and that's still a good time for a cruise."

"Oh! I didn't know you were planning a cruise for your honeymoon."

Teri blushes. "Larry said it would be more romantic."

"You're blushing," Chris laughs and says in a sing-song voice, which makes Teri blush even more.

Since their trip is short, Teri isn't able to get together with Sally and Mary Lou. She has called both of them only to be told they're out of town for Thanksgiving. She was hoping to meet them for lunch.

• • • • • • • • • • •

Saturday is spent relaxing. Plans have been made for Margaret and Clay to join Teri, Larry, Chris, and Jack for dinner that evening and then to see the show *Hello Dolly* at the Fox Theatre in Atlanta.

Standing outside the theatre, Margaret says to Teri, "You have to promise me you'll come home for Christmas."

Teri looks up at Larry; he nods yes. He is still her boss, and she doesn't want to promise something without knowing if she'll have the time off to do so.

"I'll come home, Mom."

Chris wraps her arm around Jack's back. "Good. I should be waddling by then."

Laughing, Clay and Margaret return to their car, and the others return to Jack's car.

· · · · · · · · · · · · ·

Parking in the short-term parking lot, Chris and Jack walk into the airport with Teri and Larry.

"I'm so glad you two were able to come. Larry, I'm thrilled you're going to be my brother-in-law," Chris says.

Larry smiles down at her and then squeezes Teri's shoulders. "I'm happy to become your brother-in-law."

Laughing, Jack reaches out to shake Larry's hand. "You come with her for Christmas, Larry. You're considered a member of this family already."

"Thank you, Jack. I'll see what I can do."

Picking up their carry-on luggage, Teri hugs Chris then Jack. "We better go. They'll be calling the flight soon."

Larry takes her hand in his. Waving one last time, Teri steps onto the escalator ahead of Larry and turns and waves as she disappears down the stairs.

.

Chapter 11

....

Margaret sits down with a legal pad to start listing all the things Teri needs to do for her wedding; invitations, guest list, rehearsal dinner, cake, flowers.

Does she want limos? she thinks as she jots it on her paper. Margaret is loving every second of planning this wedding. She has to admit it isn't quite as much fun as it would be if Teri was here instead of California.

"I need to call Teri and see what she thinks about some of these things." Margaret is speaking out loud as she continues with her list. Clay walks into the kitchen where Margaret is sitting at the table. "Who are you talking to?" he asks as he looks around the kitchen expecting to see someone.

"Oh, just to myself. Clay, I am so excited about Teri's wedding! Just think our youngest is getting married, and Chris is having our first grandchild. Life couldn't be better!"

"And you couldn't be happier because she's having a big wedding. You are right about life being good." Clay laughs as he gives her a peck on the cheek and leaves.

• • • • • • • • • • • •

Many phone calls have been made between Margaret and Teri. Margaret has hired a wedding planner to help with some of the arrangements. The wedding planner is disappointed because Margaret and Teri have decided the rehearsal dinner will be a very casual affair—a barbeque in Margaret's backyard. The bride's maid luncheon will be at the restaurant that overlooks the Chattahoochee River.

Teri is in her office at work when her phone rings. "Hi, Mom."

"Hi, honey. Do you have a minute to talk?"

"Yes, but not much. I have a meeting in fifteen minutes."

"I think I have found the perfect place for the reception. I think you'll love it."

"Where?"

"It's right on Lake Lanier. They just built this huge beautiful hotel, and they have a *huge* ballroom. Teri, you should see it! One wall is nothing but glass facing the lake and several beautiful chandeliers. It's gorgeous!"

"Wow, it sounds beautiful. Can you reserve it for the wedding?"

"I already have," she says laughing.

"You knew I'd like it obviously. Thanks, Mom. You're doing so much."

"And loving every minute of it! I better let you go. I'm going to e-mail you some pictures of the flower girl's dress. I found some that are really nice."

"Okay. I need to run."

"Okay. Love you, honey."

"I love you, too. I'll talk to you later. Bye."

Teri has chosen the songs for her and Larry's first dance and the father-daughter dance. The guest list has been made and Chris is helping address them, which is no small feat due to the three hundred guests to invite. Sally's five-year-old daughter, Becky, is the flower girl. Teri bought her a T-shirt with "Perfectly picked flower girl" written on the front in pink. For her five bridesmaids she has chosen a silver compact with blue, purple, and clear crystals in a butterfly design on the lid. Their name is engraved on the bottom. She hasn't decided on her gift to Chris yet, who is her maid of honor. She has helped Larry choose gold cuff links with a small diamond resting in the center of black onyx for his best man and groomsmen.

• • • • • • • • • • • •

Teri's phone rings as she sits down on the couch. "Hello."

"Teri, it's Mom. Did you get the pictures I sent of the flower girl dresses?"

"Yes. They're adorable, and beautiful!"

"Have you chosen which one you want?"

"Yes, it's the one that's described as bridal matte satin with an A-line skirt and cap sleeves."

"Oh, that's the one I was hoping you'd choose! Did you notice the satin bow that's in the back with the flowers in the center of it? It's really pretty the way it's made. What color do you want? They have it in white and champagne."

"I think I like the white one more so than the champagne."

"That's what I was thinking, too."

"Are you going to have her wear a little tiara or headband?"

"Yes. In fact I just saw one and bought it. It's satin with little pink flowers. Oh, I forgot to tell you. I have the flower basket, too. It's satin and lace. It has really pretty satin bows flowing down lace stringers from the handle. I thought we'd have rose peddles in it."

"That sounds lovely. The wedding planner has lined up the photographer and caterer."

"What kind of meal is going to be served?"

"Let's see. I have it written down right here. The salad is watercress, Frisee, and endive with coastal fruit nectar and yogurt dressing."

"Yum, that sounds good."

"The entrée is chardonnay Poached Pacific salmon with fingerling potatoes, delta asparagus, and dill beurre blanc. There will be baked rolls of course and the wedding cake for dessert."

"Oh, Mom, that sounds wonderful."

"I thought so, too."

"Has Pastor Mike said he'd do the wedding for us?"

"I really got tickled at Richard. He told Pastor Mike, quite emphatically I might add, that when he gives you and Larry the marriage blessing, he's to do it in twenty-five words or less."

Teri bursts out laughing. "Do you think he will?"

"From what Richard said, he better. Oh, I hear Clay

coming through the door so I better get off here and start some dinner. Let me know what you decide about the limos."

"Oh, Mom. I've decided not to use limos. The church is only two miles from where the reception is."

"I hadn't thought about that. But you're right. I'll scratch that off my list."

"Love you. Bye."

• • • • • • • • • • • •

Michelle has accompanied Teri to the bridal shops, and with camera in hand, she takes pictures of Teri as she poses in each dress. Teri has narrowed her favorites to three dresses and e-mails the pictures to her mother, asking her opinion.

As Margaret looks at them on the computer screen, she and Teri are on the phone together discussing their likes and dislikes, comparing each dress with the other. "Oh, Teri, I wish I could be there with you. It would be so much fun to go shopping together for your dress."

"Mom, I have a great idea! Why don't you fly out, and we can do that. The wedding is three weeks away, and I won't have to have fittings and all that."

"Oh, Teri, that would be so nice, but I can't."

"Why not? Dad won't be there. Didn't you say he had several meetings and has to go out of town next week?"

"That isn't it, honey. Chris is still having a lot of morning sickness and is absolutely miserable. That's why she hasn't been able to help much. She's planning on coming here next week so I can look after her. Jack doesn't want her to stay home alone."

"Is she okay? I mean, the baby is okay, isn't it?"

"Oh, yes. The baby is fine. She's kept all her doctor appointments, and the doctor says everything is fine."

Looking at the dresses, the long, straight skirt with its scoop neck and straps is not what either decide is right. The tight-fitted lace bodice with layers and layers of lace skirt is tossed to the side. They both agree, and it's settled. Teri's gown is satin with a floor-length and full skirt. The fitted laced bodice has a V-neck and sheer lace sleeves. The flared train is just long enough to add even more elegance without being too long. Teri has chosen a crystal and pearl tiara with a fingertip-length veil with satin lace edge. Teri can tell her mother is crying as she says, "It is so beautiful."

Teri smiles. "I know, Mom. It is really beautiful. Thank you for helping me to decide."

$$\bullet \ \bullet \ \bullet \ \bullet \ \bullet \ \bullet \ \bullet \ \bullet \ \bullet \ \bullet \ \bullet \ \bullet$$

Larry has ordered his tuxedo and asked his childhood friend, Greg, to be his best man. Four of his college friends have agreed to be groomsmen. They are flying out two days before the wedding. Greg teases Larry, "I want to make sure you get to the church on time."

"Oh, I'll be there on time. I want Teri as my wife more than anything in this world."

"Did you say Michelle and Teri are flying out on the same flight as we are, or are they leaving early?"

"They're flying out a week ahead of us. They need

to be there for the last-minute stuff. Anyway, that's what Michelle said."

"So when are we going to have your bachelor party?"

"That's up to you and whoever to decide. As far as I'm concerned, I don't want one. I don't need some skimpy-dressed woman sitting on my lap."

"Oh come on, Larry. Don't be a party pooper. Not all bachelor parties have those women."

"The ones I've attended do. They have some babe in a thong jump out of a cake or slither all over your lap. No thanks!"

"Okay, if you say so." Greg laughs as he nudges Larry's arm with his fist. "We'll keep it clean, if you insist. But it won't be as much fun."

． ． ． ． ． ． ． ． ． ． ． ．

Stepping into the courtroom, Chris is as confident as ever that she will win her case. The man that is on trial has beaten and raped an elderly woman in her home. After spending many days in the hospital, the woman is not expected to live. Her son sits in the first row. His fists are clenched and his face contorted with anger and with eyes flashing hatred as he glares at the man being brought into the courtroom. Handcuffs are in place but removed before he sits down.

Chris knows the woman's son is volatile and has worried that he may be a problem. She's talked to him and reassured him the man will be punished to the fullest extent of the law. Judge Freeman takes his seat; lifting the gavel, he pounds it down.

"This court is now in session."

The jurors have been seated, seven women and five men. The trial begins, and Chris tries to contain the nausea she feels. She's previously explained her condition to the judge, and he has graciously allowed her to have a few crackers handy to discreetly eat during the trial. She tried to recuse herself from this trial, but no other prosecutor was able to fit it into their schedule.

As the witness testimonies continue, the son of the victim can't seem to keep his anger from flaring up. "Sir, if you don't sit down and keep quiet, I will have you removed from this court! Do you understand me?" Judge Freeman says sternly.

"*If I get my hands on that scum, I'll kill him!*" The son thinks as he sits back down.

The defense attorney paints a sad picture of a man abused as a child. His summation is weak, to say the least. Looking at the jury, his final statement to them is: "He is not the perpetrator, and you must find him not guilty!"

Chris has given her summation, and the jury retires for deliberation. Jack walks up to Chris as the courtroom clears.

"Are you okay, honey? I saw you sneak a cracker."

Nodding her head yes, she suddenly makes a run for the ladies' room.

Jack is worried. *I wish she'd quit this job!*

Chris and Jack retire to the lawyers' lounge. Chris is stretched out on the sofa and has fallen asleep. Jack sits at the table drinking week-old coffee. When Chris wakes up, Jack softly asks, "Honey, can I get you anything? Do you need some crackers?"

Chris shakes her head no as her hands rest on her stomach. Chris looks up at him. "How long has the jury been out?"

Jack looks at his watch. "About six hours now."

"That isn't a very good sign considering all the evidence and witnesses. But you never can tell about juries," Chris replies.

Jack walks over to her and sits on the edge of the sofa, taking her hand. "Chris, I'm worried about you."

"You don't need to. I'm okay. Just sick to my stomach a little."

"That isn't what I'm talking about."

"Then what are you talking about?"

"The son in there. If he goes nuts, you could get hurt again."

"He's been searched thoroughly. The sheriffs are keeping their eyes on him. It will be okay."

Jack wants to tell her he wants her to quit but knows this is not the time or place. Just as Jack leans over and kisses her lightly, her cell phone rings. Jack helps her to sit up. "The jury's back. I better get back in there." Jack helps her to her feet.

"Has the jury come to a decision?" Judge Freeman asks as the defendant and his attorney stand.

"Judge, Your Honor, we are sorry to say we are deadlocked."

The son, sitting at the edge of his seat gripping the railing, is watching intently.

"Is there any possibility that a unanimous decision can be made with more deliberation?" the judge asks.

"No, Your Honor, we are hopelessly deadlocked."

"Then I have no choice but to declare this a mistrial. You are free to go."

Suddenly the son bolts over the railing, and before the deputy sheriffs can get to him, the son yells, "You'll not get away with this!"

Lunging forward, he slams Chris against the prosecutors' table, and she falls to the floor. Jack is on his feet and running to her, shoving the screaming people out of his way. "I'm getting you to the hospital now!" he says as he gently picks her up in his arms and helps her to her feet.

Chris holds her stomach and groans. The deputies have wrestled the son to the floor, and as they slap the handcuffs on him, the defendant is shoved through a door.

• • • • • • • • • • • •

Lying on the examining table, the doctor examines Chris thoroughly, placing his stethoscope on her chest and then her back, examining her arms, legs, and eyes. The doctor finally places the instrument on her now-swollen stomach, listening closely. "I want you to have an ultrasound while you're here," the doctor states as he places the stethoscope around the back of his neck. Jack is holding Chris's hand.

"Jack, I'm going to be okay. You're crushing my fingers."

Jack jerks his hand back. "I'm sorry."

"I'll set up the ultrasound right now. A nurse will be in, in a minute."

Chris doesn't know that Jack is silently praying as she is. They don't speak, but Jack wants to tell her, "That's it! I don't care if you agree or not. You are going to quit that job!"

The nurse enters with a machine. Smiling at Jack and Chris, she sets up the machine and takes the tube of lubricant, removing the cap. "This may be a little cold."

Chris and Jack watch the screen but can't make out what is there. The nurse frowns then smiles. Jack can't stand the suspense. "Is she okay? Is the baby okay?"

Chris takes his hand. The nurse begins wiping the lubricant off Chris's belly. "Oh yes. Your babies are fine."

Chris and Jack look at each other shocked and say simultaneously, *"Babies?"*

Jack suddenly feels the need to sit down, and as he's in the process of sitting, he reaches back to grab the chair only to realize, too late, the chair has been moved. Chris giggles.

"Why, yes. You have twins. Didn't you know that?" she asks as she pushes the cart through the door, gently closing it.

• • • • • • • • • • • •

Sitting at her desk, Teri is writing an evaluation on a five-year-old child named Candy. Tears fill her eyes as she leans back in her chair. She hasn't quite been able to keep her emotions under control, but she's been able to curtail them until she's in the quiet of her office. Her phone begins ringing and, quickly grabbing a tissue, she wipes her eyes and blows her nose before reaching to answer it. "This is Teri Wilson. How can I help you?"

"Hi, honey. It's Dad. Are you busy?"

"Hi, Dad. How are you?"

"I'm fine, honey. Do you have a cold? I heard you sniffling."

"No, I was just writing up an evaluation on a little girl. Oh, Dad, some of these cases just break my heart!"

"I know, honey. I don't know how you do that job. I don't think I could."

"I love helping these kids, but sometimes I can't help but just cry for them. Anyway, how are you doing? Is Mom okay? Chris?"

"Everyone is fine. I just wanted to hear my little girl's voice."

"Dad, are you sure you're okay?"

"Yes, I'm fine. There are just times when I want to hear my daughter's voice. Sometimes I just miss the heck out for you."

"I miss you, too."

"By the way, did you ever call about the guy who left the message in that bottle you found?"

"No. Darn it, Dad, I can't find the information you gave me. I have no idea what happened to it. You wouldn't by chance still have it, do you?"

"Hold on. I think I threw it in a drawer." Teri can hear him rummaging through papers and opening and closing drawers in his desk. "Oh, here it is!"

Teri writes down the information. "I'm going to call right now before I lose this again."

"Good. Let me and your mother know what you find out. That's quite a mystery you have on your hands."

"I know, Dad. I don't think I'll ever stop wondering about it until I find out. Thank you for taking the time to locate the man."

"You're quite welcome. Hang in there, honey. Larry told me you are very good with the kids, and they really respond to you."

"When did you talk to Larry?"

"When you were here the last time you gals were in the kitchen and we were all in the den."

"Oh. That was nice of him. Thank you. I needed that boost."

"Okay, honey. I love you, and I'll see you in a couple of weeks."

"Bye. Tell Mom hello. I love you both."

Picking up the paper and staring at it, Teri wonders if she should use the center's phone. *Maybe I should call Larry and ask him if it's okay. It could be very expensive.*

"Larry Martin's office, can I help you?"

"Hi, Cindy, is Larry in? This is Teri."

"Let me check. He was in a meeting, but I think he may be back now." Teri waits while holding the paper in front of her.

"Hi, honey. What pleasure shall I bestow on my beautiful bride-to-be?"

"I was just talking to Dad, and he asked if I ever called the man that wrote the message in the bottle."

"Did you tell him you lost the information?"

"Yes, and you won't believe this, but he found it in his desk."

"That's great!"

"I was wondering if it's okay if I call from here. I'll understand if you would rather I not since it will be quite expensive."

"No, no. You go ahead. I make calls to other countries all the time. It's fine. Are you going to call now?"

"Yes. I just hope it isn't three in the morning there."

"Let's see." Larry is silent for a moment. "I think it's early evening there. I wouldn't bet my life on it since I don't have my calculator handy. Go ahead, but be sure to call me back and let me know what you find out. This could prove to be quite interesting."

"Oh thanks. I will. Bye." Realizing in her excitement that she practically hung up on him, she redials only using his direct line. "Hi again. Did you forget something?"

"I love you. Bye."

After dialing the number on the paper, a woman answers the phone. From the sound of her voice, Teri guesses she's quite elderly. "Is this the Cruz residence?" Teri asks.

"Yes. Who is calling?"

The ladies accent is quite heavy, and Teri has a difficult time understanding her. "Is this Mrs. Cruz?"

"Yes, it is. Now who are you, if I may ask?"

"I'm Teri Wilson. I found a bottle awhile back with a message in it, and I'm wondering if you or your husband wrote it."

Mrs. Cruz gasps. "Why, yes! How in the world did you find us?"

Relieved, Teri begins telling her about the trip to Tybee Island and how she found the bottle.

"Oh my goodness! My husband, Harry, he's passed now, God rest his soul, threw that bottle overboard several years ago."

"I'm sorry. Do you have the time to tell me about it? I hope it isn't too late there."

"Oh no, honey, it's fine. Gee, I'd forgotten all about that." Teri waits for her to continue while trying to contain her excitement. "We were on a cruise ship. Oh, that was so much fun."

"Do you remember where you were when he threw it overboard?"

"Oh, let me think. My mind isn't what it used to be, you know."

Teri waits.

"I remember Harry found an empty bottle and thought it would be fun to put a message in it and throw it overboard. We were curious for a couple of years if anyone ever found it."

"How did you decide on what to write?"

"Harry and I spent hours trying to think of something to write. We're God-fearing people and finally settled on, oh, I can't remember what we wrote."

"It said, 'I have been lost and now I'm found,' and it gave the date and phone number."

"That's right! My, we were living in England at that

time. How in the world did you find me after all this time?"

"My father helped. Do you remember where you were?"

"Let me think. We were taking an around-the-world cruise and if—no, that wasn't it. Let me think."

Teri can hear her mumbling to herself. "Oh, I know now. It was the Indian Ocean. We'd been out to sea several days, and many of the people were beginning to get sick and grumbling about this, that, and the other. They just wanted to get off the ship and fly home. Not my Harry!"

"That must have been a wonderful trip. I'm sure you miss him."

"That I do. By the way, where did you say you found it?"

"In Georgia. There's a small island called Tybee Island, and my sister and two friends and I went there for vacation."

"That's right. You told me that. Forgive me, I'm an old lady."

"I really appreciate you speaking with me. Now I can sleep at night."

"I'm glad. When you get to my age, you won't be able to," she says and then bursts out laughing.

"Thank you so much, Mrs. Cruz. I'll cherish that bottle even more now that I know its history. I've bothered you enough."

"Thank you, honey! I can't help but wonder when I look at our pictures if anyone ever found it. I'm thrilled to know someone who seems as lovely as you found my Harry's bottle."

"Thank you again. I really appreciate you taking the time to talk to me."

"God bless you. Bye."

Teri is so excited, her hands are shaking as she dials Larry's number. Cindy picks up. "Cindy! Is Larry there?"

"You just missed him, Teri. I was stacking some papers on his desk when his phone rang. Are you okay?"

"I just have some exciting news to tell him and couldn't wait. I'll talk to him later. Thanks."

Claire walks into Teri's office, and before she can say anything, Teri starts telling her all about the bottle and talking to the wife. Her excitement is so great, she's stumbling over her words.

Laughing, Claire says, "Take a deep breath."

Teri stops midsentence, sucks in a deep breath, and blows it out dramatically then continues her high-speed telling of her story.

Calling Chris and laughing, she begins telling Chris.

"Teri, you're talking to fast! Now slow down so I can understand you."

Once again, Teri takes a deep breath and blows it out dramatically. Without stopping, she tells Chris the entire conversation with their dad, asking Larry if she can call from there, and every word of the conversation with Mrs. Cruz. Chris has listened and is now as excited as Teri.

"You really talked to her? That's pretty awesome. And she remembers all that?"

"Yes. She sounds quite elderly and had to stop several

times to think, but she was able to remember it all. She sounds like a really sweet old lady."

Chris doesn't want to horn in on Teri's excitement about learning about the message in the bottle, but she hasn't told her yet about having twins. The line is silent for several minutes.

"Chris? Chris, are you okay? Are you getting sick? I can call back later."

"No, the morning sickness is gone. Thank God."

"Then what's wrong? You were quiet an awfully long time."

"I'm fine, Teri. I just don't want to horn in on your excitement."

"What in the world are you talking about?"

"I have some news, too."

"What news?"

"Larry and I are having twins!"

Teri screams, causing Claire to come running into her office. Before she can say anything, Teri screams, "Chris is having twins!"

Claire bursts out laughing. "Teri Wilson, you're going to give me a heart attack one of these days!"

One of the counselors pops her head around Claire, "Congratulations, Teri. I just heard you scream your sister is having twins."

"Thank you. Chris, I'm so excited but I have to go right now. I'll try to call you later."

"But I didn't tell you—"

"I have to go! Bye." A few minutes later, Teri realizes

she didn't ask what sex the babies are. *Oh shoot, I'll just have to call her later.*

. . . .

Gathering in Margaret's kitchen, Michelle, Teri, Chris, and Margaret are going over the last-minute details for the wedding.

"Chris, will you pick up the cake?

"It's being delivered."

"Okay, Teri, you'll need to go to the church and speak with Pastor Mike. He said he'll be there at nine."

"Sure, Mom. Michelle, do you want to come with me?"

"I'd love to. I want to see this church you'll be married in. From what you've said, it sounds lovely."

Taking her coffee cup to the sink, Margaret says, "I'll get the flowers."

"Mom, the florist is going to deliver those," Chris adds.

Teri reaches over and lays her hand on Chris's belly. "Have you decided what you want to name them?"

Margaret interrupts, "Oh, Chris, did you have the seamstress alter your dress? You have two little darlings in there now. That dress won't fit."

Chris laughs. "Yes, Mom, I've already gone for the fitting." She places her hands on her tummy. "They'll have plenty of room to wiggle."

Laughing, the women are excited, and now things are beginning to come together. Teri stops in mid-step. "I'm so happy!" As she releases each woman from hugging them, "Just think. The day after tomorrow, I'll be Mrs. Martin."

Margaret tears up as usual. Looking at Chris then back at Teri, "One daughter is getting married, and the other is giving me two grandbabies. I'm so happy, I don't think I can stand it!"

Michelle stands smiling. *This is what a family should be like. There's so much love here.*

Teri hugs her mother again then turns to Chris. "You didn't say what you're going to name the babies. In fact, you haven't even said their sex yet!"

Chris waddles over to a chair and sits down. "I tried to tell you on the phone, but you cut me off. One is a girl, and the other is a boy."

Teri screams.

"Teri, I know you're excited, but I don't think I can take a scream this early in the morning." Margaret laughs.

Michelle sits down at the table with Chris."

"Larry and I have decided to name the girl Teresa Margaret Gordon."

"You're going to name her after us?" Margaret asks.

"Yes, Mom. You and Teri are the two that I love most—next to Dad and Jack, that is. Plus Grandma's name was Teresa. Then we've decided to name the boy Richard Clayton Gordon. Richard is Jack's father's name."

Margaret plops down on a kitchen chair. "Your father will be so honored. Chris, I am so honored that you will name your child after me, and Teri, of course. How in the world did you know Grandma's name? I wasn't sure you even knew my mother's name."

"You gave me that old album, and I went through the pictures. You had written her name under one. It was Grandma and Aunt Martha."

"Oh my, I forgot about that."

Michelle sits quietly, but she, too has misty eyes.

• • • • • • • • • • • •

Larry, Greg, four college friends, and Carl Crowl board the corporate jet. Carl Crowl, a man Larry highly respects and has been like a father to him, was the executive director before retiring. It was his direct influence that helped Larry move into the executive director position. Larry had asked him to be his best man, but he declined due to failing health.

"I don't feel right about taking the center's jet," Larry says as he takes his seat.

"Indulge an old man. I wouldn't be able to come if I had to be stuffed in one of those miserable airline seats."

The flight to Atlanta is uneventful until they come within range of Atlanta. The captain turns in his seat, looking back at Larry. "We have an engine light flashing. With the traffic up here we're going to have to divert." Thirty minutes later, the men deplane in Birmingham, Alabama.

Teri has called the hotel where Larry and the others have booked rooms, and learning they haven't checked in yet, she begins to worry. "Mom, they should have been here hours ago."

"They'll be here, honey. They may have had a late start. Larry will call you."

"I hope so. I'm really starting to get worried. You don't think he's changed his mind, do you?"

"Oh for heaven's sake, no! Larry loves you more than life itself. Go upstairs and help Chris. She's trying to make beds and clean up the rooms. Michelle is up there too. I can take care of things down here."

. . . .

Entering the operations office, Larry dials his cell phone. Looking at Greg, "I'll bet Teri is worried sick."

Margaret answers the phone. "Oh, Larry, let me get Teri. The poor woman is worried that you've changed your mind. You know how brides are just before the wedding."

"I absolutely have not changed my mind! We had to divert to Birmingham, so we're going to rent a car and drive from here. Ralph will fly into Atlanta as soon as they repair the engine."

"Let me get Teri. Teri!" Margaret shouts as she stands at the bottom of the stairs. "Larry's on the phone, honey."

Teri runs to the phone in her room. "Larry, where are you? I've been worrying about you."

"My sweet bride-to-be, I have not changed my mind! I'm in Birmingham." Then he explains what happened. Teri is so relieved. "Oh, honey, I couldn't call you from the air. We just landed. We'll be there in a couple of hours. We'll go straight to the hotel, and I'll call you from there. Okay?"

"Okay. I love you."

"I love you too. I'll call as soon as we get there."

• • • • • • • • • • • •

Teri, Margaret, Chris, and the four bridesmaids are bustling, feverishly getting dressed. The bridesmaids are dressed in pale pink sleeveless V-neck full length renaissance dresses with draped bodice and tier vertical bow with straight skirts. Chris's is similar in style but not the same, due to her pregnancy. Margaret's dress is a chiffon floor length A-line. The bodice is beaded with filigreed leaves and the matching purple long sleeve jacket adds to its elegance.

"Honey, you are so beautiful." Margaret says as she adjusts Teri's veil. Teri turns to say something to Chris when suddenly Margaret slams against her. One of the bridesmaids, in a hurry, bumps Margaret by accident and knocks her head long into Teri's flowing gown.

"Oh my gosh!" Teri exclaims as her mother plops down onto the floor. "I am so sorry, Mrs. Wilson. Oh, Lord, forgive me. Let me help you up," the clumsy bridesmaid says, reaching out a hand to Margaret.

Margaret sits stunned. Teri gently pulls the edge of her gown from under Margaret's sprawled out legs. "Mom, are you okay?" Margaret says nothing.

Chris is kneeling next to Margaret as the women peer down at her. "Are you okay, Mom?" she asks.

Margaret suddenly throws her hands over her face, howling with laughter. The tension is broken, and being reassured Margaret is okay, the others begin laughing.

"I can't believe I did that!" the clumsy bridesmaid says. Suddenly a flash lights the room.

"I wouldn't have missed this in a hundred years."

Clay laughs as he places the small camera in his pocket. The women didn't hear him knock softly at the door. He takes Teri by the shoulders and looks deep into her eyes. "Do you know how much you are loved?"

"Oh, Dad, of course I do." Tears swell in her eyes.

"I just wanted to make sure you do. I'll see you downstairs." He turns, looks at Margaret who is still laughing on the floor, smiles, and leaves the room.

Margaret is helped up and walks to the mirror to repair her makeup and straighten her dress. Teri walks to her side, "Are you sure you're okay?"

"Yes. I'm fine," she says as she begins laughing again.

Teri turns to make a last-minute check of her makeup and stops. Facing the mirror she gazes at her reflection for a long moment. Her hair is fashioned on top of her head with wisps of spiraling curls gracing the edges of her cheeks. On her leg is the delicately laced blue garter and the ruby pendant her mother loaned her has fulfilled, 'something borrowed, something blue.' Staring at her reflection Teri thinks, *Is that really me? Am I really getting married in a few minutes?*

Margaret smiles as she looks at Teri in the mirror. "Larry is a very lucky and blessed man to have you as his wife. Are you ready for the big step?"

Teri hugs her mother. "Yes, Mom. I think I've been ready since the day I was born."

Chris pokes her head around the corner of the door, "I think it's time to go down, Mom."

Larry, Greg, and his four friends look quite handsome in their tuxedos with the small rose bud boutonniere, standing at the altar waiting.

Chris, steps onto the Point-de-Paris lace patterned runner and follows the little flower girl. Little Becky, in her frilly new dress, tosses rose peddles in front of her and the smile on her face goes ear to ear. Sally, Mary Lou, Michelle, and Teri's college friends follow behind Chris. They slowly pass by dozens of pews filled with smiling faces, and decorated with white tulle and satin bows. Pearl sprays with small red and pink rose buds fill the center of each bow. Looking at the men, Chris thinks, *They really look handsome. Larry looks like he's about to burst he's so happy.* On each side of the stage stairs, a brass candelabra with seven tall white candles and green lemon grass with rose buds, white daisies, and draping satin ribbon, greet the bride.

Margaret is sitting in the front row, and like with Chris's wedding, she's tightly squeezing a hanky. Clay and Teri stand outside the doors of the sanctuary, and Clay leans over, giving Teri a kiss on the cheek.

"My little girl is all grown up now and will be starting her own family."

"Don't make me cry, Dad. I'll mess up my makeup."

The wedding march music begins. The guests all rise and turn toward the door where Teri will enter. Taking Clay's arm, they begin walking down the aisle. Whispers are heard, "Oh she's so beautiful." "My, what a beautiful bride Teri is." Margaret cannot hold the tears back and dabs frantically at her eyes. Larry sucks in a breath when he first lays eyes on her. *Dear God, she's beautiful!*

• • • • • • • • • • • •

Pastor Mike smiles broadly. Larry and Teri kneel on the bottom step of the stage and as promised, Pastor Mike says a *very* short blessing as he holds his hand closely above their heads. When he finishes the blessing, they stand and facing him, "I now pronounce you man and wife. You may kiss your bride," he says.

Larry gently takes her in his arms, and they passionately kiss. Cheers and clapping burst from the guests as Teri and Larry turn facing them.

The banquet hall is decorated with stands of flowers. A table covered with lace and satin ribbons holds the wedding cake. Each table has a place card made of a small photo frame that is embellished with hand painted blossoms, a gift for each guest. In the center of the table rose petals float in a crystal bowl.

Clay stands and gives a toast. Pastor Mike prays a short blessing over the food. Servers begin carrying plates of food to each table as soft music fills the room. When dishes are cleared, Teri and Larry enter the dance floor. Larry takes her in his arms, and as "By Your Side" by Sade plays, they glide around the floor. Everyone claps and smiles and tears express the joy in the room.

Some of the guests are gazing out the large window overlooking the lake. Twilight rays reflect off the water making it appear as shimmering glass. A small sailboat glides past the window with its sails gently flapping in the breeze. Two of the wedding guests wave back to those waving on the boat.

Clay takes Teri by the hand and walks her to the center of the floor. "Isn't She Lovely" by Stevie Wonder begins playing.

"I don't think I've ever seen you more happy," Clay says to Teri as they dance.

"This is the happiest day of my life. I love you, Dad, and thank you so much for this beautiful wedding."

As the song ends, Clay dips her slightly, and the crowd claps.

• • • • • • • • • • • •

The guests gather at the entrance of the hotel to bid the newlyweds good-bye. Teri steps to the front of the crowd and, turning her back, she peeks over her shoulder.

"Are you ready?" she shouts. Holding her bridal bouquet, an array of roses and stephanotis, she tosses it over her head. The women all shout and Michelle catches it. She starts to hand it to the woman next to her. Teri sees that Michelle caught it and realizes what she's about to do.

"Oh no you don't!" She laughs.

Larry helps Teri into the rented convertible with "Just Married" written across the trunk and tin cans and streamers attached to the bumper. Teri's veil is stretched out over the backseat as the wind gently blows it while driving to Larry's hotel room to change clothes for their flight to Hawaii.

• • • • • • • • • • • • •

Teri's parents, Chris, Jack, Mary Lou, and Sally, along with Larry's friends stand waving good-bye as Teri and Larry walk toward the gate, where they will board their nonstop flight from Atlanta to Hawaii. They plan to stay in Hawaii for a couple of days then board their cruise ship going to Tahiti and the South Pacific.

Leaving the airport and driving to Clay and Margaret's favorite restaurant, the group is gathered around a large table in a private section of the restaurant.

Michelle begins laughing. "I wonder if those two are in Hawaii yet."

Greg responds, "It's a five-and-a-half-hour flight. They probably won't be there until late tonight."

"Did they say they were staying two days then going on?" Sally asks.

Mary Lou adds to the conversation and laughingly says, "Teri said she gets really sick on boats. Maybe they should have planned to stay in Hawaii."

Laughing, Chris adds, "That's going to be one heck of a honeymoon if she has her head stuck in a toilet most of the time."

Everyone joins in the laughter, and the meals are served. Most have ordered rib-eye steak while others have T-bone and a couple have filet mignon.

"When are you leaving to return to California?" Clay asks Carl.

"We plan to leave tomorrow afternoon. That will put us back in LA tomorrow evening sometime."

Greg replies, "Yeah, some of us have to work."

Clay smiles. "One of these days, you won't have to, and then you can sit on one of those carts and ride around a golf course all day."

Laughing, Carl says, "Watch it. That's where most of my time is spent."

Everyone joins in the humor, and the dinner continues to be quite pleasant.

• • • • • • • • • • • •

Chris is stretched out on the couch. A storm is raging outside, making her uncomfortable. "I hope we don't have any tornados around," she says nervously to Jack. "I didn't see any watches or warnings on TV when I had it on a little while ago. We'll be fine."

Jack walks to her and looking down at her, he says, "Chris, we need to talk."

As Chris tries to scoot to a sitting position, Jack takes her arm and helps her up. "This sounds serious."

Sitting down beside her, Jack doesn't say anything for a minute. He's planned what he wants to say for days. *I hope she understands.* "I'd like for you to quit work. I know you love your work, but I'm so afraid you will be hurt again, and I couldn't stand it if I lost you or our babies. Chris, I love you so much, and we need to make plans and maybe get a bigger house, and I just don't want anything to happen to any of you. You can be a stay-at-home mom and take our babies for walks, and maybe we'll get a dog and the kids can have a pet and—"

Chris bursts out laughing.

Jack suddenly realizes his planned speech flew out

the window, and he's been going on and on without even taking a breath. Sheepishly grinning, "Well, what do you think?"

Expecting her to reject the idea of quitting work, he also has planned a rebuttal. Chris remains silent for a long moment, and Jack holds his breath and squirms on the edge of the couch. Chris is gently rubbing her stomach and looks at Jack while continuing to massage her stomach.

"Okay."

"What?"

Chris starts laughing. She already suspected that Jack would give a long speech trying to convince her to quit work. She hasn't said anything, but when she regained consciousness in the ambulance, she made the decision that she would not put her baby in danger again.

Jack jumps up off the couch. "That's it? That's all you're going to say? You aren't going to argue or anything?"

Chris smiles broadly. "Nope! I already turned in my resignation. They wanted me to take a leave, but I flatly said no."

Jack sits down, facing her. "Jack, when that man slammed me into my table, I suddenly realized I could lose our baby. I decided while I was in the ambulance that I would never put our child in jeopardy again."

Jack grabs her and hugs her, being careful not to press too hard on her stomach. "I love you, Christine Gordon. I should have known. I'm sorry."

"Are we really going to look for a larger house?"

• • • • • • • • • • • •

Standing beside Chris as she screams bloody murder during her final stages of delivery, the doctor says, "Push one more time."

Suddenly a little boy pops out like someone shot him out of a cannon. Closely behind him, a little girl comes forth "rather delicately," the doctor laughingly says.

Jack has held up rather well while holding Chris's hand, but when his son's head crests, he faints dead away. Chris is too busy screaming to laugh, but the attending nurses do. It isn't the first time by far that a new father has hit the floor during their child's appearance into the world. Regaining consciousness, Jack is embarrassed. He had training in delivering babies during his police academy training, but this is different. It's his babies that are being born, not a stranger's on a birthing movie in a dark room.

• • • • • • • • • • • •

Jack is holding little Richard—Ricky, they've decided to nickname him, and Chris is holding Teresa when Margaret and Clay enter Chris's room. Margaret has promised not to cry, but she just can't help it.

"My grandbabies are here!" she cries.

Jack hands Ricky to Clay, and Margaret takes Teresa from Chris's arms. Smiles and tears fill the room.

Teri and Larry shop the International Market Place, bask in the sun, play in the clear waters on Waikiki Beach, and take a guided bus tour around the island. Spending an evening at a luau, they taste poi and attend a dinner show featuring native dancers in their grass skirts and fire throwers. Tropical fruit is served with most meals each day during their four days in Honolulu. Then they board their ship.

As the ship clips across the huge expanse of water toward Tahiti and the South Pacific, Larry and Teri are enjoying the meals in the many international cafes and restaurants onboard. The days are glorious, and Teri can't be happier. The trip is like a dream, and taking a dip in the pool, a night of dancing, live theatre productions, and relaxing on their private verandah are more than she ever visualized.

Their trip includes touring Tahiti with the many shops and quiet beaches. They decide to go to Rarotonga, another island. Larry talks Teri into taking scuba-diving lessons, and her first underwater adventure leaves both she and Larry breathless at the beauty of the colorful and wide variety of fish. Larry has scuba dived for many years and is thrilled that Teri has taken to it so well.

In Aitutaki they spend the nights dancing and enjoying the cultural activities during the days. Tours around the island are available, and they take advantage of every opportunity to visit everything they can. They've learned two new foreign words: *meitaki*, which means thank you, and as they leave the islands to return home, they each say, "aere ra," which means good-bye.

Chapter 12

....

Returning to Atlanta, Teri and Larry spend two days with Margaret and Clay. Chris, Jack, and the babies arrive, and Teri can't stop gazing at them.

"Oh, Chris, they are so beautiful. We had no idea you gave birth while we were gone."

"There was no way of letting you know." Chris smiles at her children as she speaks to Teri. Larry is holding Teresa and cooing down at her. Teri looks up while holding Ricky and smiles at Larry with tears forming in her eyes.

"I can't wait until we have ours."

Chris grins and winks at Jack. "You'll have a whole new way of life, sister. These two keep us up all night, and I'm lucky to get a nap during the day."

Teri is a bit surprised at Chris's statement. "But you aren't sorry you have them, are you?"

"Oh come on, Teri! Of course we're not sorry we have them. We love these two so much that it hurts sometimes."

"I'm sorry. I just remember some of our talks."

Chris looks at Teri. "That was a long time ago. I'm

different now. I'm a mother, and there's no joy greater than that. You'll see when you have one."

Larry hands Teresa to Jack. "I think there's a puddle in a diaper."

Laughing, Larry takes the baby. Sitting down on the couch, Chris takes Ricky while Jack takes Teresa to change her diaper.

"So tell us about your trip. I'll bet it was great."

Teri begins laughing and telling about how the first day she was so sick on the ship. Then the two of them begin telling about Hawaii and their trip to Tahiti and the outer islands.

Teri and Larry spend one more day with Margaret and Clay. Just before boarding their flight back to California, Teri kisses the babies good-bye, and after giving everyone hugs, she and Larry wave as they pass through the security checkpoint.

• • • • • • • • • • • •

Teri has been back to work four months, and it's been hard having Larry gone on conference trips and in meetings until late at night at times. They speak often, and the honeymoon glow is still there.

"I miss you so much," Teri says as she talks to Larry, who is in Texas.

"I know, honey. I miss you, too."

"I wish you'd come home."

"I'm leaving in the morning. I'll be back tomorrow evening."

"I love you."

• • • • • • • • • • • • •

While sitting on the couch watching a movie on TV, Teri snuggles up against Larry and reaches for the remote control, turning the TV off.

"What are you doing? I thought we were going to watch this movie?"

"I have some good news."

"Oh, did Jimmy go home finally? That kid has made so much progress. I'm so proud of how far he has come."

Teri can't help but laugh. "No, silly. It isn't about Jimmy, although he is going home. We're going to have a baby!"

Larry says nothing for a moment. Shock is written all over his face, and suddenly before Teri can say another word, he grabs her up in his arms. Spinning around in circles, he yells, "We're going to have a baby. We're going to have a baby."

Of course the next day, Teri calls Margaret and listens to her mother scream and cry in her ear. "I'm going to have more grandbabies. Oh, you and Chris have made me the happiest woman on earth. When are you due?"

"I think we may have a Christmas baby. I must have gotten pregnant on our honeymoon."

"Oh my, that was fast."

"Mother!"

"Have you told Chris yet?"

"No. I wanted to tell you first, and now I'm going to call Chris. We're so excited, Mom."

"You have every right to be. You've wanted children even before you knew where they came from."

Teri bursts out laughing. "That early?"

Teri can tell Margaret is crying again. "Teri, I wish you and Larry lived here. I know I've bugged you forever about moving back home, but now it's different."

"I know, Mom. Maybe someday we will. Right now we can't. I need to call Chris. I love you. Bye."

As Teri gives Chris the good news, she can hear babies crying in the background.

"Teri, I'm so excited for you. I wish I could talk, but as you can hear, I have two screaming babies. I'll call you when I have them down for their nap. Is that okay?"

"Call me at the office. Claire will probably be in if I'm with the kids."

"Do you think you'll quit work?"

"I don't know. You better get to your babies before they wear out their lungs."

"You're right, bye."

As the months pass, Larry seems to travel even more than before. He isn't happy about it but has no choice due to his position with the center. Even though they now live in Larry's beachfront home, Teri spends less time walking the beach as she did in the beginning. Visiting with Michelle as much as she can still doesn't fill the emptiness of Larry being gone.

When Larry is home, they spend time walking the beach. Holding hands as they stroll down the beach, Larry sees a large piece of driftwood. Smiling and saying nothing to Teri, he guides her to the driftwood.

"Here, sit down and rest. Our baby must be tired."

Reaching down and placing her hands around her now swollen belly, "I'll bet she is."

"She?"

"Yes. The doctor told me yesterday we're having a beautiful little girl."

Teri gently sits down on the driftwood. It hasn't occurred to her yet that she was sitting, freezing to death, on a piece of driftwood when Larry proposed to her. Larry sits down next to her, and they sit quietly looking out over the ocean.

"Do you remember?" Larry asks.

Teri isn't sure what he's referring to since her mind is elsewhere. "Remember? Remember what?"

"Are you cold?"

"No." Suddenly she remembers. "Oh my gosh! We're sitting on driftwood. I was freezing, and you asked me if I wanted to go in. Then you proposed, and I almost buried you in the sand because I jumped on you so fast."

Larry bursts out laughing. "I thought you *were* going to bury me. You wouldn't get off me. Of course, I wasn't complaining."

Teri gently socks him on the arm. "I wasn't that bad."

"Teri, I've been thinking. I don't want to be traveling like I have been. You need me at home, and when the baby is born, I want to be there."

"What do you have in mind? You can't just say no to the conferences and meetings."

"How would you like to move back to Atlanta?"

"I love it here. Are you serious?"

"Yes. I've been thinking about leaving the center."

"You're serious!"

"Teri, honey, we're going to be parents." Larry reaches down and rubs Teri's stomach and speaks to the child inside, "I want to be a father and be a part of our child's life. I can't be a good father being gone all the time."

"But what will you do?"

Larry stands up and walks to the edge of the water. He doesn't say anything. Teri walks to his side. Without looking at her, Larry says, "I'm thinking about going into my own practice. You'll be near family, and I know that's important."

"You have family here. Michelle needs you, too."

"Michelle came to the office yesterday, and we talked. She's getting married but hadn't said anything yet."

Teri looks incredulously at him. "I can't believe she never said anything to me!"

"Don't get upset. You don't understand Michelle. There's a lot she doesn't tell. Ever since Mom and Dad died, she holds a lot in. She's still afraid people she loves will leave her, so she didn't say anything just in case Ralph dumps her."

"Oh, I'm so sorry. She's never talked about it other than say you looked after her."

"It's been pretty rough for her at times. I've always tried to be there for her. I think this is a good thing for her. She trusts this man, and like Chris told me when we announced our engagement, I'll hunt him down if he hurts her."

Teri stands on her tiptoes and wraps her arms around

Larry's neck, kissing him. "I really think you would, too. When is she getting married?"

"In two weeks."

"Two weeks? She isn't going to plan a wedding?"

"She said she just wants a couple of friends, you and me, and the pastor."

"Wow, and I thought Chris had a small wedding."

"I'll let her tell you about it. She said I could tell you since she doesn't get to see you much anymore. Why don't you call her and maybe have dinner together? She misses you more than you think."

"I miss her too. I'll call her when we get back."

"Speaking of which, I think we should go before you start getting cold and jump my bones again."

She and Larry turn to go back to the house as Teri bursts out laughing.

• • • • • • • • • • • •

Tomorrow is Michelle's wedding, so she and Larry sit on her patio talking late into the night. As most brides, Michelle is nervous, but her nervousness goes much deeper than the bride's usual nervousness. Teri has stayed home so they can have the privacy she knows they need.

• • • • • • • • • • • •

Pastor Johnson smiles as Michelle and Larry walk down the aisle toward him. Michelle is wearing a simple, white wedding dress. The lace bodice with a knee-length satin skirt enhances her dark tan. Her dishwater-blonde hair is styled on top of her head with a shoulder-length veil. Teri recognizes the six friends Michelle has invited. They all work at the center. Michelle asked Teri to be her maid of honor, and Ralph has a coworker friend as his best man.

"Who gives this bride away?"

"I do," Larry says and places her hand in Ralph's, kisses her, and takes his seat.

The ceremony is short, and as Michelle and her new husband walk out the front doors of the church, her guests stand in a group, cheering and throwing birdseed. As Michelle laughs, she turns her back to her friends.

Over her shoulder she says, "Are you ready?" Holding her small bridal bouquet of white daisies high, she tosses it over her head. A woman squeals as the bouquet reaches her hands. Teri has tears in her eyes, and Larry places his arm around her shoulders and hugs her close. Michelle turns, facing Larry, and then she slowly walks to him, leaving her husband standing next to the car.

"Thank you. Thank you for all the years you've been there for me. I'm happy, Larry."

As Larry releases Teri, Michelle reaches up and kisses Larry on the cheek. "I'm happy for you, 'Chel. You deserve to be happy, and Ralph is a good man. He loves you."

Michelle has tears in her eyes as she says to Larry, "I love him too."

"Well I think you better get over there to him, or he may have to spend that honeymoon alone."

Michelle bursts out laughing and runs to her husband. Waving, they climb into the car, and as the cans bounce along the pavement and the streamers fly, Teri and Larry continue to wave.

· · · · · · · · · · · ·

Teri has given her notice at work, and as she waddles down the hall to Larry's office, she suddenly bends over holding her stomach as a cramp grips her. Claire is just leaving Larry's office and runs to her.

"Oh my gosh, Teri! Let me get Larry. You stay right here." Claire runs to Larry's office and runs directly into his office, ignoring Cindy. "Larry, come on! I think Teri's in labor."

Larry has the phone in his hand and is just starting to dial. Dropping the phone in the cradle, he and Claire run out into the hall. Teri is sitting on the floor groaning. Larry runs to her and kneels down beside her. "Let's get you to the hospital!" As he helps her stand, Teri's pain has eased.

"I'm okay now."

But Larry can see fear in her eyes.

· · · · · · · · · · · ·

The doctor enters the room and examines Teri. "I think its false labor, but I want to keep you here overnight just to make sure."

Larry is holding her hand and looking down at her he nods in agreement with the doctor.

Teri looks up at him. "I'm going to be all right. I

think the doctor is right. I *hope* the doctor is right. It's too early for the baby to come."

"I think you need to stay like the doctor said. I'll call the office and let Cindy know. She can cancel my appointments for the rest of the day."

• • • • • • • • • • • •

Walking along the beach, Larry says, "I have a meeting in Atlanta next week, and if you don't mind, I'll have a Realtor start looking for a house for us. We need to talk about what you want for your new little nest."

Teri laughs and walks slowly. "Oh, Larry, this is so exciting. Mom and Chris are absolutely thrilled we're moving back. Have you gotten your replacement at the center yet?"

"I've been talking to a man who's the head of the children's unit in a hospital similar to the center. He seems to be very qualified, and I'm really leaning toward him. He's in Colorado and more than willing to move. He and his wife have two children, and he said they're more than ready to leave the cold country."

"I would be, too!"

"He's flying in tomorrow, and I'll show him around the clinic and see how it goes."

"It sounds like you've already made your decision."

"I pretty much have. How are you feeling? Are you tired? Do we need to head back?"

"I am a little. Will you pick up that shell for me? I can't see my feet, much less stoop down to get it."

• • • • • • • • • • • •

The Realtor Larry has hired calls, and Teri answers the phone. "Mrs. Martin, this is Wanda Golden, the Realtor your husband hired to find you a home. I think I have found what you and your husband are looking for. Can I e-mail you some pictures?"

"Where is it?"

"It's north of Atlanta, close to Dawsonville. Do you know where that's at?"

"Yes, my parents live out that way, and so does my sister. Would you describe the house to me?"

Wanda gives the description and more information on the location. "I have a couple more that might suit your needs too," Wanda says. "I'll send those along with the one I've described. I'll send them right away. Just let me know what you think."

"Thank you. We will."

• • • • • • • • • • • •

Mary Lou and Sally have called several times and are absolutely thrilled Teri will be moving home.

"We can't wait for you to move back!" Sally exclaims.

"I'm excited about it too. At first I didn't want to leave here. You know how I love living on the ocean."

"I know, but we can all go to Tybee Island again."

Teri bursts out laughing. "Yeah, with a bunch of kids in tow."

"You aren't having twins too, are you?!"

"No." Teri laughs. "But as big as I am, I think Gracie Marie must be half grown by now."

"How did you choose that name? I like it. It's a pretty name."

"Grace was Larry's mother's name, and of course, Marie is Chris's middle name."

"Oh, that's nice. Does Chris know?"

"Oh, yes. You know Chris. She doesn't cry very often, but she did when I told her."

"I take it you're not able to come home for Thanksgiving."

"No. The doctor says absolutely not as close as I am to delivery. We'd have to fly back, and he doesn't think that's a good idea."

"Is Michelle going to be there during the delivery? I know Larry will be."

"I doubt it. Larry is flying Mom out after Thanksgiving, and she wants to be here when the baby is born and will stay to help me. She'll go home for Christmas then."

"You'll be there by yourself for Christmas!"

"No I won't. Michelle and her husband will be spending Christmas with us. That is, if Gracie doesn't come before then."

"I just wish you could be here when the baby's born, but I understand."

"Larry just walked in the door. He said he's cooking dinner tonight, so I better go supervise. I'll talk to you later. Bye."

• • • • • • • • • • •

The turkey is in the oven, dressing is on the stove, and the sweet potatoes roasting as Michelle and Teri sing in the kitchen. Larry and Ralph are watching football on TV. Teri is feeling better than she has for the past few days. She's been rushed to the hospital thinking she's in labor, and each time, fear rises in thinking the baby will come too soon.

"Larry, Gracie can't come this soon."

"I know, honey, but it will be okay. The doctor said it's another false alarm, and he wants you on bed rest for a couple of days."

"I know, but I can't let Michelle do everything for Thanksgiving."

"You'll have time to help her."

The meal is served, and the day is going well. Everyone is laughing and joking as they watch a football game that the men are only partially interested in. Suddenly Teri bends far forward, holding her stomach and groaning loudly. Larry jumps up and runs across the room to her.

"Are you okay?"

Fear shows in Teri's eyes. "I think it's the real thing this time."

"Michelle will you start the car? Ralph, if you'll help me get her coat on and out to the car. We need to hurry."

Teri screams in pain.

• • • • • • • • • • • •

Twelve hours later, Larry is standing beside Teri as she holds their daughter.

"We need to get her in an incubator, Mrs. Martin," the nurse says as she reaches for the baby.

Michelle and Ralph are pacing the floor in the waiting room for news from the delivery room. Larry struts out and walks into the waiting room to where they're sitting.

"Gracie is here!" He grins.

Michelle flies into his arms, hugging him. "She's okay? Teri is okay? Is the baby okay?"

Laughing, Larry releases her arms from around his neck and says, "Yes, yes, and yes."

Ralph walks up to Larry and hands him a pink bubble-gum cigar. "I know you don't smoke, but I hope you like bubble gum."

Larry takes the cigar, laughing. "I love bubble gum, especially when it's pink."

Michelle tugs at Larry's arm. "Can we see her? I mean Teri and then the baby?"

"They're taking her to her room right now, and they have Gracie in an incubator. But I think they'll let us see her. I'm not sure, but we can check."

Margaret is disappointed because she wasn't there for the baby's birth. Of course Larry has called her and gives them all the good news.

"Yes, Teri is fine. She'll be home Sunday. She's doing fine, and the baby is doing great."

"I need to hop a plane right now so I'll be there for when she comes home," Margaret states.

"Why don't you wait a few days? That will give Teri time to settle in. Michelle said she'll be with her until you get here."

Margaret isn't very happy about being put off. "But what about Gracie? Who will take care of her?"

"The doctor said she's going to have to stay awhile in the hospital since she came a little early."

"Okay, if that's what you've decided. Just let me know when I need to come."

"Margaret, I'm sorry. I don't mean to sound like we're shutting you out. When the doctor says Grace can come home, you'll be the first one we call to come help."

With Larry's statement, Margaret feels better. "Thank you, Larry. I thought for a minute you may not have needed my help. I'll be praying, and I'll come when you call."

"Thank you, Margaret."

• • • • • • • • • • • •

Teri and Larry continue planning to surprise Teri's family for Christmas by having the baby clothed in Christmas attire and the three of them showing up on their doorstep in Georgia. Grace has gained weight and has just been released to come home. Teri has told her mother she's fine, and due to Christmas being just a week away, she doesn't want her to miss out on Christmas with the twins. Of course, Margaret wants to argue, but Teri has convinced her.

Deplaning in Atlanta, Teri and Larry thank the flight attendants at the door. It has been a fun flight, with the flight attendants wearing Christmas-stocking hats and handing each passenger a candy cane. Susan, the senior flight attendant, pins plastic junior wings on Grace's little red sweater. Larry has rented a car, and without notifying her parents, they pull into the circle driveway of Teri's childhood home. The house is decorated with red, green, yellow, blue, and white twinkling lights strung along the banisters and roof line of the porch. The dogwood trees lining the driveway all have lights strung throughout their branches, giving a welcoming glow. Mary, Joseph, and baby Jesus light up the hay-lined manger in the front yard. A large Christmas wreath welcomes them as they ring the doorbell.

Margaret opens the door and screams. Not knowing what in the world his wife is screaming about, Clay runs to the door to rescue his wife from whatever danger Margaret is facing.

Teri proudly says, "Hi, Mom. Hi, Dad. Meet your granddaughter, Grace Marie Martin."

Teri has the blanket pulled back from Gracie's face, and Margaret reaches for her. Margaret gently takes the baby in her arms as tears stream down her face. Clay is beaming over Margaret's shoulder and suddenly says, "Get in here before our grandchild and you freeze to death out here!"

Christmas Day is spent with grandparents and parents cooing and laughing, doting on Chris's twins and

Gracie. Gifts and gift wrappings galore are now strewn across the living room.

"I couldn't be happier," Margaret cries. "This is the most wonderful Christmas gift you could ever give me," she tells Teri and Larry. "I was so hurt when you said you didn't think I should come."

Teri walks over to her and hugs her tight. "Mom, we didn't want to spoil the surprise. I would never hurt you deliberately."

Margaret sniffles back her tears. "I know that. Oh, I am just so happy!"

Now that Christmas is behind them and the New Year is just ahead, Larry sits with Teri as she feeds Grace. "Honey, I made an appointment with the Realtor, and she's willing to show us the houses she thinks we'll like. Are you up to going today?"

"Let me ask Mom if she wants to babysit Gracie. I don't want to take her out in the cold."

Larry bursts out laughing. "Do you really think she's going to say no? That woman is so proud of her grand-children, she's almost bursting at the seams."

Teri lays the baby in her crib after burping her and laughingly replies, "You're right. That was kind of a dumb statement."

• • • • • • • • • • • • •

"Do you like this one?" Larry asks as they walk through the first house of the three they are to look at.

"I love it!"

Unlike her mother's two-story home, Teri doesn't

want stairs that could endanger her children as they grow up. This house is a ranch-style with five bedrooms and four baths. It sits on three acres and away from busy traffic.

Standing in the finished basement, Teri exclaims, "This is perfect! We can make this large room a playroom for the kids, and you can put your office down here if you want."

Larry points to the room Teri has suggested being a playroom, then the room that could be his office. "Now how much work do you think I'll get with a room full of chattering kids?" He laughs.

Wanda points out that the home is very close to Lake Lanier, which is an added attraction. "Do you want to see the others?" Wanda asks.

Teri turns to Larry. "No. I like this one!"

Larry smiles down at her. He knew she would pick this one when the pictures of the others were sent to him by e-mail. Teri had also received the pictures Wanda sent but couldn't decide which from just the pictures. Larry looks at Wanda and then back to Teri.

"You're sure this is the one?"

Teri twirls around, grinning. "Absolutely!"

Wanda laughs as she waits for Larry's answer.

"We'll take it." Larry laughs.

Back in Los Angeles, the packing has begun. Larry has had to make more out-of-town trips, and Michelle has been a tremendous help in taking care of Grace as Teri works with the movers, packing their belongings. March fifteenth is their planned moving date. The movers will load and deliver everything to their new home, and on their first anniversary, Larry, Teri, and little Gracie will be in their new home in Georgia.

Epilogue

Teri is given a welcome-home and house-warming party that Sally and Mary Lou have planned. Of course, Margaret has invited her friends, colleagues, neighbors, and anyone else she can think of. Her excitement at having her children and grandchildren "living in her backyard," as she likes to say, turns a small homecoming and house warming into a celebration that requires the three acres for parking.

Larry has had to fly back and forth to Los Angeles to train his replacement. Teri occupies her days taking care of Gracie and babysitting Chris's children when Margaret isn't available, which is seldom. She still has some special touches to do that make her "nest," as Larry likes to call it, more personal. As she and Larry relax while watching TV, Larry puts his arm around her shoulder and pulls her close.

"I think my traveling is over."

"I miss you so much when you're gone. Gracie does, too."

"I know. I miss you both, and I have Mr. Walker

trained to where he feels comfortable, and it seems everyone at the center respects and actually likes him."

"That's wonderful. So when is your last trip out there?"

"That was the last one." Teri can't help it; she squeals and hugs Larry tight. "Honey, you're choking me."

Teri laughs and snuggles closer. "So what do you do now?"

"I want to look around here and do some checking. From what I've learned already, there is a need for psychiatrists in this area. I think tomorrow I'll go look at some offices. I've already contacted Wanda, and she has a couple lined up."

"That's wonderful if you can find something in Cumming or Gainesville that would be close to home."

"That's where I'm looking."

After placing an ad in the local newspaper and creating a website, Larry has opened his office officially and already has a few clients. Teri feels she's "arrived." Being back in Georgia and near her family is more rewarding than she thought. She knew eventually she would come home. Leaving their home in California was difficult on the one hand, mainly because she loved the ocean, their walks along the beach, and sitting in the sand and watching the sunsets. On the other hand, she knows she would never be totally happy living so far from her family.

• • • • • • • • • • • •

Chris knocks on the door, and as Teri places Grace in her toddler swing, Chris opens the door, and little Ricky and Teresa toddle in.

"Hi, there's my two sweethearts. How are my little sugar plums today?" Teri asks as she gives each a hug.

Gracie reaches out to Chris as Chris kneels down. "And who is this little sugar?" Chris asks as she lifts Grace from the swing and tickles her tummy.

"Would you like some coffee, Chris? I made a fresh pot."

"Sure, if you already have some made. Why don't we take it downstairs and let the munchkins play?"

"Grace is getting really good at putting her toys back in the toy box," Teri says as she lowers Grace to the floor.

"I wish my two would. They seem to like having them scattered all over the house."

"Gee, I wonder whose fault that is."

While the children play, Teri grins. "I have some news."

"You're pregnant."

"Yes. Isn't it exciting?"

"My two are enough for me. How many do you two want?"

Laughing and holding up ten fingers, "A bunch!"

"You're kidding!"

"Yes, but I wouldn't mind having that many. We've agreed on four. Don't you want more, Chris?"

"No. Jack and I both think two is enough. He's going for a vasectomy next week. We don't want any surprises."

•   •   •   •   •   •   •   •   •   •   •   •

Larry's practice is very successful. Teri and Margaret spend hours planting flowers, shrubs, and blooming trees. The landscaping wasn't bad when they bought the house, but Teri wants to make it more welcoming. Plus Grace and Candice are old enough now that they can use their little toy shovels, toy lawn mowers, and little plastic spades to help. Larry walks up to them as they're digging in the dirt, making a new flower garden.

"You two are a sight for sore eyes." Larry laughs. Teri looks up, and Margaret bursts out laughing. "You have dirt all over your face, Teri."

Larry reaches down and wipes a smudge off Teri's nose. "The material for the gazebo will be delivered this afternoon. Where have you decided to put it?"

Teri points to an area back from the house in the center of the two acres they have cleared. "Right over there. I want to eventually make it similar to how Mom and Dad's is."

Larry glances at the area she's pointing out then back at her. "With the path and all the flowers?"

Margaret emphatically says, "Of course! That's what she and Chris grew up with, and my grandchildren will love it too."

Larry looks at Teri. "Is that what you have planned? That's a lot of work and may take years."

Teri glances at Margaret then grins. "Yes. Do you want some iced tea? I'll go get some. Mom, do you want some too?"

"You go ahead. I want to finish getting this rose bush in the ground."

Larry and Teri walk to the house, with the kids still helping Grandma plant flowers.

Teri pours their ice tea, and taking it out to the patio, Teri smiles. Larry recognizes the expression on Teri's face.

"What is that gleam in your eye?" Larry asks.

"Oh, I don't know. Maybe it's because we're pregnant again."

Larry isn't stunned this time. He suspected it when Teri kept getting up early and running to the bathroom with her hand clamped over her mouth. He played like he was still asleep.

"I know." He laughs as he walks around the table and hugs her. "Maybe we can produce a boy this time. I don't know how to act around all these women."

Teri's surprised at Larry's comment. "What if it's another girl? Will you be disappointed?"

"Absolutely not. I was just kidding, Teri! You know I love our daughters. If we have a girl, I will love her just as much."

"I'm sorry. It must be the hormones again."

• • • • • • • • • • • •

Standing beside Teri in the delivery room, Margaret holds her hand as Larry instructs her to breathe. They've decided not to learn the baby's sex, so the doctor and nurses haven't revealed it to them. Margaret has constantly tried to convince Teri otherwise.

"But we won't know what color clothes to buy or how to decorate the room."

A blood-curdling scream rips through Teri as little Mathew, "Mat" for short, enters the world. Three minutes later, Jeremiah follows. Larry and Teri picked out a couple of names for both sexes. Mathew is after Larry's father, and Jeremiah "is just a nice name." Larry laughed. Linda or Susan had been chosen if it was a girl.

Larry enters the waiting room where Chris, Jack, Clay, Mary Lou, and Sally wait. They all jump up in expectancy as Larry walks across the room. His face shows signs of exhaustion. Teri was in labor twenty-three hours.

No one says anything, waiting for Larry to speak. Sitting down, Larry puts his head in his hands for a moment.

"Larry, what's happened?!" Chris demands. "Is Teri all right? What about the baby?"

Larry runs his hands through his hair. "They're all, all right."

"All?" Clay asks.

Larry looks up with tired eyes. "Twins!"

"But Teri didn't say she was having twins!" Chris says as she plops down on a chair, shocked.

"We didn't know. She's always been pretty big through the pregnancies, and since we told the doctor we didn't want to know the sex, he assumed we didn't want to know it was twins."

Clay bursts out laughing. "Well I'll be."

• • • • • • • • • • • •

Mary Lou and Sally sit with Teri on the patio as they watch Teri's four children and Sally's two playing on the swing set. Chris drives down the long driveway, and as soon as the car stops, Ricky and Teresa jump out and run to join the others playing.

Teri asks Chris as she sits down, joining them, "Do you want something to drink?"

"Do you have any sweet tea? I need sugar!"

Laughing, Teri enters the house and returns with a large tumbler filled with the drink.

"I've been thinking," Sally says.

"Oh, that can be dangerous," Mary Lou says.

"The kids are old enough now. Why don't we take them all to Tybee Island? We all need a vacation."

Chris bursts out laughing. "Yours, mine, and Teri's. Eight kids and you call that a vacation!"

"Sure, we'll put all of them in one room, and we'll each have a single so we can rest and have a great time." Sally laughs.

"It sounds good to me, but I don't think we have enough money to pay the hotel for the kids' damage to their room when we leave." Mary Lou interjects.

"Let's make a plan to go, and then we can present it to our husbands. Not that they'll have much say about it if we make up our minds to go." Chris laughs.

· · · · · · · · · · · ·

As the kids in their swimming suits jump the waves that roll onto the beach and build sand castles, the women relax on their lounge chairs under two large umbrellas. Surprisingly, the kids have been very good. No crying, no fighting, and by bedtime, they fall asleep before their heads hit the pillows.

· · · · · · · · · · · ·

Rising early, the women have fed all the kids, and everyone is clad in their bathing suits ready to go to the beach. Teri reaches for her water bottle and holds it out, looking at it thoughtfully.

"Are you coming?" Chris asks.

"Remember my bottle with the note?"

"Yes. What about it?"

"Why don't we put a message in this water bottle and throw it off the end of the pier as far as we can?"

"I suppose we can, but that's awfully close to shore. Someone will find it before we can even walk away."

"Not if we can throw it far enough and with the wind and tide, there's no telling how far it will go."

"Okay, if that's what you want to do."

Teri drinks the last of the water and sets the bottle on the counter to dry. They all leave for the beach.

Upon returning to their rooms, Teri checks to see if the bottle is dry and, satisfied that it is, picks up a pen and paper.

"Come on, kids. It's time to go." Sally says as the trunk of the car is closed. Teri reaches into her bag and pulls out the water bottle. "I'm going to run over to the pier and throw this out into the water. I'll be right back."

When she returns to the car, Chris asks, "What did you write on the note?"

Teri smiles broadly, "God loves you!"

Lightning Source UK Ltd.
Milton Keynes UK
UKOW06f1124110216

268163UK00010B/145/P